Riders to
Moon Rock

Also by Andrew J. Fenady
in Large Print:

A Rebel: Johnny Yuma
Double Eagles
Claws of the Eagle
The Man with Bogart's Face
A. Night in Beverly Hills

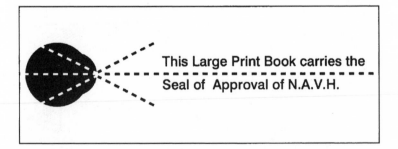

Riders to Moon Rock

Andrew J. Fenady

Thorndike Press • Waterville, Maine

Published in 2005 by arrangement with Leisure Books, a division of Dorchester Publishing Co., Inc.

Thorndike Press® Large Print Western.

The tree indicium is a trademark of Thorndike Press.

The text of this Large Print edition is unabridged.
Other aspects of the book may vary from the original edition.

Set in 16 pt. Plantin by Christina S. Huff.

Printed in the United States on permanent paper.

Library of Congress Cataloging-in-Publication Data

Fenady, Andrew J.
    Riders to Moon Rock / by Andrew J. Fenady.
       p. cm. — (Thorndike Press large print westerns)
    ISBN 0-7862-8011-5 (lg. print : hc : alk. paper)
      1. Ranching — Fiction. 2. Texas — Fiction. 3. Large
type books. I. Title. II. Thorndike Press large print
Western series.
PS3556.E477R53 2005
813'.54—dc22   2005016380

Dedication

with a bow to
    Emily Brontë

for every
    Heathcliff and Cathy
    Shannon and Heather

and for the only
    Mary Frances

As the Founder/CEO of NAVH, the only national health agency solely devoted to those who, although not totally blind, have an eye disease which could lead to serious visual impairment, I am pleased to recognize Thorndike Press* as one of the leading publishers in the large print field.

Founded in 1954 in San Francisco to prepare large print textbooks for partially seeing children, NAVH became the pioneer and standard setting agency in the preparation of large type.

Today, those publishers who meet our standards carry the prestigious "Seal of Approval" indicating high quality large print. We are delighted that Thorndike Press is one of the publishers whose titles meet these standards. We are also pleased to recognize the significant contribution Thorndike Press is making in this important and growing field.

Lorraine H. Marchi, L.H.D.
Founder/CEO
NAVH

* Thorndike Press encompasses the following imprints: Thorndike, Wheeler, Walker and Large Print Press.

Prologue

There is a place in Texas where the vagrant west wind weaves through the buttes, threading toward a mystic formation known as Moon Rock.

It is a place holy and horrible, serene and savage, and — like the ever-changing moon — bleak and beautiful.

Cut like a towering cathedral over a desolate diocese, rising as if not of this earth. From another time and space. Alone and alien. Trying to tear itself out of a troubled Texas earth and seek the calm of some faraway forgotten harbor.

It has been said that Moon Rock has been struck by lightning more times than any other place on earth. But wind and rain out of a seething sky, thunder and lightning with all their fury, have failed to wear down or tear apart this place known as Moon Rock.

Tales are told, mostly whispered, of ancient sacrificial blood rites — of death

7

chants and pagan oblations — of forbidden moon-bathed meetings by young lovers — of secret births and unmarked graves.

But no tale of Moon Rock is more rent with love and violence, passion and jealousy, desire and revenge, than that of a boy and girl who grew up in its shadow, grew up amidst the carnage of a civil war. Their voices sometimes can still be heard: the man and woman called Shannon and Heather — riders to Moon Rock.

Chapter One

It was the cold, wind-whipped Texas winter of 1847.

Three hunched-up cowboys, forked onto their shaggy ponies, had gathered up more than a score of gaunt strays, longhorns who had wandered into Ghost Canyon — too far from winter grass and too close to Kiowas, but still on land that belonged to Shannon Glenshannon.

Glenshannon's spread was one of the biggest in Texas — or anywhere. Dull, flat, monotonous in places where the Lord had stomped the dust off his boots, in other places verdant with vales in thirty shades of green, and in still other places, craggy with jagged cliffs and red stone monuments — all of it the domain of one man.

One of Glenshannon's cowboys, an amateur geographer, once observed that it would take a man on a good horse a lot of breakfasts to circle it. Nobody had ever tried.

But there were those, especially in the

early days, who did try to invade Glenshannon's domain. Indians. Mexicans. Bandits. Rustlers. All now dead and buried or banished.

Glenshannon Hall and everything around it still belonged to an Irishman who had crossed the Red River a quarter of a century before.

The three cowboys, Chet Williams, Dobe Carey and Judd Gibbs, moved the stiff-legged herd toward the mouth of Ghost Canyon and in the direction of Glenshannon Hall.

That noon, the sun was a cold orange ball and hung like a full autumn moon at dusk.

On the spine of the west canyon wall, a dozen mounted Kiowas, with scraggy, weather-worn hides and hungry faces, watched and waited.

Their leader, Seccoro, was an older man who carried the coup stick of a Kiowa chief. At Seccoro's side was a young boy of indeterminate years — maybe ten, or months more. The boy, astride his Indian pony, looked and was dressed like a Kiowa.

Seccoro's clear eyes moved from the herd below to the boy he called Tamonito — which meant Little Brave One in Kiowa — and spoke to him in the language of the tribe.

10

"Tamonito, you will watch and remember. It will not be long until you ride at your father's side."

Running Bear, one of the other Kiowas, the tallest and broadest, mounted near Seccoro, looked at the scrawny youth with unmistakable contempt.

"He's not your son, Seccoro, and he'll never be a Kiowa."

Seccoro touched the boy's shoulder with the coup stick and let it rest there.

"Tamonito's as much a son as any of my dead sons were — and more Kiowa than you."

Seccoro raised the coup stick from the boy's shoulder.

"And one day this will be his."

Unspoken hatred blazed in Running Bear's eyes — hatred he had nurtured for the boy since the Kiowas came upon the two wagons with white families nearly five years before.

Only one man prevented Running Bear from doing what he had thought about many times during those five years. The man was Seccoro. The thought was killing the boy.

But Seccoro was old, his strength waning. Running Bear was young, his strength still waxing — and patient and cunning.

11

The Kiowas were poorly armed, most of them with bows and arrows, and a few, including Seccoro and Running Bear, with revolvers and rifles they had taken from lifeless bodies of white enemies.

Seccoro, holding high the coup stick, gave the command to attack. The ragged band picked up the yell and raced down the slope, leaving the boy behind to watch and wait.

This was a far cry from the bold and bloody charges that the great chief had led in the almost three decades since Seccoro had assumed command of his tribe. When, instead of a dozen scrawny warriors, he was followed by hundreds of screaming Kiowa braves, the finest light cavalry since the Mongols galloped from the Far East to conquer half the known world.

Seccoro had had more than his share of conquests — over Comanches, Apaches, Arapahos, Mexicans and the whites. But not lately. As he grew older his followers seemed to melt away to join new chiefs, bolder chiefs, such as Santanta, Guipago and Setangya.

Since both of Seccoro's sons were killed in battle, one by Comanches, the other by the First Dragoons of the U.S. Cavalry, the great chief seemed to have lost his ferocity, his thirst for conquest. He seemed almost content to survive instead of prevail.

Still, when in order to survive, to provide food for his hungry clan, it was necessary to lead a raid, Seccoro was ready to meet the challenge and maybe death, as in the glory days of his reign.

Seccoro and the Kiowas charged down the loose shale of the canyon slope toward the herd and three cowboys below.

Chet Williams, Dobe Carey and Judd Gibbs were better armed — with Colt Walker revolvers and Hall Breechloader carbines — than their attackers, but were outnumbered and outmaneuvered by the charging Kiowas.

Williams was hit and killed in the first volley, his body trampled by the startled steers. Carey and Gibbs fired and dropped two of the Kiowas, then simultaneously decided on the intelligent course. They rode away.

The Kiowas did not pursue. They had accomplished their mission — food. The successful raiders began to round up the scattered beeves.

Seccoro lifted his coup stick and waved to the boy up above. The boy waved back.

But Seccoro's victory was short-lived.

In the distance, from the mouth of Ghost

Canyon, more riders appeared with superior numbers and fire power.

There were twenty of them including Carey and Gibbs, led by a tall, thick-trunked, imposing man — gray-haired, with a frontier face and buffalo shoulders.

Shannon Glenshannon.

As they galloped they fired a barrage of bullets from rifles and revolvers. The Kiowas were doomed — half of them dispersed or killed, the other half in panic.

Seccoro gave the command for what was left of his force to retreat. As he looked up toward the rim of the canyon wall where the boy watched, a shot tore into Seccoro's chest. The old warrior slammed onto the cold, hard ground and lay still, the coup stick still in his hand.

Running Bear, one of the few survivors, reached down from his horse as he raced by Seccoro's body and snatched the coup stick from the dead chief.

Shannon Glenshannon reined up, raised the hand that held his Colt .44, and spoke in a slight brogue to the riders around him.

"That's enough, men. Let 'em go."

As always, Shannon Glenshannon's cowboys followed his orders, although Gibbs was sorely tempted to fire a few more shots. Instead he rode up to his boss.

14

"Thanks, Mr. Glenshannon. Lucky for us you happened to be this far out."

"One of the boys spotted unshod pony tracks headed into the canyon. Then we heard gunshots."

"They killed Williams."

"We killed more of them. That old one looks to be their chief." Glenshannon nudged his horse closer to Seccoro's body, then turned toward the pony and rider racing down from the canyon hillside.

The boy riding recklessly toward them was unarmed.

He lept off his pony and cradled the dead chief's face in his thin arms.

Glenshannon dismounted and walked toward the boy and the body. In a sudden savage surge the boy sprang up and pounded at the chest and arms of the big man, crying — and speaking in English for the first time in years.

"You killed him. You killed my father! You killed my father."

The big man grabbed the boy by the arms and steadied him. Gibbs, Carey and a couple of the other cowboys started toward the boy but Glenshannon waved them off and spoke in a calm but commanding voice.

"We defended what belongs to me."

With savage, hard-as-a-bullet eyes the boy looked up into the weathered face of Shannon Glenshannon.

"His people are hungry." The boy's gaze went down to the dead chief.

To Glenshannon the boy looked hungry too. Hungry and grieved . . . and there was something else.

"I'm sorry, lad . . ." Glenshannon looked deeper at the strange boy. With his hand, as gently as possible, he turned the boy's head away from the fallen Indian and toward him.

"He can't be your father . . . you're not an Indian."

"Secorro is my father."

"Secorro?! So that's him, is it? He was once a great chief . . . a great warrior. I'm sorry, lad."

"That you killed him?"

"That I didn't know him sooner. Things might have been different. How long have you lived with the Kiowas?"

"As long as I want to remember."

"How did you come to them?"

"There were two families . . . two wagons . . ."

"Attacked by Kiowas?"

"By fever. I was the only one alive."

"Poor lad. No more than a puppy and

twice orphaned. Well, you'll come home to Glenshannon Hall and stay with us."

Some of the other cowboys glanced at each other, some in disbelief, others in disapproval. But they all knew it was not an unexpected gesture on the part of their boss.

The boy looked directly at Glenshannon and spoke one word.

"No."

"I think you will." Glenshannon smiled.

"No," the boy repeated.

"What kind of life would you go back to?" Glenshannon's head nodded toward the dead chief. "And without him?"

The boy knelt at the side of Seccoro's body. With his hand he wiped the blood and dirt from the dead man's face.

The words echoed in the boy's brain.

"What kind of life would you go back to? And without him?"

His mind swept back to another time, another place, another life, barely remembered.

The first light of that distant dawn — two wagons motionless, as still as death. Death that was in the air and in the wagons. Two families moving West together — out of southern Illinois to St. Louis and from St. Louis across the Mississippi, through Missouri, the northwest border of Arkansas,

17

into Texarkana and across the Red River into Texas. Two wagons carrying all the earthly possessions of two families, and something else besides.

Fever.

Both families afflicted. The Johnsons — husband, wife and three children. And the boy's family — his mother, father and sister, one year younger than the boy.

A campfire — cold. As cold as the bodies in and around the wagons. Bodies that not long ago burned hot with fever, now cold and still and stiff.

A Kiowa hunting party, thirty mounted warriors led by Seccoro followed closely by Running Bear, charged into the camp to raid and kill the sleeping occupants.

But death had preceded them.

It appeared that all the white travelers would travel no farther. Seccoro, Running Bear and some of the other Kiowas dismounted.

Seccoro held the coup stick of the chief in his hand. He approached the first wagon but made a sudden stop.

From behind the wagon a boy staggered into sight. In his trembling right hand, barely able to carry it, was a Colt Paterson five-shot cap-and-ball revolver.

The boy shuddered. His eyes were hazy.

18

He breathed a deep breath and tried to raise the revolver but couldn't.

Seccoro smiled. But Running Bear was not smiling. He said something that the boy could not understand, but his intent was unmistakable and so was the look in his narrow eyes as he drew the knife from the sheath on his right side and moved toward the boy.

As Running Bear took the second step, the boy raised the Colt, held it with both hands as steady as he could and fired.

The impact from the Colt staggered the boy and he almost fell.

Running Bear's left hand went to his side and his palm turned up red, smeared with blood from the slight wound just below his rib cage.

Some of the other Kiowas smiled. A few even laughed.

Seccoro's face was expressionless, but not Running Bear's. The wound was not as painful as the humiliation inflicted by a sick infant white boy.

Again Running Bear spoke. He raised the knife and came toward the swaying boy.

Then it was Seccoro who spoke. The Kiowas listened to their chief as he pointed the coup stick toward Running Bear.

"You will not touch the boy."

"I will kill him."

"Not before I kill you. He is brave and worthy to live. He will live with us . . . in place of my dead sons."

"I will —"

"You will say no more . . . and do nothing to hurt him."

"He will die from the sickness."

"I don't think so."

Seccoro smiled and went to the boy. The boy dropped the Colt as Seccoro put his arm around him. The chief picked up the revolver and led the boy to his horse. Seccoro mounted, then reached down and lifted the boy onto the animal.

The boy pointed to the sky. Already the birds had begun to circle around the scent of death below.

Seccoro gave a command and half a dozen Kiowas stayed behind to bury the dead as the chief, with the boy in front of him, led the others away.

And as they moved off, Running Bear was no longer close to Seccoro.

The boy did not die from the sickness but Running Bear never stopped thinking about killing him.

So long as Seccoro was chief, all Running Bear could do was think about it and wait for the time when Seccoro was no longer strong enough to lead his people. And there was something else Running Bear could do — mercilessly taunt the boy when Seccoro was not near enough to see and hear. Running Bear knew that the boy would never complain to Seccoro. That would be a sign of weakness. No. The boy would never do that.

In the years that passed, Seccoro taught the boy the ways of the Kiowa. To track. To scout. To survive. The boy was an eager pupil, and eager to prepare for the day when he had to face Running Bear alone.

And now that day had come. Seccoro was dead. But the boy was not yet old enough and strong enough to challenge the warrior who now carried the coup stick of a Kiowa chief.

"What kind of a life would you go back to? And without him?"

The boy, his face a silent lamentation, looked up at Shannon Glenshannon and spoke barely above a whisper.

"I'll go with you."

Glenshannon smiled and nodded.

"But first," the boy said, "I will bury my father."

"Alright, lad."

"I will bury my father like the chief he was."

"Will you let us help you?" Glenshannon asked.

"Why not?" the boy replied. "You killed him."

Unlike the Sioux, the Cheyenne and other tribes, the Kiowas did not bury their dead in trees or specially built altars. They buried their dead in caves or in the ground.

The body of Seccoro was buried in the cold, hard earth of Ghost Canyon.

Chapter Two

"Poor lad, no more than a puppy and twice orphaned."

As they rode out of Ghost Canyon, the terrain became less bleak and melded into darker, richer ground with trees, a trail and even a stream and willow grove. The air seemed warmer and friendlier — but not to Chet Williams, whose dead body was wrapped in a blanket and tied over his horse.

The boy couldn't help looking at the big man he rode beside. A man who commanded respect, with eyes the color of a December sky and a crooked smile creased on his face, a face fashioned like the prow of a powerful ship, wind-chased and confident.

"Twice orphaned."

The boy had no clear recollection of his real father. Seccoro had become his father and the boy had become an Indian.

Indian braves did not grieve outwardly for the dead. Unlike the squaws who beat and cut themselves and wailed in their grief, the men made no show of emotion and never even mentioned the names of the dead.

The boy would never speak Seccoro's name again. That too would be left in Ghost Canyon along with the Kiowa chief's body.

The Kiowas were hunters and wanderers. They did not raise crops or cattle. They stole cattle and horses and wives and anything else they coveted, just as those same chattels were stolen from them by other tribes — Comanche, Apache, Sioux, Cheyenne.

The borders of Indian territories were ill defined and belonged to whoever was the strongest at that time and place.

The boy knew or remembered little, if anything, of a country called the United States or a place called Texas.

Texas. A bountiful land, but also a time-worn battlefield — and worth fighting for. Rich soil, ample forests and deep harbors. Claimed and conquered by Indian tribes — Kiowa, Comanche, Cherokee and Apache — with arrows and tomahawks. Then came the conquerors with gunpowder — Spaniards and Mexicans. And then the unyielding, unending procession of Americans — men like Austin, Sam Houston, Jim Bowie, William Travis, Davy Crockett, Sam

Mavrick and Shannon Glenshannon. Pioneers, all born somewhere else, who came to live and die in Texas.

The boy had no idea that the man he rode beside was born in a place called Ireland, had become a Texan and was now an American citizen — ever since December 29, 1845, when U.S. President James Polk signed legislation making Texas the twenty-eighth state of the United States.

Nor did the boy know that at the present time, since April 25, 1846, the United States was at war with Mexico in a conflict that would define the southern boundary of Texas.

There was a different kind of conflict within the boy, a different kind of war — between two worlds. The world of the Kiowa and the world he had years ago left behind and was once again crossing into.

Chapter Three

As they rode, the boy saw more cattle than he had seen since he was born. Enough beef to feed Seccoro's tribe and twenty other tribes for a dozen years.

Glenshannon Hall was not a ranch. It was an empire. Vast, variegated and self-sustaining.

The ruler of that empire sat not on a throne, but on a saddle next to the boy. No crown. No cape. No sword. A broad-brimmed hat. A corduroy jacket. A Winchester in his saddle boot and a Colt on his hip.

The boy wondered how one man could come to command such an empire. That was just one of the many things he wondered, one of the questions he wanted to ask. How had this man become chief? The boy knew that some of the Indian chiefs inherited their title. Others conquered or killed the inheritors and declared themselves ruler of the tribe.

The boy didn't think the man he rode next to was an inheritor. He seemed more like a conqueror, strong but not severe.

And as they rode the boy found himself thinking not in the Kiowa tongue, but in the language he first learned to speak.

And then the boy saw it. From a distance it looked like a huge stone bridge over dry land, arching high and wide across the broad trail they had been following.

But it was not a bridge. It was an entrance. A proclamation. Across the top of the arch were carved two words:

GLENSHANNON HALL

Glenshannon reined his horse to a stop. He turned to the boy.

"This is where you'll live, lad."

The boy said nothing.

"But only as long as you want to stay. I hope it'll be a long time. Let's have a look."

There was much to look at.

As they rode under the arch and toward the headquarters the boy beheld a sight unlike any he had ever seen or imagined.

The main building was an imposing Spanish-style two-story structure with a tile roof and a wide veranda. Nearby there were corrals and small buildings, bunkhouses for

27

the cowboys. A stable. All in excellent repair. Bright and gleaming even in the hazy winter sun.

For the boy who was used to huts, hovels, lean-tos, teepees and caves, it was beyond comprehension.

Closer to the headquarters, on a smoothly sloping hillside, there was rooted a magnificent, almost mystical oak tree, and beneath it, framed by a white picket fence, was a lone grave with a large white marble headstone.

The other cowboys peeled away to their respective places and duties, leaving only Glenshannon and the boy moving on toward the main building.

As they rode there was a variety of animals, many of them running loose near and around the barns, stables and corrals. Pigs, chickens, goats, cats and dogs — even a three-legged dog, blind in one eye, with a chunk of his right ear chewed and flopped over, and missing part of his left hind leg. Lost in a fight with a wolf, Glenshannon told the boy. One of the cowboys was going to shoot the dog, but every time the cowboy took aim that dog would hop away. So they had decided to let him live. That was four years ago and Lucky was still living, still hopping.

Glenshannon dismounted. The boy stayed on his pony.

As the front door of the main building opened, Glenshannon lifted his arm to help the boy off the saddleless pony, but the boy glided off gracefully and both moccasined feet landed softly on the ground.

"Father! Father!"

A beautiful little girl, maybe a year younger than the boy, bounded out from the front door. Her eyes, bluer than her father's. Her long curled hair darker than a raven's wing. Her complexion white as new snow. Her face lovely as a Christmas cake. But her pink lips pouting.

"Father! Hadley's hidden my needlepoint and won't tell me where it is . . ."

"Heather . . ."

"Please make him tell . . . please."

Glenshannon lifted her in his hawser arms and kissed her cheek laughing.

"Heather, my darlin', never mind Hadley, give your father a hug, a welcome-back hug, and tell him how much you missed him while he was gone."

"Oh, I did, but please make him tell where he hid it, please . . ."

By now there were three other people on the porch. Glenshannon's son, a few years older than the boy. A well-worn cowboy in his early fifties who canted a little to the left as he stood, and even more when he walked.

A handsome woman with a strong face and able body, her auburn hair streaked with gray and pulled back tight to a bun.

Glenshannon set Heather gently on her feet and turned toward the porch.

"Hadley, I've told you not to tease your sister."

"Awww, who cares about her dumb knitting." Hadley possessed a pinched face, feline eyes and a recessive chin, but somehow, all put together, the sum of his features added up better than the parts.

"Well, then," Heather asked, "where is it?"

"I forget."

"Hadley," Glenshannon said, "you'd better remember and fast."

"It's in the kitchen."

"*Where* in the kitchen?" Heather puffed.

"In the wood box." Hadley smiled a malevolent smile. "With the spiders!"

"I'll fetch it for you, Heather." The man on the porch cast a beetling look at Hadley. "Wouldn't want one of them spiders to bite Hadley and die."

"Thank you, Pepper." Heather giggled.

Hadley took a step closer, but still on the porch, and pointed with bemusement at the boy.

"What's that?"

"The lad's come to live with us." Glenshannon smiled at the boy, then turned to make the introductions. "That's my son, Hadley." He brushed the little girl's cheek. "His sister, Heather. Ol' Pepper, who's the real boss of the outfit, and Hannah Dean, who takes care of all of us."

Pepper stepped off the porch.

"Appears you run into some bit of a dustup out there." Pepper had been peering out of a window and had spotted the dead body tied to a horse.

"Ghost Canyon. Kiowas after beeves. Williams is dead."

"What about the Kiowas?"

"I'll tell you later."

"Always later."

Hadley had produced a pocket knife from his pants. He walked off the porch, picked up a piece of wood and started stroking slices off too close to the boy.

"Kiowas, huh? So he's nothing but a dirty little savage and —"

"Hadley." Glenshannon's voice was firm.

"We don't want no dirty little Indian beggar around us!" Hadley spat out.

"Hadley." Glenshannon's voice became even firmer, dangerous. "I decide who stays at Glenshannon Hall and who doesn't."

Glenshannon calmly but firmly grabbed hold of Hadley's arm, took the knife away

31

from him and snapped the blade from the handle. He let both pieces fall to the ground. Hadley instinctively moved a step back.

"And he's not an Indian." Glenshannon addressed not only Hadley, but all the others. "When we get the dirt off and some food into him he'll be just like the rest of us."

"What's his name?" Heather's eyes had been studying the boy.

"Probably something like Howling Wolf," Hadley snickered.

"What is your name, lad?" Glenshannon asked.

The boy did not answer.

"Well, never mind." Glenshannon smiled. "You're starting a new life and you'll have a new name. Now, I'm called Shannon Glenshannon and I'll give you one of my names. From now on you'll be Shannon. That's, if it's alright with you."

Neither Hadley nor Heather seemed particularly pleased as the boy looked up at Glenshannon and nodded.

"Well, then." Glenshannon put his arm around the boy's shoulder. "Let's go inside. Hannah, is there anything to eat?"

"Anything you can name that doesn't have hair on it. But first, I'd suggest" — she

looked at the boy now called Shannon —
"I'd suggest a good scrubbing and some civilized clothes."

"Good idea." Glenshannon nodded and
led Shannon toward the front door.

The rest of them followed — all but
Hadley, who picked up the two pieces of his
broken knife and held them in the palm of
his soft, pale hand.

Pepper poured a bucket of water over
Shannon's head as the boy sat naked in a
huge tub inside one of the rooms of the
main house — a house of thick walls, tall
and ample windows and tile floors.

"Keep scrubbin', boy. You got two, three
more layers to go."

Shannon rubbed the bar of lye soap
across his chest, producing a brownish foam
that dripped into the tub already thick with
grime. His dirty Kiowa clothes lay in a pile
next to the tub.

"Well, I guess that'll do for now," Pepper
said after another ten minutes. "You'll have
to peel the rest of it off some other time. My
innards are commencin' to growl." He
tossed Shannon a towel. "Pull on them
duds I brought in for you." He pointed to a
shirt, pants and other items laid out on a
bench.

As Shannon stepped out of the tub and dried off with the towel, the door opened and Hadley came into the room. He looked at Shannon in disgust, then spotted the clean clothes on the bench.

"These are my clothes." Hadley picked up the pair of pants.

"Not anymore," Pepper said. "They're too small for you. Your father said to give 'em to Shannon."

Pepper took the pants away from Hadley.

" 'Sides, you got more pants than you and six like you could ever wear."

Hadley started to leave the room but turned back to the bench, bunched up the clean shirt and threw it into the dirty tub.

After Hadley left, Pepper went to the tub, pulled out the shirt and began to twist it so the dirty water would drip off.

"He sure as hell ain't his father's son . . . nor his mother's . . . I think he hatched out of a buzzard egg."

Shannon, wearing Hadley's clothes hanging loose over his rope-thin body, stared with ravenous anticipation at the food on the dinner table. A huge platter was overloaded with steaks, another platter piled high with boiled potatoes, and other containers brimming with vegetables — winter peas, corn and okra — along with a plate heaped with fresh-baked biscuits.

The six people at the table included Heather, Hadley, Hannah, Pepper — and at the head of the oblong oak table, Shannon Glenshannon, whose face was bowed as he said grace.

"Bless us, oh Lord, and these thy gifts which we are about to receive from thy bounty through Christ, our Lord . . . and bless our beloved Marni, my wife and mother of our children, who is in heaven with you. Amen."

As Glenshannon raised his head, smiled and nodded, Shannon's right hand thrust out, grabbed one of the steaks, then with both hands holding on to the still-hot meat, began biting and chewing and devouring until, within moments, he realized something was amiss.

Nobody else had moved. They sat, some — Heather and Hannah — in embarrassment, some — Glenshannon and Pepper — in amusement, and Hadley in utter disgust.

Shannon didn't know the word, but he sat cloaked in humiliation.

His first instinct was to get up and run away. But he would not give Hadley that satisfaction. He put what was left of the meat back on the platter and looked at Glenshannon.

"Good God!" Hadley croaked.

"That'll be enough, young fellow," Glenshannon said.

Pepper lifted the steak platter and passed it around. The diners helped themselves, all avoiding the steak that had been partly devoured, until the platter got back in front of Shannon. He had been watching the procedure of his dinner companions.

For the first time since he could remember he picked up a fork, stabbed it into the chewed-on steak, and placed the meat on the plate in front of him.

He smiled with satisfaction, then lifted the platter of potatoes and passed it to Pepper.

Progress, Glenshannon thought to himself, and smiled.

Hadley was not smiling.

Chapter Four

Glenshannon opened the door to a small room just down a narrow hall from the kitchen. He struck a match and lit an oil lamp on a dresser.

"Come in, Shannon."

The boy stepped into the room and looked around. Beside the dresser there was a bunk bed with a small table next to it and a straight-back chair.

"This'll be your room. We'll get you whatever else you need tomorrow. Now get some sleep. It's been a long day and you've got a lot to get used to . . . and so have we, lad." Glenshannon walked to the door. "Good night."

The boy lifted his right hand slightly in acknowledgement and gratitude. He couldn't bring himself to say anything . . . not yet.

Still clothed, Shannon lay in the bunk bed, looking through the window at the floating moon, full and amber.

Only last night he had looked at the same moon in the same sky, but from a different world.

The world of the Kiowa.

A world of bow, lance and shield, of tomahawk and buckskin, paint and feathers, of Sun God, peyote plant and polygamy. A nomad's world where all possessions were moveable. Where wealth was measured in horses and wives, where there was sun and sky and field and little or no confinement. A world without thick walls, fireplaces, tile floors, tall windows and kitchen stoves. An outdoor world. A world much bigger than this room.

Shannon couldn't remember the last time he slept in a bed.

He got up, went outside and lay on the ground under a tree.

Shannon fell asleep as soon as his eyes closed.

At first light a shadow passed across his face. He bolted into consciousness and looked at Shannon Glenshannon. The big man smiled.

"I said there'd be a lot to get used to. It'll take time, lad."

Glenshannon walked back to the horse he had left a few feet away, mounted and rode in the direction of the oak tree and grave on the side of the hill.

Shannon Glenshannon knelt near the large marble tombstone at the head of the grave. The tombstone was engraved.

Maureen	Shannon
Glenshannon	Glenshannon
1802–1837	1795–
Beloved Wife	Beloved Husband
and Mother	and Father

At Rest Until The Life To Come

He took off his hat and touched the marble marker.

"Well, Marni, a lot has happened since I was up here yesterday morning. Indians again. Kiowas. Raided our cattle that had wandered over to Ghost Canyon. If I had known how hungry those Kiowas were I'd have given them enough beef to get by. But those Kiowas won't talk to us. They're too proud to ask for anything . . . so they go to stealing.

"There's some of 'em that won't steal anymore. Among 'em, an old chief named Seccoro. He was once a great warrior.

"We lost one of our hands. You didn't know him. Came to work here just over a year, year and a half ago. We'll see to it he gets a proper burial.

"And Marni, there's something else. We always talked about having three kids, but . . . but you went to heaven when Heather was born. Well, it seems that maybe the Lord sent us another son.

"He's about ten or twelve years old, I'd say . . . hard to tell, he's so undernourished. Lived with the Kiowas, but he's white. There's somethin' about him that's sad, but strong. You would've liked him, but then you liked everybody and everybody liked you.

"But I loved you, Marni, from the first time I saw you . . . green eyes sparklin', red hair blazin' in the Irish sunlight . . . and I always will.

"Oh . . . I named the boy Shannon. I'll tell you more about him when I get to know him better."

Later that day Pepper gave Shannon a haircut while Heather watched.

After supper, in front of the fireplace, Shannon and Heather sat together on the tile floor while she read aloud from a book, the story of Cinderella and Prince Charming by the brothers Grimm.

Glenshannon sat in his oversize leather chair, smoking a curved pipe and listening to Heather's voice.

40

Hannah was knitting. Between puffs on a cigar, Pepper worked on a leather belt he was making for the boy. Hadley was nowhere in sight.

When Heather finished the story, Glenshannon knocked the ash out of the pipe, pulled the gold watch from his vest and nodded toward Heather and Shannon on the floor.

"Better get to bed. Tomorrow's a big day. Shannon, you're going to see a horse race like you've never seen before. The finest animals in the territory and the best riders."

That night Shannon slept inside on the bunk bed.

Chapter Five

Over a year earlier, four of Glenshannon's best riders and top hands had left the ranch. They also left Texas, along with Captain Jack Hays of the Texas Rangers, and joined up with Zack Taylor. They were with the general when he took Monterrey in the Mexican War — part of a fierce force, so fearsome it was dubbed by the opposing army *"Los Diablos Tejons."*

But there were still some of the finest horsemen in Texas — maybe not counting Indians — riding the range for Shannon Glenshannon.

Every year at this time Glenshannon put up a one-hundred-dollar prize for the winner of a two-mile race, and this year was no exception. Dozens of spectators came from other ranches and from the nearest town, Gilead, to see the contest and, not incidentally, to make bets.

This year there were nine contestants. The three favorites were Sam Carson, Judd

Gibbs and Buck Jenkins, the foreman. Carson had won last year and was odds on to win again this year.

The start and finish line was near the stable.

Glenshannon, Heather, Pepper, Hannah, Shannon and the other spectators watched as the riders mounted and lined up their animals.

"Father," Hadley said to Glenshannon, "I'll bet you a new pocket knife Carson wins."

"Hell, yes, he'll win," Pepper said. "He's got the best horse."

"I'll give you two lengths," Hadley said, ignoring Pepper.

"Now let me get this straight, son," Glenshannon said. "If I lose you get a pocket knife. But what do I get if you lose?"

"I'll leave that up to you, Father. I know you'll be fair and honorable."

"Never heard of such hogwash," Pepper mumbled.

"Alright, Hadley." Glenshannon smiled. "You have a bet, m'lad."

"Listen here, everybody," Dobe Carey shouted, holding a pocket watch in his left hand and a .44 in the other. "This race for a grand prize of one hundred dollars, coin of the realm — put up by our boss and bene-

43

factor, *Señor* Glenshannon — is going to start in exactly one minute promptly as soon as this gun goes off!"

"Shannon, I . . ." Heather turned to speak to Shannon, who had been standing next to her, but he was gone. She caught sight of him as he disappeared into the stable.

Dobe Carey fired his .44 into the air and the riders blasted off like nine simultaneous cannon shots.

But in the next instant there was an additional, if unlikely, rider.

Shannon, aboard his saddleless pony, vaulted out of the stable entrance and streaked toward the larger, more formidable animals.

Glenshannon, Heather, Hadley, Hannah, Pepper and the entire crowd stood in frozen amazement as the bareback rider held the rope reins in his hands, leaned forward and commenced to close the gap between himself and the field.

It had been a long time since the boy had smiled, had been happy, and now he was not just happy, he was fulfilled, exultant as the horse responded in perfect harmony with the rider, shortening the distance between them and the horsemen ahead, horsemen who were now aware that there was another contestant in the race.

"By God, that boy can ride!" Pepper yelled, and slapped the back of Hadley's shoulder, almost knocking him off his feet.

The spirited pony moved up closer to the cowboys, but Carson was well in the lead, Gibbs second and Buck Jenkins almost next to him as they were just a couple hundred yards from a pole with a fluttering banner marking the turn-back toward the start and finish line.

Shannon and his pony passed the last-place rider, then the next. They were neck and neck with two more.

At the turning point, Shannon wheeled his pony close to the pole and started back, leaving another horseman in his dusty wake.

Shannon tore past another rider, caught and passed Buck Jenkins, then Judd Gibbs, leaving only Carson ahead of him — far ahead.

Carson looked back in disbelief but felt he had it won. The race and the hundred dollars.

Carson's horse, a red Arabian stallion he called Colorados, was one of the biggest and strongest of its kind in Texas, measuring close to seventeen hands, with long sturdy legs and rippling muscles that bunched and stretched under his gleaming crimson coat.

But Colorados carried a hundred-eighty-pound rider who straddled a saddle that added another forty or fifty pounds.

Shannon had never been weighed but he likely tipped the scales at less than a hundred, and there was no saddle to burden his pony. He leaned closer to the flowing mane of the little animal. Both boy and pony were Kiowas again and Shannon urged the horse on in the language both of them understood. The pony's nose nodded up and down, his ears flattened and he clipped away even more ground.

None of the spectators had bet on Shannon and his pony because nobody knew that they would be in the race. But there was something so heroic about the effort of horse and rider, that more and more of those who watched the race began to cheer for him and even make some fast bets as to the outcome.

"Ride, Shannon, ride!" Glenshannon shouted. "Get him, lad!!"

"Don't let him catch you, Carson!" Hadley screamed. "Use your spurs!!"

"Come on . . . ," Heather yelled, ". . . come on, Shannon."

Hadley shot her a look of contempt commingled with disgust, and she stuck her tongue out at him.

46

"Shannon!" she repeated. "Shannon! Shannon!"

"Catch him, boy," Pepper yelled. "Catch him!"

"He will," Hannah added confidently.

Shannon gained ground until he pulled alongside Carson and the pounding Arabian. Carson whipped his long, leather reins across the back of his horse's neck and dug his spurs again and again into Colorados's flanks.

Shannon just loose-reined his pony and kept talking Kiowa to the incredible little animal, who responded by taking the lead, forging ahead by a nose, a neck — then a length, two lengths, then three.

Carson's face was grim and desperate. He was spurring, yelling and whipping, but his horse fell farther and farther behind.

With a hundred yards to go, Shannon was almost ten lengths ahead but his horse hit a gopher hole, tumbled and crashed with a terrible, sickening impact.

Heather screamed, turned away, and burrowed her head into her father's side as he put an arm around her.

A dirgelike silence fell across the rest of the spectators — all except Hadley.

"Carson!" Hadley jumped off the ground

and yelled again and again. "Carson! Carson!"

Shannon rolled over on the ground where he fell, and looked for his pony, who lay snorting in pain as Carson raced past them and across the finish line.

The rest of the horsemen veered away from Shannon and the pony as Glenshannon and Pepper ran toward the fallen forms on the ground.

Shannon staggered to his feet, rubbed the dirt out of his eyes and off his face, made his way to the pony and knelt beside it.

He touched the animal's head. The pony's eyes were afire with pain, his mouth frothing and twisted.

Shannon Glenshannon knelt close to the boy and pony. Slowly he pulled his gun from its holster, looked at Shannon and then at the shuddering animal.

"No," Shannon said.

"I'm sorry, lad," the big man replied. "It's got to be done."

"I know . . . my father gave him to me . . . I call him Pony That Flies . . . I'll do it."

There was a pause. Glenshannon nodded. He handed the boy the gun, rose and walked away as Shannon patted Pony That Flies.

From a distance Glenshannon stood and watched and heard the sound of a gunshot.

He waited until the boy approached and stood next to him.

There were no tears in Shannon's eyes, but they were elegy eyes. He held out the gun.

Glenshannon took it. Shannon walked away. The big man holstered his gun and followed.

Shannon walked past Heather without looking at her and did not reply when she spoke.

"I . . . I'm sorry, Shannon."

As Glenshannon put his arm around Heather, Hadley appeared and stood next to them.

"Father . . ."

Glenshannon looked at his son.

"You owe me a pocket knife," Hadley said.

Chapter Six

In the two days and nights since the race, Shannon hadn't spoken a word. He either nodded or shook his head, no more than he had to, when anyone asked him a question or tried to make conversation, but he made no audible sound.

He came to the dinner table but did not eat.

He slept outside.

Shannon Glenshannon had paid Carson the hundred-dollar prize money.

"I'm sorry, boss," Carson had said, "things turned out the way they did. I don't feel proper takin' the money. Why don't you give it to the boy?"

"He wouldn't take it," Glenshannon replied.

"Suppose we split it?"

"Money doesn't mean anything to the lad. But you're a good man, Carson. I'll tell him of your offer."

Glenshannon had also paid off his bet to

Hadley, who had no qualms about accepting.

After the third breakfast that Shannon did not eat, Pepper lit up a cigar, blew about a half dozen smoke rings while Heather and Hannah left the table, then looked at Glenshannon, who was finishing his third cup of coffee.

"I'm worried."

"About what, Pepper?"

"About that boy. I've heard some Indians have been known to deliberately starve themselves to death."

"In the first place, he's not an Indian."

"Does he know that?"

"In the second place, you just made that up."

"Maybe I did, but I'm still worried that he's gonna do somethin' like . . ."

"Like what?"

"I don't know . . . maybe run away."

"On foot?"

"Well . . . he's liable to . . . to . . ."

"What?"

"I don't know . . . maybe steal a horse."

"I've got a better idea."

"You have?"

"I have."

"Well . . ."

"Well, what?"

"It's about time."

51

★ ★ ★

Hadley sat on the stoop of the front porch whittling on a piece of birch with his new knife.

Heather walked out from the doorway holding an apple in each hand. Hadley didn't speak to her and she said nothing to him as she moved past and toward the corral and Shannon, who was looking through the rail at a remuda of horses inside the enclosure.

When she walked up beside him, she took a bite out of one apple and extended the other toward him.

"Hello, Shannon."

No answer.

"Would you like an apple?"

He barely shook his head.

"You haven't eaten anything since . . . Shannon, you ought to eat something. You're just skin and bones to begin with . . . you hear me?"

No answer.

"Are you ever going to eat again?"

No answer.

"Are you ever going to talk again . . . in your whole life?"

Silence.

"Okay, then. But this apple is delicious. Let me know if you change your mind."

Glenshannon walked out of the front door followed by Pepper.

Hadley stood up, still holding the knife.

"Oh, Father . . ."

"Yes, what is it, Hadley?"

"I just wanted to thank you for the knife. I didn't expect a John Henry — that's the best knife made."

"That's why I gave it to you."

"Oh, and I just wanted to ask you something."

"Go ahead."

"What would you have wanted me to give you if I'd lost?"

"Maybe you'll know . . . someday."

"I . . . I don't understand."

"Maybe you will . . . someday."

Glenshannon started off, followed by Pepper, who turned back to Hadley.

"I don't think so," Pepper said as he gimped away, blowing smoke from the cigar.

Heather took another bite of the apple and waved as Glenshannon and Pepper approached the corral.

"Hello, Father."

"Hello, darlin'." Glenshannon smiled. "Looks like you've grown awfully partial to apples."

"This one" — she held up the apple still in

her left hand — "I offered to Shannon but he doesn't want it. He won't eat anything or say anything."

"Is that so?" Glenshannon frowned.

"You know it is. Go ahead, Father, try to make him say something."

"Oh, I don't think I will, but Shannon" — he looked at the boy, who continued to gaze straight ahead at the horses in the corral — "Shannon, it occurs to me that you can't be of much help around here on foot. You'll be needin' a horse."

Shannon turned and looked up at the big man, who was smiling.

"You said your father gave you a horse. Well, your new father's going to give you a new horse."

By now Hadley had approached and could hear what Glenshannon was saying.

"Take your choice of any one in the corral."

"Any one?" Shannon spoke for the first time.

"Point him out and he's yours."

"The black," Shannon said without hesitating. He pointed at his choice — little more than a yearling, indigo-black and spirited, green-broke. "The black," he repeated.

Glenshannon laughed.

"Does that mean I can't have him?" Shannon asked.

"It means . . . that you know your horse-flesh, lad."

"Father." Hadley stepped between the two Shannons.

"What is it, my boy?"

"That's the best horse of the lot."

"Sure . . . and that's why he picked him."

"But that's the horse I was going to pick. It's not fair."

"You got the best knife. He got the best horse." Glenshannon smiled. "Seems fair enough."

"But I want him. He's mine!"

"No, he's not. I told Shannon he could have his choice and he's chosen. Besides, that's too much horse for you."

"But not for him?!" Hadley pointed with his knife at Shannon.

"I don't think so, not after that race." He turned toward the boy, who was still gazing at the black in the corral. "But Shannon, I've got to point some things out about that nipper you picked."

"What?" There was apprehension in the boy's voice, afraid of what he was going to hear.

"He's a lot different than that little pony you had. This fellow's going to be big . . .

55

maybe bigger than Carson's horse. This one's shod and you'll have to learn to saddle ride. Looks to me like a one-man horse. You think you can be that man? Groom him. Train him, take care of him. You think you can, lad?"

Shannon nodded.

"Then he's yours." Glenshannon put out his right hand.

Shannon didn't understand the gesture.

"This seals the bargain." Glenshannon placed the boy's right hand into his own. "When we shake hands the deal is done and done."

They shook hands — the boy as vigorously as he could.

"Why don't you go and shake hands with your horse?" Glenshannon nodded toward the black and grinned.

Shannon started through the fence of the corral, but stopped. He turned back, took the uneaten apple from Heather's hand and stepped into the corral.

As Shannon entered, the horses took notice and reacted. Some of the horses retreated, some moved off to the side along the fence. The black didn't move. He stood his ground and leveled his wide-set eyes as Shannon approached, not fast, not slow, but steady.

Then the black's head bobbed and the muscles in his strong young body bunched and loosened. His right hoof pawed at the ground and his broad head twisted just a bit, with gleaming eyes still aiming at the boy who now stood directly in front of him.

The animal was nothing but black. From head to hoof. From nose to tail. Not a spot or mark on him. Black as ten feet down.

The boy took a bite of the apple. Then another.

As he chewed, Shannon extended his hand and the apple, stopping just an inch from the horse's mouth and nostrils.

The black took a sniff, then a bite.

Shannon gently placed what was left of the apple into the animal's mouth and patted his head.

Horse and boy looked at each other and chewed.

Glenshannon, Heather, Pepper and Hadley all stood at the corral fence and watched. By then Hannah had also come outside, walked to the corral and stood next to the group.

So did a half dozen cowhands, including Carson.

"I'll tell you one thing, boss," Carson said.

"What's that?"

"Some time from now, I wouldn't want to race against them two."

"They look wonderful together," Heather said and smiled.

"Just what the boy needed," Pepper added.

But Hadley had the last word.

"I hope the little beggar breaks his neck."

Chapter Seven

There's nothing as good for the inside of a man as the outside of a horse

The old saying was true enough in the case of Shannon and Black. That was the horse's new name.

And no horse was ever better cared for and no boy was ever happier.

In the months that followed there were many changes in the country and at Glenshannon Hall.

Nine years after General Antonio Lopez de Santa Anna overwhelmed the Alamo, which had been under the command of Lt. Colonel William Travis and Jim Bowie, and then was himself overwhelmed by Sam Houston, who commanded a much smaller force than Santa Anna's at the Battle of San Jacinto, Mexico and the United States went to war.

Actually, it was the United States who went — went into Mexico after an American contingent of sixty-three was ambushed near Nueces when the Mexican army crossed the Rio Grande and attacked.

Both countries were looking for an excuse to fight and the United States was looking for a way to extend its borders.

The House and Senate authorized President Polk to go to war and President Polk authorized General Zachary Taylor to go to Mexico with an army that included a detachment of Texas Rangers led by Captain Jack Hays.

Taylor invaded from the North and won a string of victories in a succession of bloody encounters.

President Polk then put General Winfield Scott, hero of the War of 1812, in command of an army of 12,000 men. They landed near Vera Cruz with orders to take that port, fight their way to Mexico City and force Santa Anna to surrender.

It would take until February 2, 1848, and the Treaty of Guadalupe Hidalgo, to officially terminate resistance and hostilities. In the meantime, there was an outpouring of gunfire and blood — from the successful siege of Vera Cruz to the 260-mile march toward Mexico City and the battles of Buena Vista, Cerro Gordo, Jalapa, Contreras, Churubusco, El Molino, and Chapultepec, where on September 14, Mexico City's mayor surrendered to General Winfield Scott while a band of dragoons played "Yankee Doodle Dandy."

The United States was further along the way to its Manifest Destiny.

Captain Jack Hays and his Texas Rangers had played an important part in the victory over Mexico and now the Rangers were back across the Rio Grande and home in Texas. Four of Glenshannon's hands had joined up, including Buck Jenkins, the foreman. Two came back. Buck Jenkins didn't and Carson became foreman.

Shannon had known little or nothing about these events when his world was with the Kiowas. When they came to an end, his world was Glenshannon Hall. And in that world he was thriving.

It was hard to tell who was thriving more — Shannon or Black.

Both were gaining weight, height and muscle. Since the race, all the cowboys on the ranch looked at the boy with growing respect — and not just because he could ride. He was eager to help in any way he could. If a feisty cow ran away from the herd, it was Shannon on Black who, with some fancy maneuvering, got the rascal back. Shannon would lend a hand wherever and whenever needed.

Heather looked on him with pride, Pepper with satisfaction, Hannah with confidence, Glenshannon with gratification, and Hadley with smoldering jealousy.

There wasn't anything the interloper couldn't do better than the older boy, heir to Glenshannon Hall and all that went with it.

Hadley continued to be caustic and demeaning in his treatment of Shannon, but never in the presence of his father.

He would lie awake some nights fantasizing schemes — all ending unhappily for Shannon and the horse that should have belonged to him.

Some day he would take revenge. On the boy, the horse, or both.

But Hadley was nobody's fool. He wouldn't risk doing anything that could be blamed on him. Now more than ever, he had to cultivate his father's appreciation and good will. He recalled a line he had read from Shakespeare: "Smile and smile, and be a villain."

Midafternoon seemed more like dusk. Dark clouds rolled across the painted sky and drifted east.

The searchlight of the sun did its best to break through the heavy sky but failed to penetrate the moving veil clinging above the Texas landscape.

Shannon had started out riding Black to nowhere in particular, but after a time he began to realize that nowhere in particular was turning out to be in the direction of Ghost Canyon.

And as he rode he had the feeling that he was not alone, that he was accompanied by some unseen presence — ahead, above, or behind him. He looked behind and could see no one — above, only the troubled sky, and ahead, the mouth of Ghost Canyon.

While he vowed he would never say the name, he couldn't help thinking of Seccoro and of Seccoro's tribe — and of Running Bear. The memory of his Kiowa days would always be with him, and especially his memory of Seccoro.

But other events had begun to crowd his mind with more recent memories, and while the Kiowa days would never completely disappear, they were already beginning to fade.

He would not jar those fading memories back into focus by visiting Seccoro's grave. Shannon decided to turn and ride toward Glenshannon Hall and his new life — and as he did he saw her.

A couple hundred yards away, Heather sat astride her pony, Buttermilk. She seemed tiny, as if he were looking through the wrong end of a telescope.

Shannon galloped toward her and reined Black in alongside.

"Hello, Shannon." She smiled.

"Hello? What do you mean, hello?"

"What else could hello mean, except hello?"

"What *I* mean is what are you doing way out here all alone?"

"But I'm not all alone. I'm with you."

"You weren't with me . . . not up until now."

"Yes, I was. You just didn't know it. And I thought all Indians were so . . . so . . . what's that word? Perceptive, yes, that's it, perceptive about things like that."

"Things like what?"

"Like being followed."

"I had things on my mind."

"What kind of things?"

"You ask a lot of questions."

"Well, you don't give many answers."

"Your father's going to be awful mad when he finds out."

"Finds out what?"

"That you rode out all this way alone."

"But I told you . . . I'm not alone. . . ."

"Don't start that again . . . what're we going to tell him?"

"What I always tell him, the truth."

"I don't want him to blame me."

"If I tell him the truth, he can't blame you."

"Well, we'd better start back. It still looks like it might rain."

"Okay, but I want to show you another way back."

"Is it shorter?"

"It's better."

"Better in what way?"

"You'll see. Follow me. Okay?"

"Okay, I guess. You've been following me long enough."

"Not *this* close." She smiled.

It didn't rain.

They rode back for over half an hour.

"Why did you follow me?"

"Because I wanted to see where you were going."

"Why?"

"Just curious."

"Don't do it again unless you tell me."

"Why not?"

"Well, because . . . you might get lost."

"I won't get lost. I grew up around here."

"Oh, so now you're growed up."

"*Grown* up. And you know what I mean."

"I'd like to know what makes this way back better than the other."

"You'll see soon enough. As a matter of fact, you can see right now . . . look!" She pointed to the northwest. "Shannon, have you ever seen anything like it in all your life?"

Shannon hadn't.

Just over half a mile away, ripped up from the earth, was a bleak and desolate rock formation, jagged, and jutting black out of the brown, harsh ground surrounding it. As if it had escaped upward from hell, cracked, then torn the earth's shell. In savage grandeur, it towered defiant and dominant over everything it surveyed.

Against the molten sky it looked like a black moon waxing or waning at the three-quarter mark, but with ridges and peaks — a sawtooth cradle, forbidding and dangerous.

"It's a magic place," Heather said. "Like in those stories I read to you . . . well, have you ever seen anything like it?"

"No." Shannon shook his head. "I haven't."

"Isn't it beautiful?"

"I'm not sure."

"What do you mean?"

"There's something about it that's . . ."

"That's what?"

"I don't know."

"You're not scared of it, are you, Shannon?"

"Of course not. What's there to be scared of? It's just a place. There aren't any dragons or monsters up there, like in your fairy stories."

"I don't know. I've never been up there."

"Well, why should you? Why would you want to go to such a place?"

"I don't know. Maybe because there's no other place like it."

"That's a dumb reason. What do they call that place?"

"Moon Rock."

"Moon Rock . . . Yeah, I can see why."

"Why don't we go up there together?"

"When?"

"Now."

"Are you crazy? What about your father?"

"What about him?"

"It's going to get dark pretty soon and he's going to be mad."

"He won't be mad at me . . ."

"I'm not worried about you. He'll be mad at me and I don't blame him."

"Will you promise to take me up there some other time? It'll be our magic place. Will you, Shannon?"

"Will you promise never to follow me again?"

"I'm not sure."

"Well, neither am I. Now let's get back."

He wheeled his horse and rode toward Glenshannon Hall.

Heather followed.

". . . 'Magic place,' " she heard him mutter.

Chapter Eight

"I was just about to send out a search party for the two of you," Glenshannon said.

They did get back before dark. Just before.

There were five people on the veranda waiting for them. Glenshannon, Pepper, Hannah, Hadley — and Carson, who was going to lead the searchers. Over a dozen hands were mounted near the stable.

Glenshannon, Pepper, Hannah and Carson were obviously relieved at the sight of the two youngsters.

Hadley did his best to mask his disappointment.

Not that he necessarily wanted harm to come to his sister — she was harmless. But if getting rid of the interloper meant losing her in the bargain, he would bear up with brotherly bravado. He would have preferred that Shannon had been bitten by a snake, scalped by Indians, or just run away, and that Heather had come back alone. But unfortunately, both of them were back without serious consequences.

In fact, Heather seemed content. Even more than content — pleased and happy.

Hadley hoped that his father would not be happy and would mete out harsh punishment to Shannon.

"Alright, Carson. You can call the men off."

"Yes, sir. And I'm glad everything turned out . . . the way it did."

"We all are," Glenshannon said.

He couldn't read Hadley's mind.

Carson headed for the stable, waving to the men to unsaddle.

"Alright, lad, you and I are going to have a serious talk." Glenshannon looked at Shannon. "I thought you had better sense than this."

"He does," Heather said as she dismounted. "Don't blame him. He left by himself. It was my idea to follow him and he was awful mad when I caught up with him over at Ghost Canyon."

"Awfully angry," Hannah corrected, her hand covering a smile.

"Ghost Canyon?" Glenshannon adjusted the brim of his hat. "What were you doing out that way?"

Shannon made no answer. Glenshannon understood, or thought he did.

"Well," he said, "it took the both of you long enough to get back."

"I had to show him something."

"You had to show him something?"

"That's right."

"What, may I inquire, was that?"

"Something you showed me . . . a long time ago. Remember? A magic place."

"Are you talking about Moon Rock?"

Heather smiled and nodded.

"Well, you'd better dismount, lad, and stable the horses. It's getting late. Hannah, is there anything for supper?"

"Dear Mister Glenshannon, may I remind you that you pay me to — among other things — supervise the kitchen where we have in our employment not one, but two full-time cooks to see to the culinary needs of this household?"

"Is that so?"

"That's so. And tonight for supper this household can ingest any and everything from soup to salad, chicken-fried steak to fried beefsteak, mashed potatoes to —"

"Alright, Hannah, I am duly reminded and chastised. Let's all clean up, have supper and thank God" — he looked at his daughter and Shannon, who now stood next to Heather — "that things all came right."

"Amen, brother," Pepper said.

71

But things hadn't all come right. Not for Hadley.

After supper they all sat in the great room, warmed by yellow and blue flames dancing upward from the huge stone fireplace into the chimney draft.

Glenshannon smoked his pipe, Pepper a cigar. Hannah was knitting by rote and thinking of only she knew what. Hadley sat on a miniature version of his father's chair, staring at the flames, silent and sullen. For the time being, he had forgotten the advice he had gleaned from Shakespeare — to smile and smile. Heather and Shannon sat on the floor playing a game of checkers. One of Heather's kings jumped Shannon's last two checkers and the game was over. Neither Shannon nor Heather said a word about the outcome, which was the same as most of the other checker games they had played.

"Father." Heather looked up toward Glenshannon. "Tell us about it."

"About what?"

"About the magic place."

"Moon Rock? You've heard all about it before."

"Shannon hasn't."

"Well, *I* have — and who cares?" Hadley said, still looking at the fire. "It's just a big pile of ugly rocks."

"It is *not,* Hadley," Heather exclaimed. "It's beautiful."

"Well, I guess it all depends on how you look at it," Glenshannon said. "There's an old saying: 'Beauty is in the eye of the beholder.' "

"How do you behold it, Father? You own it," Heather asked.

"I'm not so sure . . ."

"About how you behold it?"

"No — whether I own it."

"What do you mean?"

"Well, the old Spanish land grant was a little vague about that part of the boundary."

"Oh, you must own it, Father. I'm sure you do."

"If he does," Hadley said, "you can have my share of it, little sister."

"I'm not sure anybody owns it." Glenshannon puffed on his pipe. "Or ever did — oh, maybe a long time ago, some lost tribe worshiped or even lived there."

"Worshiped those rocks?" Hadley grunted.

"Well, in a way," Glenshannon said, "it does sort of look like the remnants of a great cathedral."

"Not to me," Hadley grunted again.

"No, I guess it wouldn't, Hadley. It's been said that Moon Rock has been struck by lightning more times than any other place on earth. The Indians thought it was the gods talking to them. They went up there to perform sacrificial blood rites. It was a secret meeting place for young braves and maidens, and sometimes a burial place with unmarked graves of those who had broken tribal law. And so, like many other places and people, it all depends on how you look at it — or *want* to look at it."

"I don't want to look at it at all," Hadley said. "Or go anywhere near it."

"I do." Heather beamed. "Will you take us there sometime, Father?"

"And whom do you mean by *us*?"

"Shannon and me, who else? Will you?"

"Shannon, would you like to go there?" Glenshannon asked.

The boy just shrugged.

"Of course he would. You should have seen the look on his face when he first saw it."

"I remember the first time we went up there," Pepper said. "Don't you, boss?"

"Never mind."

"Tell us about it, Pepper, please," Heather urged.

"We was trailin' a couple of would-be horse thieves who decided to make a stand there."

"What happened?" Heather asked.

74

"Oh, they're buried up there along with them other Indian lawbreakers."

"You mean you killed them?" Hadley sat forward.

"It come down to them or us. Killin' 'em wasn't as hard as buryin' 'em, up there in them rocks . . . but we got both jobs done, didn't we, boss?"

"It sounds like a lovely spot for a picnic," Hannah said, and kept knitting. "You want me to fix a basket for next Sunday, Mister Glenshannon?"

"Would you, Hannah?" Heather smiled.

"I was only joking, child, for heaven's sake!"

"Oh . . ." Heather was disappointed, but persisted. "Well, would you take us up there sometime, Father?"

"Maybe. When you're a little older."

"Next month?"

"Maybe next year."

"You hear that, Shannon?"

Shannon nodded.

Hadley wished the three of them would go up to Moon Rock and that the gods would talk and lightning would strike — at least one of them.

Chapter Nine

There were still some lanterns lit within Glenshannon Hall. Outside, the buildings were illuminated by a hunter's moon. Most of the hands were asleep or at least in a horizontal position.

Early to bunk, early to rise.

Activity would begin with first light and the clarion call of Caesar, the red rooster, announcing that it was time to commence with the work scheduled for the day.

The German grandfather clock in the hall had just struck ten times and all the occupants were in their beds. All except one.

It was a ritual with Shannon. Every night before going to sleep he would pay a visit to the stable, say goodnight to Black and bring him a snack. An apple, a couple of carrots or a handful of sugar. Shannon would light one of the lanterns, stroke the horse's neck or flank and brush away any speck of dirt he might have missed when he had curried the animal earlier.

Sometimes he would whisper things, thoughts he couldn't, or wouldn't, express to humans during the day. Thoughts about his benefactor, Shannon Glenshannon. About Heather and Pepper, whom he liked more and more . . . and about Hadley, whom he liked less and less.

For some reason he couldn't look at Hadley without thinking of Running Bear. Hadley was not nearly as deadly or dangerous, but there was that same smoldering look in his eyes.

Shannon continued to whisper to Black. The other horses in the other stalls didn't seem to mind. Most of them stood sleeping and occasionally snorting.

Otherwise all was quiet. But at the next moment, Shannon heard something and turned.

Pepper stood just inside the stable, a rifle in one hand and an oil cloth in the other.

"Hello, boy."

"Pepper."

"Tuckin' Black in for the night?" Pepper said.

Shannon shrugged and patted the horse's neck.

"I see you come in every night."

Pepper didn't sleep in the main house, although Glenshannon had time and again invited him to take one of the spare rooms.

"Nope. I like it where I am," Pepper always replied.

Where he was, was in the bunkhouse nearest the main building, but not in a room with the other cowboys. Pepper had two good-sized rooms, well-furnished with items accumulated over the past twenty years or more, including an impressive collection of artillery.

Everything from eighteenth-century dueling pistols to Colt Dragoon revolvers, from Hawken rifles of the early frontier to the newest Spencer seven-shot rifle, which he held in his hand.

"I never saw that gun before." Shannon pointed to the Spencer.

"Just got it. The boss ordered one for himself and one for me. I was just wipin' it clean. Do it every night . . . just like you do with your horse."

"Can I see it?"

"You're lookin' at it, aren't you?"

"No, I mean can I hold it?"

"I 'spose." Pepper handed Shannon the rifle. "But be careful, boy. It's loaded."

Shannon turned the rifle over, admiring the gleaming barrel, the breech made of shiny golden brass, and the handcrafted wooden stock. He lifted the Spencer to his shoulder and pointed it up toward a beam in the ceiling of the stable.

"I come in here because there's somethin' I wanted to mention to you. . . ."

Pepper was about to say that he just wanted to make sure that Shannon would not take Heather alone to Ghost Canyon, or Moon Rock or any other far place unless somebody older and abler was with them. Heather was the apple of the boss's eye and — he had prepared the speech and was about to make it, but he never did.

There was a terrifying sound, then sounds.

Frenzied, shrill, skirling. A shattering cacophony from outside.

Animals. Not just hogs, chickens and goats snorting, cackling and croaking, but a savage, screaming, life-and-death clash.

Shannon, still carrying the rifle, ran out of the stable with Pepper gimping after him.

The cougar had already torn the throat from Lucky, and the dog lay dead on the ground. The supple beast, now with a fat hen in his jaws, vaulted over the chicken coop fence and sprang with leaping, supple strides directly toward Shannon, who stood in its path.

Shannon swung the Spencer to his

shoulder, cocked the lever and fired again and again — three times.

The first shot missed. The second and third shots found their marks: the cougar's shoulder and then his head, where the bullet lodged in his brain. The cougar dropped, quivered, then lay motionless with the mangled chicken in its bloody, gaping jaw.

Lanterns were lit inside the main building and the bunkhouse. People streamed out of both places, some of them carrying guns and rifles, and most of them dressed in whatever they slept in.

Suddenly a sheet of silence fell over the moon-splayed ranch.

Silence and stillness.

Nobody spoke, nobody moved. Not the animals in the pens, corrals, barns, stables, or on the grounds — and not the people.

For that moment, death had called a halt to everything and everybody and only the smell of death prevailed.

But only for a moment.

Carson, Gibbs and Carey all approached the lifeless cougar to make sure that it was lifeless.

Almost simultaneously, Gibbs's boot pressed against the cougar's leg and the point of Carson's rifle nudged its shoulder.

Limp and lifeless.

Then there were murmurs and stirrings — the assembled cowboys looked from the cougar to the boy with the rifle, and to Pepper.

"You mean to tell me," Carson gawked at Pepper, "that this little shaver shot and killed that panther all by hisself?"

"You don't see Dan'l Boone around here, do you?" Pepper smirked.

"That cat weighs more'n he does!" Gibbs scratched his head.

Glenshannon, Heather, Hannah and Hadley all stood close together, all in their nightclothes, but Glenshannon held a revolver in one hand. He reached out with the other and touched Shannon's shoulder.

"Are you alright, lad?"

Shannon nodded.

"What happened, Pepper?"

"Well, you see, folks, we was inside the stable where I was teachin' this here boy the fundamentals of firin' a rifle, when we heard the ruckus out here, so we run out and the boy applied the lessons I had just taught him to that there thief in the night lyin' dead right over there . . . and that's about the long and short of it — ain't that so, boy?"

"Yeah, I'll just bet." Gibbs snickered.

"You doubtin' my say-so, Gibber?"

"Hell no, Pepper. Sounds logical — logical as hell."

All this time Heather avoided looking at the dead cougar and was trembling.

"You'd better get her inside, Hannah," Glenshannon said. "We'd better all get inside . . . but first you two" — he pointed at Carson and Carey — "you two drag that carcass out of here and cover it with somethin' 'til we can bury it in the morning — along with ol' Lucky."

"Yes, sir," came the double reply.

"You're sure you're alright?" Glenshannon looked at Shannon again.

And again Shannon nodded. He looked from the big man to Pepper.

"Can I keep it?" Shannon asked.

"The rifle?" Pepper said.

"No. The pelt." He pointed to the cougar that was being dragged away.

"Don't know why not, lad." Glenshannon smiled. "We'll have it skinned for you."

"I'll skin it," Shannon said.

"By yourself?" Glenshannon asked.

"Why not?" Pepper remarked. "He shot it by hisself. Gimme back my rifle, boy."

Shannon handed Pepper the rifle and smiled for the first time that night.

"Be careful," Shannon said, "it's loaded."

They all laughed. All except Hadley.

Fate had brought forth an instrument of danger, this time in the form of a deadly cougar, that could have eliminated the interloper.

Once again the interloper had prevailed.

Chapter Ten

Lucky was buried. So was the cougar — but skin naked.

Some of the cowboys, including Pepper, had watched as Shannon went to work on the carcass with a flensing knife.

Living with the Kiowas, the boy had skinned other animals, or had helped to skin them. Rabbit, raccoon, goat, antelope, steer, even buffalo. But never before a cougar. He went about it silently and efficiently while the cowboys looked on.

"What the hell is it," said Gibbs, pointing to the place nearby where Lucky was buried, "that prompts a mangy, half-blind, crippled, flea-bitten cur to stand up to the fang and claw of a prowlin' panther? That damn fool dog could've just run away and let that cat have its supper."

"Maybe," Pepper said, "it's the same thing as prompts a boy to stand up to that same cat, with a rifle, while it's leapin' at him with that same fang and claw . . . you ever think of that, Gibber? Some call it guts."

"That ain't what I call it," Gibbs said. "I call it crazy."

"That's why I'd rather cross the river with that boy than with you," Pepper said.

"You two can cross whatever you want. Me, I'm goin' to work." He pointed to the hillside in the distance with the oak tree and marble tombstone where a figure knelt at the graveside. "Boss'll be back pretty soon," Gibbs added. "Wouldn't do for him to see us all standin' around jawin'."

Shannon Glenshannon placed the cactus rose at the head of the grave.

"Well, Marni, my darlin', we had us some more excitement last night. And it had to do with that young boy I've been tellin' you about. He acquitted himself well. You would've been proud of him. Just as if he had been our own son. I wish I could always say the same about our son, Hadley. I try to see you or me when I look at him, but mostly I see a stranger.

"It's not like looking at Heather, she's you all over again, Marni. Of course, she hasn't got your red hair, but she's got your blue eyes and the way you tilted your face and looked at me — she does that too, when she's surprised or disappointed or pleased. Sometimes it's hard to tell which. But she's smart like you, beautiful, independent, sassy sometimes, but always loving and . . . well, she's you all over again. You gave your life when she was born, but you go on living — here and in heaven.

"I love you, Marni."

The cougar pelt, a gleaming, burnished, lustrous bronze in the sun, was tacked up on the side of a barn to stretch and dry.

Pepper had helped Shannon with that part of the procedure.

Heather had stayed away, as far away as she could, during the bloody business of skinning the carcass, but now that the pelt was detached and stretched, she decided to take a look. And so did Glenshannon, who held her hand as they approached Shannon, Pepper and the pelt.

"Well, lad" — Glenshannon smiled and pointed to the pelt — "I see you got it done."

"And he done it by hisself," Pepper said. "I just helped him hang it up."

Glenshannon nodded. "It's beautiful," he said. "Isn't it, Heather?"

"Well . . ." Heather tilted her head slightly and looked at it like it was a painting hanging on a wall, trying to make up her mind about it. ". . . I'm not sure."

"What're you going to do with it,

Shannon?" the big man asked.

"I don't know . . . anymore."

"What do you mean, *anymore?*"

"I know what I was going to do with it . . . but now I'm not sure."

"Why not?"

"Because" — Shannon looked at Heather — "I don't know whether she'd want it."

"You were going to give the pelt to Heather?" Glenshannon smiled.

"Thought she might put it on the floor of her room, but . . ."

Heather's eyes opened even wider, looking at the pelt — looking at it now in a different light.

"Well, Heather, what do you say?" Glenshannon nodded toward the pelt.

"What does she say about what?" Hadley inquired as he approached.

"Shannon just offered the cougar pelt to Heather as a gift." Glenshannon smiled.

"Good God! I'd sooner have a —"

"Never mind what you'd sooner," Glenshannon said. "He didn't offer it to you. Well, what do you say, Heather? Do you want it? Because if you don't . . ."

"I want it! I want it! I'll put it in my room and keep it always — and think about how brave Shannon was. Please, Shannon, may I have it?"

Shannon nodded.

"In our family," Glenshannon said, "it's customary when we receive a gift to give a gift in return."

"But I don't have anything like that to give him. . . ."

"Why don't you give him one of your dolls?" Hadley grinned.

"That's enough, Hadley," the big man said. "You'll see, Heather. It doesn't have to come from you, but from our family. We'll think of something."

"I got an idea I'll toss out to you later, if it's okay with you, boss."

"That's fine, Pepper. And in the meantime, if you three young ones want to go for a ride — a short one, mind you, no farther than Willow Creek — why, go ahead and give your horses some exercise."

"No, thanks, Father," Hadley said. "I've got better things to do than waste time with children." He turned and walked away.

"Well, what about it . . . 'children'? Do you have better things to do?" Glenshannon asked.

"I don't." Heather smiled.

"You, Shannon?"

"I'll saddle up the horses," Shannon said.

"I'll help you," Pepper remarked. "Matter of fact, I just might ride along with you in Hadley's place. And maybe we'll take a couple fishing poles along with us."

Willow Creek ran through the Glenshannon ranch just about a mile from headquarters.

And just about an hour later Shannon and Heather sat along the south bank, each of them holding a fishing pole extended over the clear water flowing downstream.

Pepper sat on the grass, legs stretched out, his back leaning against a willow tree, smoking a cigar with his eyes nearly shut.

In just about anywhere else in the United Sates or most other places, Willow Creek would not have been called a creek — a stream, maybe, or tributary, or channel, or estuary or maybe even a river.

But this being Texas, where things and people were measured in different terms, it was considered just a creek.

In the short time that they had been there, Shannon seemed content to sit, looking at the string attached to his pole bending with the current, but otherwise inactive.

Heather did not seem at all content. She was pouting with impatience and waving the pole so that sometimes the end with the string attached would disappear beneath the surface of the water.

"Pepper!"

"What is it, girl?!" Pepper's eyes flashed open and the cigar nearly dropped out of his mouth.

"Are you sure that there are fish in this creek?"

"Just as sure as sundown."

"Have you ever seen any?"

"Yep."

"Have you ever *caught* any?"

"Yep."

"Without using a pole?"

"Sometimes. Why I recall the occasion when I was just sittin' here whistlin' — right here where I am now — and this ol' fish jumped out like a snake from a basket and landed right in my lap."

"Pepper!" she said. "I don't believe that."

"I've got a witness."

"Who?" Heather asked.

"Why, my horse. Same horse that's standin' right over there."

"Why don't you whistle one up for us right now?" Shannon said.

"Wouldn't be fair . . . wouldn't be teaching you two the fundamental principle of fishin'."

"What's that?" Heather asked.

"Patience."

"Patience?" she repeated.

"Patience." He nodded, and relit his cigar. "There's no shortcut to fishin'. You'll find that out as you grow older."

"I think," Shannon said, "we're going to grow a lot older before we catch any fish around here."

"Shannon," Heather asked, "have you ever caught fish in other places when you were living with . . . before you came here to Glenshannon Hall?"

"Sure. Lots of times. Only, Kiowas fish with spears."

"With spears? You mean you stabbed the fish?"

"I guess that's what you'd call it."

"Where?"

"Where what?"

"Where did you fish like that?"

"All over. Wherever we went and there was water."

"Did you travel very much?"

"Indians don't stay in one place very long, they keep moving."

"Why?"

"Why?"

"Yes. Why? Don't they have houses and stables and —"

"No. Most of the things they have, they can take with them. They go where the game is . . . where the weather . . ."

"And you traveled with them?"

"Of course."

"I've never traveled off Father's land."

"You haven't?"

"Why should I? We have everything we could ever want right here, or else father has it brought in. I don't see any reason to leave here as long as I live."

"What about school?" Shannon asked.

"Hannah teaches me. She knows everything."

"No, she doesn't."

"Everything I need to know. So I'll just stay right here."

"No, you won't, little lady." Pepper sat up and leaned forward from the tree.

"What makes you say so?"

"Well, because you are just a little lady. And as you grow older, you'll want to see other places and people. You'll want to get married and some Prince Charming will come along like in those stories you read and you'll leave here and go and live in his castle and raise a family."

"Why can't he live here?"

"Because that's not the way it's done. In the Bible, Ruth says to her husband,

'Whither thou goest, I will go. Whither thou lodgest, I will lodge. Your people will be my people.' "

"But what if I want to stay here with Father?"

"Well, in the first place, girl, your father's not going to live forever. Nobody does. And in the second place, when the boss is buried up there on the hillside next to your mother, all this will belong to Hadley . . . and things'll be different around here — a lot different, I suspect."

Heather sat frozen. In the last two minutes her entire future had changed as the import of what Pepper had said sank in.

And what he had said was meant as much for Shannon as it had been for Heather.

All their lives — even his in some ways — hinged on the mortality of one man.

Shannon Glenshannon.

In the months since his father gave first choice to Shannon, Hadley had been riding half a dozen horses trying to make up his mind which to choose.

By that afternoon he had narrowed the possibles down to two.

"Carson," Hadley asked, "which one would you pick?"

"That's not the point."

"What do you mean?"

"Well, one man's pick is another man's poison." He nodded at one of the two animals. "Now that Arab's got a lot of spirit and a lot of bottom. . . ."

"Is that the one you'd pick?"

"Maybe. But we ain't talking about me. A horse and a rider, they got to hit it off — be what they call compatible, have the same sort of outlook. You've ridden him. What do you think?"

"He rides well enough, but . . ."

"A little bumpy maybe?"

"Well, that wasn't the word I would've used but . . . yes."

"Now, that there gelding" — Carson nodded toward the other animal — "is one of the finest horses on this here ranch. Strong, intelligent, cooperative. He sure makes his rider look good."

"You think so?"

" 'Course, that's only one man's opinion. . . ."

"Thank you, Carson. I'll think it over."

"You bet." Carson walked away. He knew that Hadley had already made up his mind.

That night after supper, they were all sitting in their usual places in the great room and as usual a haze of cigar and pipe smoke added to the wood-burning scent of the fireplace.

Heather was unusually quiet and from time to time glanced over toward her father and recalled what Pepper had said that afternoon at Willow Creek.

"Your father's not going to live forever. Nobody does . . . when the boss is buried up there on the hillside next to your mother . . ."

Her mother's death held little meaning for Heather because she never knew her mother. She couldn't picture her mother alive. She couldn't picture her father dead. He meant everything to her.

She wanted to spring up and run to him. Put her arms around him and say, no, not say — beg. "Please, Father, don't die. Don't ever die. Stay here with us — with me — stay here forever."

"What's the matter, darlin'?" Glenshannon said. "You seem awfully pensive this evenin'."

"What does pensive mean, Father?"

"Oh, thoughtful — melancholy. What were you thinking about?"

"Oh, about something somebody said."

"Who? Hannah?"

"No."

"Shannon?"

"Not Shannon. He doesn't say much."

"Well, that just leaves Hadley, Pepper or me."

Pepper hoped that Heather wouldn't choose to quote what he had said about the boss's mortality and Hadley's inheritance. Maybe he shouldn't have said it. But it was too late to do anything about it except hope that Heather wouldn't repeat it now — or else change the subject before she spoke up.

"I meant to tell you somethin', boss," he said.

"What is it, Pepper?"

"Uh . . . well, come to think of it . . . it makes no never-mind."

"I've got something to tell you, Father," Hadley announced. "I've made up my mind."

"About what?"

"About my horse. I've picked it out."

"Good," Glenshannon said. "Which one?"

"The gelding. And I'm going to call him Bucephalus. That was the name of the horse that belonged to Alexander the Great."

"That's right, son," Glenshannon said. "He conquered the world on that horse."

"Well," Hannah remarked, "he died trying."

"I think you've made an excellent choice, my boy," Glenshannon said. "We all wish

96

you the best of luck with him. And now" —
he looked at Pepper, then at Shannon — "I
think it's about time, don't you, Pepper?"

"If you're thinkin' what I think you're
thinkin' then I think so."

Glenshannon rose and walked to the
gunrack against the stone wall. The rack
held nine rifles. A chain extended from one
end of the rack through the rifle trigger
guards to the other end — secured by a
strong lock.

Glenshannon removed a key from his vest
pocket, unlocked the chain and selected one
of the rifles.

"Shannon, come here."

Shannon rose and went to the big man.

Glenshannon had selected a seven-shot
Spencer, an exact duplicate of Pepper's rifle
that Shannon had used to kill the cougar.

"I said it's an old family tradition. A gift
for a gift. You gave Heather the pelt, and in
return our family presents you with this gift.
We already know that you know how to use
it. Take it, lad."

Glenshannon extended the rifle.

"I . . . I . . ." Shannon could not speak. His
eyes welled and his hand trembled as he
took the Spencer and tried again. "I . . .
I . . ."

"There's no need to say anything, lad. We

97

know how you feel. It was Pepper's idea. . . ."

"Yeah, boss," Pepper said. "But it's your gun."

"Not anymore. And there's a saddle boot that goes with it. You can have that tomorrow."

"I . . . I . . ." He still couldn't speak.

"I think," Heather said, her face now brightened, "I think he wants to thank you."

Shannon managed to nod.

"Be careful." Pepper grinned. "It's loaded."

"Well" — Glenshannon smiled — "I think it's the end of a pretty fair day. Hadley got his horse and Shannon got his rifle."

But Hadley didn't think it was a pretty fair day . . . at least not the end of it.

Chapter Eleven

Later that night, Shannon's Spencer leaned against a bale of hay as he fed a second carrot to Black and patted the horse on the neck.

When Black was finished chewing, Shannon walked to the nearby bench, sat, reached out and took hold of the rifle with both hands. He turned it over again and again as he had done with Pepper's rifle.

But this one was his, as Black was his. He had a place to live, and all the food he could eat — or wanted to eat. He didn't have to hunt for food and go hungry when there was no game to kill. If it was cold outside there was always a place here at Glenshannon Hall where it was warm.

And he thought of Seccoro's tribe, the way they lived, the way they struggled to live — and the way he had lived with them.

They were still out there, Running Bear and the rest of them — what was left of them. Could he ever live that way again — did he ever want to?

Could he ever be Tamonito again? Even if Seccoro were alive and Shannon Glenshannon were dead?

"What're you gonna do, boy? Sleep with that gun and that horse?" Pepper stood by the double-door entrance to the stable.

Shannon smiled and shook his head no.

Pepper walked to the stall across from Black and petted the muzzle of the gelding.

"Nice horse, ol' Alexander the Great picked. 'Course he don't near match up to yours."

"Who was he?" Shannon asked.

"Who was who?"

"Alexander the Great. Was he from Texas?"

"Nope. Some far-off country across the ocean."

"And did he have more land than . . ."

"Than who?"

"Heather's father."

"Oh, I reckon he did."

"It's hard to believe that anyone could."

"Well, nobody around here does."

"You know, Pepper, I find it easier to talk to you than to anybody else here."

"Well, boy, I take that as right friendly."

"Can I ask you something, Pepper?"

"Don't know why not."

"How did he come to get it? I mean, all this? Do you know?"

100

"Well, I ought to. I was with him when he done it. You want to hear about it?"

Shannon nodded.

Pepper sat on a bale of hay near the bench.

"Well, the tellin' of it calls for a good ceegar." He pulled a cigar from his pocket, then another one. "Have one yourself."

"I . . . I . . ."

"Now don't go to stutterin' again. Anybody old enough to own a rifle is old enough to smoke a good ceegar."

Pepper struck a match, lit his and then Shannon's.

"Now don't go swallowin' the smoke. Just let it roll around in your mouth and let it out gentle — like this."

When it came to smoking, Shannon proved to be a good pupil — and a good listener as Pepper told the story:

First time I seen him was at the Emporium, that was a saloon over in Gilead. It still is. I'd done a hitch with the Texas Rangers and was recoverin' from an encounter with a couple of waddies, one of which put a slug into my left shoulder shortly before he passed from this world on to the next. His companion decided to come along peaceable.

My left arm was still in a sling while I

was leanin' against the bar nibblin' on a drink and watching a high-stakes poker game.

There were six players in the game and more money on the table than there is in some banks.

The most colorful fella called hisself Franchot Dupree, wore a fancy hat and everything that went with it, includin' a pearl-handle pistol, more fit for a woman.

He also had more money in front of him than any of the other gents, and they all were gents — ranchers, a lumberman, a steamship owner and I don't know what else.

This Dupree, most of his mouth was on the left side of his face. He had hawk eyes and a narrow nose that almost drooped over his pink upper lip.

So, I was watchin' 'em. Mostly watchin' the Frenchman when he walked in. Big, good-lookin' fella, and he come up to the bar next to me. Even before he opened his mouth there was a lot about him that said Irish.

"Shannon Glenshannon," he said, and put out his hand. "Can I buy you a drink?" I took his hand and the drink. "Name's Pepper."

"How about buying me a drink? My

name's Cherrie." The pretty saloon girl spoke with a Creole lilt. She was young and didn't need all that war paint to go with her orange hair.

"Alright, Cherrie, just one."

He ordered the drinks and turned his attention to the game where the Frenchman had just gathered in a sizeable pot and was about to deal another hand.

Cherrie drank her drink, said thanks and approached another customer down the bar.

Glenshannon never took his eyes off the game. After a while one of the gents who no longer had any money in front of him got up from the table. "Well, that does it for me," the gent said and went out the door minus a couple of thousand.

"I'll see you, Pepper," Glenshannon said, and took a step toward the table.

"Just a minute, son," I said. "You ain't thinkin' what I think you're thinkin' — are you?"

"I wouldn't, mister." Cherrie was back. "Those boys don't play for marbles and chalk. I've seen a lot of card games in New Orleans, but this one . . ."

"Listen, son," I said, "I been watchin' that game and . . ."

"I been watching it, too, Pepper. And I

thank the both of you," he said to Cherrie and me, then moved away.

"That poor cooked calf," I remarked to Cherrie, and swallowed another whiskey.

"Is that chair open, gentlemen?" Glenshannon inquired.

It didn't take but a second or two for all the players to look up and qualify the questioner.

"This game ain't for jaspers," one of the players said, "and it takes cash to get an invite."

"Is a thousand in cash enough to get that invite?" Glenshannon removed a stack of bills from the shirt he had just unbuttoned.

"Sit down, stranger." The Frenchman smiled a crooked smile. "We play five-card draw, jacks or better to open."

Nobody bothered with introductions or small talk. They went right to work with the cards.

After about a half hour Glenshannon had at least doubled his poke. The Frenchman's pile also increased and the rest of 'em were suckin' eggs.

Glenshannon seldom went up against the Frenchman, who from time to time removed his hat, wiped with a handkerchief at his brow and the hatband, then went back to winning.

Well, it came down to this — the other players went bust and Glenshannon and Dupree each had over five thousand stacked in front of them.

At the time I had no notion as to how the immigrant could do so good against this kind of competition. I was to find out later on.

"Well, stranger," the Frenchman said, "it seems that you and I are the two survivors."

"So it seems."

"You have won a lot of money."

"So have you."

"I'm used to winning."

"I'd like to get used to it, myself."

"You can't do that — unless you keep winning. But to keep winning, you have to keep playing."

"Sounds logical — up to a point."

"The point is we can call it a day with two survivors and a healthy profit, or . . ."

"Or what?"

"Keep playing — until there is one survivor with a huge profit. What do you think, mon ami?"

For the first time Dupree went to French.

"It's your game, bucko." Glenshannon came back with an Irish term. "I'm just sitting in."

"Very good, but . . ."

"But what?"

"This could go on for a long time, unless . . ."

"Unless what?"

"One hand for the whole pot."

Dupree put the deck on the table.

"High card deals."

Glenshannon nodded and cut. A jack. Dupree drew a king, shuffled and started to deal. Nobody else in the Emporium moved or hardly even breathed. There'd never been a pot this size on the table. Maybe twelve thousand — one winner, one weeper.

Dupree dealt five to Glenshannon and five to himself. Each man read his hand.

"Cards?" the Frenchman asked.

"Two."

Dupree dealt.

"Dealer takes one."

He dealt himself a card, took off his hat, put it on the table, drew a handkerchief from his pocket, wiped his brow, then the inside band of his hat, put it back on and looked at his cards.

"Well, mon ami, for the pot what do you have?"

"Just a minute," the Irishman said. "You've two choices . . ."

"What are you saying?"

"I'm saying, you can fold without showing your hand or . . ."

"Or what?"

"Or play the hand that's in your hatband, because that's the hand I'm callin'. Take your choice."

You coulda' heard a feather fall. The air was heavy as paste and nobody budged.

"In that case . . ."

Dupree went for his pearl-handle pistol but he was already looking into the barrel of Glenshannon's cannon.

"Mine's bigger," Glenshannon said.

"Then I have no choice!"

He got up, and the son of a bitch sort of bowed to everybody, then started for the batwings.

The crowd commenced to stir and make some comments and as Dupree reached for the batwings with his left hand he drew that same pistol with his right hand again and whirled back toward the table.

"Look out," I hollered and cleared leather, but the Irishman was already ahead of both of us. His shot hit Dupree in the right side of the chest, and he dropped like a shot buffalo. His hat fell off and spilled out five cards.

"Is he dead?" somebody asked.

"Nope," somebody else answered.

"Couple of you carry him over to Doc

Swiezgood up the street," ordered Baldy, the owner of the Emporium. Evidently this wasn't the first time somebody layed flat and bleedin' on the Emporium's floor.

After they carted out the Frenchman I walked over and picked up the five cards. Cherrie tagged along.

Glenshannon was stuffing money into his pockets.

"Three deuces," I said.

"That left him one short," Glenshannon smiled.

"He's gonna have trouble dealing with that right arm." Cherrie also smiled.

"This is yours." Glenshannon handed her a hundred-dollar bill.

"What for?"

"For advising me not to get into the game."

"It wasn't very good advice."

"But you didn't know that . . . and you, Mr. Pepper . . ."

"Just plain Pepper and don't go offerin' me any money."

"How about a drink then?"

"That offer, I accept."

Well, sir, after that drink I didn't see him for about a week or so. I had just about recovered from that slug in the shoulder, thanks to Baldy's good whiskey, and was thinkin' about ridin' over to Ranger head-

quarters and signin' up for another hitch —
there wasn't but a few coins left in my purse
— when in he comes strollin' and smilin' like
he's just had a good breakfast.

I asked him what he'd been up to and he
said he'd like to show me somethin' if I had
some time. I allowed as how I had the time,
then I asked him if he'd made up his mind
what he was goin' to do with all that money
and he said he'd already spent it, or most
all of it.

As we rode along I asked him how he got
so good at cards. He said his father, Brian,
was a hard-workin' farmer all his life,
worked seven days a week and when he
died and was buried in the ol' sod, he was
still in debt. But Brian's brother, Tim, Shannon's uncle, never worked a day in his life
and lived in relative comfort all his days just
playin' cards at the pubs. Tim made sure
not to win so much that the losers would
quit playin' with him, but enough for all his
needs. He was a natural with numbers, had
nimble fingers that could deal seconds and
thirds and taught his nephew a few tricks
unbeknownst to Brian.

By the time Glenshannon was thirteen he
could count the cards at blackjack, by fifteen he was a poker master — but never
played for money while his father was alive.

He married his sweetheart, Maureen Dolan. They sailed to Boston where she was stayin' with relatives while he came west with just over a thousand dollars to make his fortune and send for her.

He pointed in the distance to what is now Glenshannon Hall and said, "There it is" — ten thousand dollars' worth of adobe, sticks, bricks and thousands of acres of land.

He'd just bought it from the widow of Don Miguel Alverez, Dolores, who wanted to return to her birthplace in Mexico, Tacatecas, and had left two days earlier.

Glenshannon had the deed to the old Spanish land grant the widow had signed over to him in his pocket.

He also had something else. Company.

Three caballeros stood on the porch of the otherwise deserted main building and ranch. They were armed with pistols in their holsters and one of 'em carried a rifle to boot.

Glenshannon introduced himself as the new owner.

"Not yet, señor, not until we get our share of the money."

"Who are you?"

"We are Don Miguel's brothers."

"The ranch belonged to his wife, and I bought it from her."

110

"We don't think so."

"This deed in my pocket thinks so."

"A thousand pesos apiece would do it."

"Got no pesos — or dollars — for you."

"Gold? Silver?"

"Just lead."

"We don't believe you."

"Ride away, Pepper," he said.

I didn't.

"So I guess we have to kill you and find out."

Two of 'em drew, the third one raised his rifle.

I shot one. Glenshannon shot one. And we both shot the other one. I stayed here instead of goin' back to the Rangers. And that's how Shannon Glenshannon come to own all this.

Pepper puffed on his cigar as he had been doing while telling the story.

Shannon hadn't taken a puff since Pepper's story began.

"And you've been here ever since?" Shannon asked.

"Not quite. I left for a spell back in '36 — met up with an old friend. We had a piece of work to do. When it was done, I came back."

Pepper rose and pointed to the Spencer still across Shannon's knees.

"You take care of that there rifle, boy, and it'll take care of you."

Shannon nodded.

"Well," Pepper said, "that's enough confabulatin' for tonight. See you in the mornin' — oh, I'll see that you get cartridges for that there thunder stick."

Pepper gimped out the barn door.

Shannon would never look upon either Glenshannon or Pepper in the same way again.

While living with the Kiowas, around the tribal campfire at night, he had listened to countless stories told time and again of the heroic deeds of dead Kiowa chiefs in long-ago encounters with other Kiowa chiefs or leaders from other tribes, or in battles with white enemies. About how they won victories and claimed hunting grounds.

But they were all like the stories Heather read about people in the distant past, people he never knew or saw.

Tonight he had heard the story of the place he was living at — and the people he was living with. Of the danger and death it took to acquire that place — and keep it.

No. He would never look upon either Glenshannon or Pepper in the same way again.

Chapter Twelve

What Pepper hadn't told Shannon — among other things — was that when he left the ranch for a spell back in '36, it was just after the massacre at the Alamo by Mexican forces led by General Antonio Lopez de Santa Anna — and the old friend he went to meet up with was Sam Houston.

In 1836, when Texas declared its independence from Mexico, Houston had been named commander in chief of the revolutionary forces. President Jackson had sent him to Texas to make peace with the Indians and, if necessary, war with the Mexicans.

That war became necessary when Santa Anna's army crossed the Rio Grande to teach subservience to the upstart Texans.

The Texans didn't want to be taught subservience or anything else by Santa Anna.

Houston needed time to organize his army. He ordered Colonel William B. Travis to buy him that time by defending the Alamo against the advancing Mexican army.

Travis and the Alamo defenders bought that time, but at a terrible and fatal price.

After thirteen bloody days came the final assault by 4,000 Mexican troops on March 6, 1836. All 183 Texans were killed but so were over 1,500 of Santa Anna's soldiers.

Santa Anna ordered the bodies of the Texans to be burned. But rising out of those flames came a battle cry: "Remember the Alamo."

Pepper responded to that battle cry by leaving Glenshannon Hall to join up with Houston, whom he had met and fought beside in an encounter with hostile Cherokees when Pepper was still a Texas Ranger.

"How are you, Pepper?" Houston offered his hand. "Figured you'd show up."

"You figured right, General," Pepper said as they shook. "What do we do first?"

"Retreat."

"How's that?"

"You said *first,* didn't you?"

Houston's army amounted to little more than scattered bands of settlers who had come to make a new start in Texas, but they were all anxious to fight and avenge the Alamo.

Too anxious — almost rebellious when Houston ordered retreat after retreat.

Pepper was not among the rebellious.

Pepper had faith that Sam Houston knew what he was doing — and how to do it at the opportune time and place.

That time and place was April 21, 1836, at San Jacinto, when Sam Houston, with Pepper at his side, led 800 Texans into one of the most significant battles of American history — a surprise attack that caught Santa Anna's army of more than 1,250 during their siesta, killing more than 600 and capturing the rest, including a bewildered General Antonio Lopez de Santa Anna.

And it was at San Jacinto that Pepper saved Sam Houston's life when Houston's horse was shot from under him and he was pinned beneath the animal. As a Mexican lieutenant raised his saber to make the kill, Pepper made his.

But in the battle Pepper received a wound in his left leg that left him with a limp for the rest of his life.

"Glad you showed up, Pepper," Houston said to him at the field hospital.

"Things was pretty dull around the ranch the last few months, general."

Pepper went back to Glenshannon Hall and Sam Houston went on to become the first President of the new Republic of Texas — and after Texas became the twenty-second state of the United States in 1845, he was elected to the nation's senate.

Another thing that Pepper didn't mention to Shannon was that every year since San Jacinto a courier arrived at Glenshannon Hall with a letter that always read just about the same — dated April 21.

Dear Pepper,

Another year has gone by and I'm still living and breathing.

I thank you. My wife thanks you. Our children thank you — and I reckon Texas thanks you.

As always,
Sam Houston

Chapter Thirteen

During the months that passed, in what was probably his thirteenth or fourteenth year — Shannon didn't know just what year he was born — he became a cowboy's cowboy. Pound for pound, the best cowboy on the ranch.

He could do, and did do, anything any other ranch hand was capable of doing. Rope and wrestle down calves, even steers, and brand them. Round up strays. He worked with Svenson, the blacksmith at Glenshannon Hall, and learned to fashion and nail on horseshoes. He had four legs and six hands and made music when he worked.

And when he wasn't working, he read, devouring book after book in Glenshannon's library. Mostly biographies, from Alexander the Great to Napoleon to George Washington. And the great authors and poets: Shakespeare, Milton, Johnson, Byron, Shelley, Keats. And sometimes in the great room by the fireplace, it was now Shannon doing the reading out loud while Heather and the others listened — all but Hadley.

"Lad," Glenshannon said early one morning, "Pepper and I are taking the buckboard into town on some business. How about coming along?"

"I don't think so."

"Oh, come on, lad, it's about time you saw some civilization."

"Isn't this civilization?"

"I mean a town with people besides cowboys — with streets, businesses, a bank . . ."

"And saloons," Pepper added.

"Come along, lad."

"If I come, can I bring my rifle?"

"You won't need it" — Glenshannon smiled — "but if that's what it takes, bring it."

South of the Red River and the Oklahoma Territory, west of the Sabine that separated Louisiana and Texas, and east of the Brazos that flowed toward Galveston and the Gulf of Mexico, Gilead sprouted in a patchwork of buildings, adobe and wood — once a part of Mexico, later the Republic of Texas and now a speckle in the United States of America.

The two-up buckboard hitched to a pair of matched whites rolled into Gilead while the sun was still on the rise. Pepper held the reins, Glenshannon sat next to him, and Shannon was on the floor of the buckboard leaning against one side — except now he was leaning forward wide-eyed, absorbing a setting he had never seen before.

He had read about villages, towns and cities, but this was the real thing, with real people going about their business on the boardwalks of both sides of Main Street.

Stores, shops, a hotel, a newspaper office, a sheriff station, a general store, a saloon, a barber shop, a combined livery stable–blacksmith shop housed in one barn-like building, and the most formidable structure — a brick edifice with a prominent, perfectly lettered sign.

FIRST NATIONAL BANK
OF
GILEAD
AMOS HIGGINS
PRESIDENT

Many of the citizens waved at the occupants of the buckboard and Shannon knew that the salutations were not meant for him but for the two occupants of the seat in front of him who both waved back or nodded at the parade of citizens.

Pepper pulled the buckboard to a stop near the bank, which was also not far from the Emporium Saloon.

Shannon jumped off, still holding the rifle, and reached onto the floorboard up front, lifted the anchor, attached it to one of the whites' bridles and let it drop on the street.

As Glenshannon and Pepper were debarking they both turned and reacted to a voice.

"Hello, strangers!" Cherrie emerged from the batwings of the Emporium and walked toward them grinning.

Since that fateful card game over twenty years ago, she had added some balast and bosom, her hair was an even more brilliant orange, but her face under the war paint was still bright and inviting.

"Hope you two don't mind being seen in public with a disreputable old saloon girl, but when I saw —"

"Cherrie," Glenshannon said, smiling. "You are more than likely the most reputable citizen in this benighted community and it's an honor to be seen with you anywhere." Both men removed their hats.

"Still have a bit of the blarney, I see, Mister Glenshannon. And Pepper, you're getting gray. I can give you something for that if you like." She looked at Shannon. "Who's this strapping specimen, your new foreman?"

"Not yet," Glenshannon said. "But he'll get there. Name's Shannon."

"That's a coincidence." Cherrie smiled.

"No, it's not." Glenshannon put his hat back on. "I've got some business with Amos Higgins but I'll come in afterward and have a drink. Understand you now own a piece of the place."

"That's right. It took twenty years but I've got twenty percent of the Emporium. At this rate I'll own the joint outright in another eighty years."

"How'd all that come about?" Pepper asked.

"Baldy started sitting in on his own poker games. Kept losing. My line of work is still paying off — if you can believe that — so I just kept nibbling in. How about you, Pepper? You got business with Banker Higgins?"

"Hell, no!"

"Shannon, you want to come with me to the bank?"

Shannon shook his head no.

"Well, you're not going into the Emporium, lad." Glenshannon smiled.

Shannon hopped onto the back of the buckboard, still carrying his rifle.

"Alright, you stay here and soak up some civilization; I'll be back in just a few minutes, lad."

"And in a few years, he's going to be a real heartbreaker," Cherrie said. "I pity the poor ladies."

She and Pepper strolled toward the Emporium and Glenshannon made his way to the bank.

"Amos," Glenshannon said to the overdressed, overweight, middle-aged president of the First National Bank of Gilead, "I've got some business to talk over with you if you've got the time."

"For our biggest depositor and best friend we've got all the time in all the clocks in town," Banker Higgins proclaimed.

As Shannon sat in the bed of the buckboard with the Spencer barrel pointed upward between his legs, looking from one side of the street to the other, the two Krantz brothers, Kurt and Burt, stood close by on the boardwalk watching him.

It was easy to discern that they were brothers because both had pig eyes and faces that went with the eyes. They were both oversized for their ages — fifteen and sixteen born nine months and ten days apart.

Kurt nodded to Burt, then they both swaggered over to the side of the buckboard.

"Who you, boy?" Kurt grunted.

"Never seen you before." Even their voices sounded the same.

Shannon didn't speak. He looked across to the other side of the street.

"Hey, you, boy, you look at your betters when they're talkin' to you — hear me?"

"Maybe he can't hear," Burt said. "Maybe he don't talk. Maybe he's a dummy."

"You a dummy, boy?" Kurt grinned. "Yeah, that's it, he's a dummy."

"What's a dummy doin' with a gun like that?" Burt pointed to the rifle. "I never seen a gun like that!"

"Hey, dummy." Kurt took a step closer to the wagon. "Let's take a look at that there gun. See how it hefts."

"Yeah." Burt made a fast move to grab the Spencer.

But Shannon moved faster.

He let the rifle fall into the bed of the wagon and leaped off flying onto both Krantzes.

All three landed on the ground and became a pinwheel of flailing fists, elbows and feet, punching, kicking and even biting.

Shannon drew first blood, knocking two front teeth out of Kurt's mouth and splitting the bone of Burt's nose. But Burt managed to pin back Shannon's arms while Kurt plunged his fist into Shannon's ribs, then face — until Shannon kicked Burt in the groin, wheeled and slammed Kurt against the side of the buckboard and ripped a right again and again into Kurt's distorted face until he dropped.

That's when Sheriff Joe Fox and a sizeable contingent of other citizens appeared — including Pepper, Cherrie, then Glenshannon and Amos Higgins.

"What the hell is goin' on here?" Sheriff Fox stood between the bleeding brawlers.

"He . . . he . . ." Kurt pointed at Shannon while rubbing his own crotch. "He's got a gun in that wagon and was pointin' it at us . . . gonna shoot us for no reason at all . . ."

"Not true," came a deep voice out of the crowd. The voice belonged to a thin, tall man dressed in a black frock coat with a flat-crowned hat. The voice seemed much too deep for his narrow chest. "I saw what happened."

"Well, then, tell us what happened, Reverend Groves," Sheriff Fox said.

"This young fellow was minding his own business when these two . . . bullies accosted him for no reason except that they are . . . bullies."

"That's good enough for me, Reverend," said Fox. "Now everybody go about your business, and you two" — the sheriff pointed to the brothers Krantz — "better go get some medical attention." He turned to Shannon. "You alright, son?"

"I'll say he's alright!" Cherrie smiled. "And then some!"

Shannon reached in and took hold of the rifle with one hand and with the other, wiped some leaking blood from his mouth.

"Well, lad," Glenshannonn chuckled, "I think you've seen enough civilization for one day."

Chapter Fourteen

By the time Pepper repeated — more than once — the episode involving Shannon and the events that occurred in Gilead, to the entire population of Glenshannon Hall, the episode had assumed more heroic proportions than any story ever recounted by any other recounter — with the possible exception of an ancient Greek named Homer.

The two Krantz brothers multiplied threefold and young Achilles emerged triumphant against the field of felled opponents.

Glenshannon smiled as Pepper related the encounter to Heather, Hannah and Hadley. Heather was enthralled, Hannah just a trifle skeptical, and Hadley just plain contemptuous. Like Achilles, the interloper had to have some spot of vulnerability — and someday Hadley would find it.

As good a shot as Shannon was with his rifle, he wanted to be even better. Rather than practice near the buildings at the ranch where he could be seen and the shots heard, he would ride a considerable distance away on Black, dismount, set up stick targets and fire away.

One warm, clear morning under an azure sky, he was doing just that, when two riders heard the shots and rode toward the sound of gunfire.

Shannon had stuck seven sticks into the ground. After seven fast shots, six of the seven were blown apart and the remaining target was nipped, but still stood.

He started to reload the Spencer when he heard the hoofbeats. Glenshannon pointed to the standing stick and smiled.

"Looks like you missed one, lad."

Shannon shrugged.

"I would've missed more than that — and so would anybody else on the ranch." The big man grinned.

Shannon smiled.

"Shannon?" Heather asked. "Would you teach me how to shoot a rifle?"

Shannon's answer was to look at her father.

"Well, darlin', maybe someday," said Glenshannon.

"Someday! Someday!" she sulked. "That's all you ever promise! There are some things I'd like to do today!"

"Now Heather, you can do some other things today, but shooting a rifle isn't one of 'em."

"Alright then, there *is* something else you promised that we can do today."

"What's that?"

Heather pointed and smiled triumphantly. Moon Rock was what she pointed to.

"You promised you'd take Shannon and me to Moon Rock, and that was a long time ago. We're not very far. It's right over there!"

"Well, darlin', I guess you've got me." He motioned to Shannon. "Mount up, lad, and we'll go have a look-see."

"Right over there" was over a mile away, but within the hour the three of them had left behind the flat, fertile terrain and had made their way through the ominous out-crop of rocks scaling upward to the black cradle that gave Moon Rock its name.

The three of them dismounted and stood outlined against the delft blue sky. They were surrounded by a limitless horizon with a clear vision of the vast domain that circled the bleak, forlorn formation towering over the earth below.

"It *is* magic!" Heather proclaimed. "Just like I knew it would be!"

"I don't know about magic, darlin', but it is like nothing I've ever seen before."

"I could stay here forever!" she said. "Shannon, don't you think . . ." But she was alarmed, almost frightened by the look on Shannon's face. A look she hadn't seen since the first day he came to Glenshannon Hall. Forbidding. Primal. "Shannon, what's wrong?"

His eyes were open but unseeing, or maybe seeing what Glenshannon and Heather could not — seeing a specter from out of the past, or a portent of the imminent future.

But it was not what he saw. It was what he felt that made him shudder.

"Let's leave!" he said. "Now."

"What is it, lad?"

"I don't know. I'm not sure . . . but it's something . . . I can't explain . . . but I know we've got to leave."

Glenshannon remembered Ghost Canyon and the look in the boy's eyes as he touched the dead body of Seccoro — it was again as if the boy were touching the dead. Glenshannon didn't need or want further explanation.

"Alright," he said. "We'll leave now."

Even as they started to make their way from the heights of Moon Rock, the sky began to darken, to evolve from azure to cobalt. Clouds formed like a rolling sea, brewing, then overhanging, roiling within until they could not, or would not, contain the pent-up fury.

The rain came first in spurts and splashes around them as they rode faster away from the buttes and toward the level land below. And as they descended they seemed to leave behind the worst of the cloudburst, but could hear the drumbeat of thunder that warned of what was to come.

When they had reached the flat table of land that was almost dry, they instinctively turned back at the crackling sound from Moon Rock.

Crooked white shafts pierced the seething clouds above the stone cradle, and lightning struck the spot where the three of them had stood minutes ago.

"What was it, lad? How did you know what was coming?"

"I didn't know what it was. I . . . I just know something told me that we had to get away from there. . . ."

"Maybe" — Glenshannon looked back at Moon Rock as the clouds that had huddled there were dissipating, making the slick crest visible again — "maybe it was the spirits that hover there. Whatever it was, I think we've all had enough of Moon Rock to last for the rest of our lives."

"No," Shannon said.

"What do you mean, lad?"

"I'll go back again . . . sometime."

"But why?"

"I'm not sure . . . but I know I'll go back."

"Yes, well, right now I think we'd better go home. Heather, are you alright?"

She smiled and nodded. And something inside told her that someday, when Shannon went back to Moon Rock, she would be with him.

To Heather, Moon Rock was still a magic place.

Even more now.

Chapter Fifteen

Everyone at the ranch had heard about what happened at Moon Rock, and what almost had happened.

And, of course, everyone was pleased at the outcome — almost everyone.

Hadley knew that their escape from Moon Rock would make the bond between his father, sister and Shannon even stronger.

If Hadley couldn't break that bond, at least for the time being, there had to be some way to make Shannon suffer.

He made sure that no one saw him go into the stable where all the prize horses were kept, including Bucephalus. He slipped a halter rope onto Black's head and tied the other end with a double knot onto a post.

He struck a kitchen match and set fire to one of the bales of hay inside the stable.

Shannon walked across the yard from the bunkhouse where he had been talking to Pepper and headed toward the front entrance of the main building.

He saw Hadley hurrying from the stable to the rear of the headquarters and Hadley realized that he had been seen by Shannon, who thought nothing of it at the time and kept walking.

But before Shannon went much farther he discerned something was wrong — and in the direction from which Hadley had been running.

Smoke had begun to seep through the boards of the stable and from the entrance.

Inside, flames leaped from the hay-strewn floor and from the bale close to Black. The other horses whinnied — eyes dilated, nostrils flared. They reared and bolted out of their stalls toward the double doors in front.

As the fire and smoke swept closer, Black tried to rear but was held fast by the halter tied to the post with the double knot.

Shannon, Glenshannon, Pepper, Carson, Gibbs and some of the other hands headed toward the stable as more than a dozen horses, including Bucephalus, but not Black, charged out of the double doors and galloped past them to safety.

Shannon realized his horse was not among the fleeing animals. He started toward the stable but the big man grabbed him.

"What're you doin', lad?"

"Black! Black's still in there! He didn't come out. . . ."

Glenshannon shoved him at Pepper, who took hold with both hands.

"Keep him here, Pepper!" Glenshannon was racing to the stable. "I'll get him out, lad."

"You stay put, boy." Pepper tightened his grip and Carson also clamped onto Shannon, who was still trying to break loose.

Suddenly Shannon stopped struggling. He had spotted Hadley standing on the porch, behind Heather and Hannah.

Even from this distance Shannon could see the hollow look in Hadley's eyes as he watched the stable burn. There was no doubt in Shannon's mind as to how the fire had started.

Glenshannon grabbed a blanket from one of the stalls and waved away the smoke as he made his way toward Black, who was still tied. He reached the horse and pulled at the rope to no avail.

He dropped the blanket and pulled the halter over Black's head, freeing him. Glenshannon whacked the horse's flank.

"Get out, boy!"

The animal needed no urging. Black ran

past Glenshannon through the smoke and fire, toward the stable door.

Glenshannon picked up the blanket and flapped it in front of him as he started past a huge burning pile of hay in the middle of the floor. The hay had reached as high as the loft above and someone from that loft had left a pitchfork on top of the pile.

Part of the burning haystack began to collapse and sent the pitchfork sliding on a swift, deadly descent.

The look on Glenshannon's face confirmed the impact.

Just after Black galloped through the framework of fire, Glenshannon walked out of the stable door. Except he wasn't exactly walking. Staggering, wobbling — then falling forward with the prongs and the pitchfork still impaled in his back.

Shannon, Carson, then Pepper reached the fallen man. Pepper wasted no time, he grabbed the handle and pulled the pitchfork free from Glenshannon's back.

"Carson, ride for the doctor!"

Carson was already on his way to the post where his horse was hitched.

Shannon knelt with both knees beside the big man.

"Gibbs! Carey!" Pepper ordered. "You two help me lift him into the house."

"Let me help," Shannon pleaded.

"No, son, you just walk on ahead of us. We'll get it done."

They lifted Glenshannon and carried him up the steps toward the door. Heather's face was buried against Hannah, and as Shannon looked at Hadley, Hadley's eyes lowered until all that was left were closed lids.

Chapter Sixteen

Dr. Zebuleon Barnes had done all he could, but it wasn't very much and it wasn't enough. Shannon Glenshannon was going to die. The bed he lay in would be his death bed, and soon.

One of the pitchfork prongs had penetrated a lung and there was no way to staunch the internal bleeding.

The doctor had given his patient laudanum and was standing helplessly near the bed along with Shannon, Heather, Hadley, Pepper and Hannah.

He had been born on a rock-ribbed patch of land across an ocean and came to a new country with a new wife and no more than he could carry in his pockets. He had left that wife near the east coast of the new country and made his way west alone. Across the Allegheny and the Monongahela, the Ohio, the Mississippi, the Red River, and into a tempestuous territory that belonged to Mexico.

He had gambled every cent he possessed and won. With the use of his brains and gun, and guts, he had carved out an empire and held it against would-be invaders, red, brown and white, while the woman he loved was with him and bore him a son, and then, in bearing a daughter, had died.

Even with that son and daughter, and all those others around him — Pepper, Hannah, Carson, Gibbs, Carey, the dozens of ranch hands, and more recently, Shannon, the strange young lad who somehow had become the third child he and Maureen never had, with all those people near him most all of the time, there had been a void that could never be filled, or even start to be filled, since the departure of his beloved Marni.

And now, after having conquered all the other dangers and challenges, he lay on his deathbed because an unseen hand of fate had plunged a pitchfork into his body and was draining that body of life.

But there were two people in the room who knew that the imminent death of Shannon Glenshannon was not due solely to that unseen hand of fate, but to another unseen pair of hands.

Shannon Glenshannon opened his eyes and barely managed to move his right hand.

"Heather, my darlin' . . . Hadley . . . Shannon . . . come closer. . . ."

The three of them came to the edge of the bed. Glenshannon's hand reached out and took hold of Heather's hand as she wept.

"Don't cry, Heather . . . I'm going to be with your mother . . . Pepper and Hannah will . . . will help you until Hadley is old enough to run the ranch . . . I want the three of you to stay together. I love you all and want you . . . to love each other . . ."

Those were Shannon Glenshannon's dying words — and his last wish.

The doctor lifted the sheet and covered the face of the corpse.

They all had gathered on the hillside around the tombstone and the freshly dug grave that held the plain pine coffin, an exact duplicate of the coffin that held the remains of Maureen Glenshannon, next to whom he would sleep the last mortal sleep.

Father Francis Shaughnessy had come to speak the words that had been spoken for nearly two thousand years over the faithful departed. Words that would be listened to by Heather, Hadley, Shannon, Pepper, Hannah and more than a hundred others as they had been listened to by millions through the ages, at other times and other places.

Father Shaughnessy had more the face and body of a coal miner than those of a priest, but his voice was caramel-mellow and his presence comforting. He was all in black except for the white band at his throat. He held a Bible in a rough-hewn hand but spoke the words from it without ever opening the book.

"And he opened his mouth, and taught them, saying 'Blessed are the poor in spirit for theirs is the kingdom of heaven. Blessed are they that mourn; for they shall be comforted. Blessed are the meek for they shall inherit the earth.' "

Hadley couldn't help thinking, as he heard those words, that while he hadn't inherited the earth, he would now inherit a portion of it. As men measure it, a damn good portion — and all that went with it. It would all be his by the law of primogeniture, no matter what his father's last words were.

"Ask and it shall be given to you. Seek and ye shall find. Knock and it shall be opened unto you . . ."

It had been given to him — Glenshannon Hall.

"Rejoice and be exceedingly glad for great is your reward in heaven."

Hadley wasn't thinking about his reward in heaven.

He was exceedingly glad about his reward here on earth.

He couldn't help looking from the hillside at all the land around it.

All his.

"The Lord giveth and the Lord taketh away. Blessed be the name of the Lord."

Nobody was going to take it away. Not even the Lord.

"Hail Mary, full of grace. The Lord is with thee. Blessed art thou amongst women, and blessed is the fruit of thy womb, Jesus. Holy Mary, mother of God, pray for us sinners, now and at the hour of our death. Amen."

Hadley wasn't thinking about the hour of his death.

As far as he was concerned, he had just begun to live.

As Hadley thought those thoughts to himself, the thoughts of Pepper, Hannah, Carson, Gibbs, Carey and all the ranch hands were only of Shannon Glenshannon, of his fair-handedness, his honesty, his dignity, his strength, his goodwill and his favorable effect on all their lives.

Heather was inconsolable. Pepper's words had come true. Her father wouldn't live forever. But the words had come true too soon. Much too soon.

Hannah Dean loved Shannon Glenshannon more, and in more ways, than anyone knew or suspected.

Though he did his best not to show it, Shannon's grief was the deepest, and he somehow knew his life would be the most affected. But it was not of himself he was thinking. It was of the man he had met at Ghost Canyon, and had come to love.

Shannon had lost his third father.

His closest father — and friend.

Chapter Seventeen

All the principal parties involved were gathered in the great room.

Hadley sat in his father's chair. Hannah was there, and Shannon and Heather.

Amos Higgins, who besides being a banker, was a lawyer, the only one in Gilead, was summarizing the sum and substance of Glenshannon's will — the will Glenshannon had sketched out on paper the day he and Pepper took Shannon for his first visit to civilization.

On that paper, Glenshannon had left five hundred dollars to each ranch hand who had been with him for five years, a thousand for ten years or more.

Hannah received two thousand and employment at her present salary as long as she stayed at the ranch or went with Heather when Heather married.

Pepper collected three thousand and would continue to receive ten percent of the profits from the ranch for as long as he lived.

Shannon was to receive a thousand dollars, stay on the ranch as long as he wanted and take the foreman's position after he reached the age of twenty-one, and it became available.

Heather was to receive ten thousand dollars on her twenty-first birthday and twenty percent of the profits if the ranch were sold.

Amos Higgins was named as trustee until Hadley reached the age of eighteen.

There was only one drawback to this will that was written in Glenshannon's hand and was now held in Amos Higgins' hand.

It was not legally binding because Glenshannon had written it as a draft for Higgins to look over but had never actually signed it, and until a document is signed, no matter whose handwriting it is in, it is not legally valid.

So had a circuit court ruled, and so it was up to Hadley to determine which part or parts of Glenshannon's document he would honor and which part or parts he would not recognize.

They were all there at Hadley's behest. He had made his decision and was ready to make his announcement.

"All parts of the document" — Hadley spoke in as deep and somber a voice as he could summon — "will be immediately rec-

144

ognized except the part that refers to the boy called Shannon. That part I will hold in abeyance until I deem it a proper time to decide."

There were murmurs from Pepper and Hannah. Heather stood up and pointed at her brother.

"Hadley, I think you . . ."

"That's all I have to say at this time, so all of you leave the room before I change my mind about a few other things — all except you, Shannon. I want to talk to you."

Hadley was already beginning to assume airs befitting Alexander the Great as he sat on his throne and waited for the room to be empty of everyone except Shannon and the new master of Glenshannon Hall.

Hadley held his father's curved pipe in his hand as he looked at Shannon and spoke.

"First of all, you are not going to receive one thousand dollars — or one red cent. But I'm going to be more generous than you might think. You can keep Black. The stable is being rebuilt. If you want to stay, you will stay in the stable and take care of the horses. And you can forget about ever being foreman of Glenshannon Hall, or anything but a stable boy. If you decide to stay, you'll stay under those conditions. Or you can leave — now, or anytime. That's all."

Shannon turned and walked out of the great room into the hallway where Heather stood. She had heard Hadley's terms.

"Shannon . . . ?"

He looked at Heather as he walked past. She knew he was going to stay.

Chapter Eighteen

The decade that followed Glenshannon's death proved to be the prelude to the bloodiest drama of a country not yet a century old.

The cause for some would be "states' rights." Others used the word that became the shame of a nation: "slavery."

Under the U.S. Constitution all men were created equal — but not all free. The tolerance for slavery was part of the glue that allowed the states to remain united after the American Revolution. It made for an essential but uneasy unity — with increasing rumblings of disunity.

Rumblings that had their origins as early as 1619 when a Dutch ship with twenty African slaves aboard landed at the English colony of Jamestown, Virginia.

But more than a century before that, black plantation slavery had begun in the new world when Spaniards started importing slaves from Africa to take the place of American Indians who had died of over-work, undernourishment and exposure to disease.

In 1820 the Missouri Compromise had provided for Missouri to be admitted to the Union as a slave state and Maine as a free state, and Western territories north of Missouri's southern border to be free soil.

Texas had entered the Union in 1845 as a slave state.

Abolitionists vowed to awaken the conscience of the entire nation — at least the northern half — by sounding the Liberty Bell day and night, until enough citizens would listen and respond with new laws, or with a battle cry and gunfire.

But during that decade there was no sound of a Liberty Bell at Glenshannon Hall. While there were no slaves at the ranch or anywhere nearby, the ranch was part of a slave state and there was little question on which side of the issue Texas would come down.

And during those years, the closest thing to a slave at Glenshannon Hall was a stable boy called Shannon.

He groomed and watered the horses in the rebuilt stable.

He held the stirrup while Hadley mounted Bucephalus after Shannon had curried the animal.

He cleaned the manure from the stable as Heather watched from the doorway and smiled and held her nose.

He ate alone in the stable while Hadley, Heather and Hannah dined in the dining room, where Hadley sat in Glenshannon's chair. Pepper took his meals with the ranch hands, and sometimes with Shannon.

Shannon visited the graves at the hillside and left flowers there — and sometimes even tears.

One Sunday morning, he chopped some wood and carried it to the fireplace where Hadley sat in his inherited chair, smiling. Shannon struck a match, lit the fire, looked at the flames, then at Hadley — who was no longer smiling.

"That's enough! Get out of my house!" Hadley ordered.

There were times when Hadley went into town, or slept late — since his eighteenth birthday he had begun to enjoy the bottled companionship of bourbon or rye more and more each night. During some of those times Shannon would ride Black, giving vent to the pent-up turbulence within him.

On that Sunday morning he rode, and rode fast, with Heather far behind him. They both knew where Shannon was going — where Heather would catch up to him.

They sat on the throne-like stone at Moon Rock.

She had begun to blossom. Her eyes blue as an angel's. Her face not as round as it used to be — and her body beginning to round. But she still harbored her juvenile fantasies.

They sat in silence for a long time, each remembering the first time at Moon Rock.

"Shannon," she finally said. "I don't know why you stay. . . ."

"Don't you?"

"But I'm glad that you do, and I'm sorry for the way Hadley treats you."

"I don't want to talk about Hadley."

"Alright then, we'll talk about you." Her face brightened as she began her storybook fantasy. "Do you know what you are?"

"I'm a stable boy."

"No — you're a prince."

"A prince of the manure piles . . ."

"A Kiowa prince."

"Ha!"

"Don't laugh. And someday — someday, Shannon, you'll go back to the Indians. You'll lead all the tribes and get back all the lands that were taken from them. . . ."

"Including Glenshannon Hall?"

"Including everything. You will be king of all the Kiowas and all the Indians" — she stood up and curtsied — "and I will be your queen. May I be your queen, King Shannon?"

"Sit down. Indians don't have kings."

Heather remained undaunted.

"They will. You'll be the first one. And you'll build a castle here at Moon Rock . . . and we'll . . ."

"Live happily ever after? Is that what you were going to say?"

"Why not?"

"Because, Heather, you read too many fairy tales about Cinderellas and Prince Charmings. It's about time that you see the world as it really is, not like in story books. . . ."

She fell silent and looked away from him.

"I . . . I'm sorry, Heather. I didn't want to be . . . well, not nice to you . . . to hurt your feelings . . ."

"You didn't really." She suddenly smiled. "I know you never would. Since Father died, you . . . I don't exactly know how to say it, Shannon, but since you and Father and I came up here that day . . . well, it was sort of . . . magic . . . wasn't it?"

Shannon nodded.

"We'd better get back before Alex the Great sends somebody after us."

"But we will come back to Moon Rock again, won't we, Shannon?"

"Well, I will," he said. "And if you want to come up at the same time, I guess I can't help that."

"Neither can I." She smiled.

And as the months went by, they did come back — more than once.

Early on another Sunday morning Pepper asked Shannon to mount up and come with him. After about half an hour, Pepper reined up and dismounted.

"I reckon this is as good a place as any."

Shannon also dismounted.

"For what?"

Pepper reached into his saddle bag and pulled out a belt and a holster with a gun in it.

"It's about time you strapped on one of these. The belt and holster's had some use, but the gun's brand new — Remington revolver, a lot smoother and faster on the draw than a Colt. Tie it on, son, it's yours."

"Pepper . . ."

"Don't say nothin'. You can't go on carryin' that rifle every place you go. It ain't civilized. Go ahead, strap it on."

He did.

"Boy, you're a natural born rifleman, but a handgun's different. You ever use one?"

Shannon shook his head.

"Well, you're gonna learn how now. That's right, it's loaded. There's them who keep the hammer on an empty chamber. I'm not one of 'em, might need that extra cartridge. Now the most important thing is this: Never, never squeeze the trigger unless you're willing to kill. Understand?"

Shannon nodded.

"Because if you're not willing to kill without hesitation, you could be killed, because the other fellow probably won't hesitate. And that's the difference between the quick and the dead — that one split second of hesitation. Understand?"

Shannon nodded again.

"And don't do anything stupid like aiming to wound. That lets him get off two shots and maybe kill you. So you aim to kill. Got that?"

"Yes."

"Good. And don't go aiming for the head."

"Why not?"

"Too small of a target and moves quicker than the rest of the body. The chest, boy, that's the place, broader and slower and where the heart is. Right there."

Pepper's forefinger tapped Shannon's chest twice. "Now speakin' of that, don't give him a good target by standin' square on. The less he has to shoot at, the better your chance of comin' out alive."

"Alright."

"And forget that crap about watching his eyes. Nobody shoots with his eyes. He shoots with his thumb and trigger finger. When he starts to move, you move — unless you figure he's faster and you decide to move first."

"That's not exactly fair."

"Sometimes it's exactly necessary. Don't worry about being fair . . . worry about being alive."

"Yes, sir."

"So don't squeeze unless you've got a damn good reason to kill . . . otherwise they'll probably hang you. Ever see anybody hang?"

Shannon shook his head.

"It ain't pretty. Now let's give it a try." He pointed at the Remington on Shannon's hip. "Hook. Draw. Fire. See that tree over there with that branch hanging down?"

"I see it."

"That's a man who wants to kill you . . . and that branch is the bastard's heart. When I say 'now,' the bastard's hand is commencin' to move. You move too. Hook. Draw. Fire. Fast but not too damn fast or the barrel won't be level. You ready?"

154

Shannon nodded.

"So's he. *NOW!*"

Hook, draw, fire is what Shannon did. The branch split and fell to the ground. Shannon fired again, tearing the branch apart.

"How was that?"

"Overkill . . . but good. You sure you ain't ever fired a pistol before?"

"Never."

"Well, son, your hand was made for the trigger — so was your eyes. But it's a heap different facin' a man with a gun. Keep practicin' and you'll be ready, but I hope the time don't come. By the way, I told Hadley I was givin' you this gun."

"What did he say?"

"Didn't seem to care much, one way or 'tuther."

"Pepper . . ."

"Yeah?"

"Thanks for the gun . . . and the lesson."

Chapter Nineteen

Pepper and Carson stood talking in front of the bunkhouse when they heard the gunshots. So did everybody else around headquarters.

Ranch hands came out of the bunkhouse, Hadley out of the main building followed by Heather and Hannah, and Shannon ran out of the stable.

Gibbs was riding hard and fired twice more as he reined up.

"What the hell is it?" Pepper asked.

"Indians!" Gibbs caught his breath and repeated, "Indians! Three or four Kiowas cuttin' out a few steers on the north range."

"Bastards!" Hadley spat. "Thieving bastards."

"Look here, Hadley," Pepper said. "I heard your dad say that if they were hungry, he didn't mind if they —"

"Well, I do mind. Let them get away with a few and they'll be back for more."

156

"What do you want us to do, boss?" Carson stood ready.

"Take a half dozen men and go after them. Kill them and they won't come back."

"Yes, sir," Carson said. "Carey, you and your team saddle up. Gibbs, get a fresh mount. I'm going with you."

"Yo!" Carey was already on the move.

"Hadley." Shannon took a step.

"What do you want?"

"Is it alright if I go too?"

Hadley thought about it, but not for long. There was always the chance that the Kiowas might shoot and even kill the interloper and that would be a fitting fate as far as Hadley was concerned.

"Why not? Go ahead." Hadley smiled.

Pepper knew why Hadley was smiling.

Heather started to say something but thought better of it.

In spite of the start Carson and the other ranch hands had, Shannon and Black were the first to reach the north range and first to see the rustlers in the distance.

Three mounted Kiowas were herding a half dozen recalcitrant beeves.

One of the Kiowas spotted Shannon and fired from his single-shot rifle, a shot that was far wide of its target.

Shannon slowed just a little, pulled the Spencer half out of its boot, then quickly changed his mind. He decided to go with the handgun.

The other hands were up to him now and blasting with long guns and pistols. Shannon had yet to fire.

One of the Kiowas was hit and fell from his pony. The ranch riders rode past him and pursued the other two fleeing red men.

But not Shannon. He reined up a few feet from the Kiowa facedown on the ground.

Near the Indian there lay a coup stick and as the red man slowly turned faceup holding his side where he had been wounded, but not badly, Shannon already knew the face would be that of Running Bear.

Shannon's gun pointed directly at Running Bear's heart.

Running Bear realized it was Tamonito who held the gun — not the unarmed boy of years past, but a man, near full grown, whom he would kill in an instant if the situation were reversed.

Running Bear looked with dead man's eyes and waited for his executioner to fire point-blank.

The executioner pointed at the coup stick, then lowered his gun hand to his side.

Running Bear reached out and picked up

the coup stick, thinking that Tamonito would wait until he held it in his hand, then kill him, so he would die as a chief. He rose to his feet holding the wound at his side with his left and the coup stick with the other, waiting for Tamonito to raise the gun and point it at his heart again.

Shannon did raise the gun and this time pointed it toward Running Bear's pony that stood nearby. He motioned from the pony to Running Bear then back to the animal.

Far in the distance the ranch riders were heading back toward the two men.

Running Bear nodded a perfunctory acknowledgment — as close as he could come to giving thanks for his life — then sprang toward the pony, mounted, and galloped away from Shannon and the oncoming riders.

Shannon fired three shots toward the rapidly departing Kiowa.

All three shots missed.

"Looks like they all got away," Carson said without a trace of disappointment. In fact, Shannon thought he detected a trace of a smile on the foreman's face.

"Looks like." Shannon nodded and leathered the Remington.

"Well, at least we saved Hadley's cows," Carson added.

Shannon nodded again and thought to himself that if things had gone different at Ghost Canyon years ago, he might have been one of the rustlers.

Chapter Twenty

With the election of Abraham Lincoln as President of the United States in 1860, it was no longer a question of if, but of when.

When would the issues of states' rights and slavery versus the principle of a strong Union and freedom for all bring forth the clash of resounding arms and with it a bloodbath never before seen or even imagined by either side?

During the 1850s President Franklin Pierce's attempt to compromise, and balance the teeter-totter of North and South — freedom and slavery — fell asunder in "Bleeding Kansas" and he failed to gain renomination by the Democratic Party. Instead, the convention of 1856 nominated James Buchanan of Pennsylvania.

Buchanan defeated John C. Fremont, the Republican candidate, in 1856, but Buchanan proved even more spineless in the matter of slavery and a strong Union than his predecessor, Pierce.

The country had had enough equivocation and straddling.

Abraham Lincoln stood for a strong Union and against slavery.

The country — at least most of it — stood with Lincoln.

During these years, the changes in the country were evident, and so were the changes in Shannon and Heather.

The only time they could spend together was when Hadley left the ranch and they could get away. Then they would ride away separately and meet at Moon Rock — a rendezvous they managed once, sometimes twice a month during the years after Shannon Glenshannon died and Hadley became the lord of Glenshannon Hall.

And now as they rode back from Moon Rock, there was little resemblance to the boy and girl who had ridden up to Moon Rock with Shannon Glenshannon nearly a decade ago.

Shannon was now a strapping, hard-shouldered, handsome young man, with brooding eyes the color of a clear December sky, a lean, tapered face framed by coarse, unruly lamp-black hair, a countenance that seldom smiled and was never seen to laugh.

And Heather was now a beautiful flourishing young lady. With a lovely face, fresh as a spring garden, and a blossoming body.

In the years he had worked at Glenshannon Hall, mostly in the stable since his benefactor died, Shannon's earthly possessions consisted of his horse, his rifle, and a handgun.

Not only had he not received the thousand dollars mentioned in the unsigned will that Glenshannon left behind, Hadley had decided that Shannon would receive no monetary compensation for work performed. His only remuneration was food and the shelter of the stable.

But for Shannon, there was another, far more important compensation. The meetings at Moon Rock and the occasions at the ranch when he could look at Heather, and when she might be able to glance back at him and smile.

His clothes consisted mostly of store-bought presents given to him by Pepper at Christmas. Besides clothes, Pepper made sure that Shannon never ran out of cartridges for his Spencer and Remington.

Everything Shannon wore smelled of the stable and — scrub as he might — so did he.

Heather didn't mind it at all.

Months ago Hadley had met Wade Rawlins at Amos Higgins' bank in Gilead.

Higgins had introduced Rawlins as a new depositor, a recently arrived Virginia gentleman who had purchased a ranch near Gilead and decided to settle in Texas.

The two men had gone to the Emporium for a drink and had an amiable conversation. Snob that he was, Hadley was pleased to meet another gentleman in contrast to the riff-raff on the ranch and — with the exception of Higgins and a dozen or so others — most of the residents of Gilead and its environs.

Hadley had invited Rawlins to come to Glenshannon Hall for drinks and a visit. Rawlins said he would be happy to do that as soon as the dwelling they were constructing at his new ranch was completed, or nearly completed, and didn't require his constant presence.

Evidently Rawlins had made enough progress to take Hadley up on his invitation.

Wade Rawlins' elegant black carriage, hitched to a handsome blood-bay, stood by the front entrance of the main building.

The two men sat on the veranda at Glenshannon Hall.

Even though it was the middle of the day, Hadley was in the middle of a bottle of bourbon that stood on the table between the two men.

Rawlins had been sipping, Hadley gulping.

Hadley's face was lined beyond his years, his eyes glassy, his complexion sallow, his flesh flaccid.

Rawlins dressed, looked and spoke like the Southern gentleman he was.

Hadley poured another four fingers of bourbon for himself and tipped the bottle toward Rawlins' glass.

"Thank you." The visitor smiled. "No more."

Hadley lifted his glass in a toast.

"We've been talking about the Confederacy, Mr. Rawlins. Well, here's to Kentucky's great contribution to the cause . . . the best damn bourbon in the world." Hadley smiled and drank.

"I'm not so sure that Kentucky would come in on the side of the Confederacy."

"No? Too bad. Then I'll have to lay in a supply."

"We can still joke, Mr. Glenshannon, but war will come. Lincoln's election makes it inevitable and my former residence, the Shenandoah Valley, will suffer greatly."

"What makes you so sure of either — or both?"

"As for the first, Lincoln will try to abolish slavery. The South must stop him

— or try. Their economic survival depends on it."

"And the second?"

"The Shenandoah Valley?"

Hadley nodded.

"Unfortunately, it is the ideal avenue of approach between the armies of both sides, North and South. A passport to victory or defeat."

"Is that why you left?"

"Perhaps it was the hand of fate."

"How do you mean?"

"After more than a hundred years, our home burned to the ground. We suspected arson."

"By slaves?"

"We had no slaves."

"A Virginian without slaves?"

"There are a great many of us who don't believe in slavery — and we are not looked upon with favor by other Southerners."

"I didn't realize that."

"So I sold the land and came west."

"Well, Mr. Rawlins, I'm sorry for your troubles, but pleased for your companionship."

"Thank you, Mister Glenshannon, I'm sure that we'll be friends."

"Why not? You're one of the few cultured gentlemen within a hundred or so miles around. As for the war, let it come. The South will triumph, Lincoln will be hanged and we can" — Hadley took another drink — "go about our business."

"That seems to be the outlook of most Southern gentlemen."

"Do you have a different outlook, Mister Rawlins?"

"I don't think it will be that simple. War never is."

Hadley rose abruptly and slammed his glass down hard on the table, spilling most of what was left of the bourbon.

Rawlins flinched, and for the moment sat startled, unaware of the cause of Hadley's bewildering behavior.

Hadley rose without saying a word and walked to the edge of the veranda as the two riders approached.

"You! Wait a minute, you scum! I told you I don't want you riding out with my sister!"

Shannon dismounted and was about to help Heather.

"Get away from her, you stinking savage."

Heather quickly dismounted and took a step forward.

"Hadley, we didn't ride out together. I just happened to meet Shannon as I . . ."

"I don't want to hear any of it. Not from

you and not from him. You!" He pointed at Shannon. "Get to the stable where you belong and rub down the horses . . . and keep your dirty face out of my sight."

Shannon stood straight and received the abuse without a word, without a change of expression or a sign of emotion.

He took the reins of both horses and led the animals toward the stable.

"Heather, you come up here." Hadley turned and moved back toward Rawlins, who was obviously uncomfortable about what he had seen and heard.

Wade Rawlins was also obviously aware of the beauty of the young lady who walked up the stairs and smiled as Rawlins rose and anticipated an introduction.

Hadley took hold of the bottle and spilled more bourbon into his glass. He did his best to assume a warm and friendly attitude again.

"Rawlins, I want you to meet my sister. Heather, this is Mister Wade Rawlins, late of Virginia. Mister Rawlins is going to be our new neighbor."

"I am honored, Miss Heather." Rawlins removed his wide-brimmed hat and bowed slightly.

She brushed the hair from her face and nodded — a ravishing young lady who favorably filled out her riding clothes. She moved erect, but free, with lively, inviting eyes shining out of her oval face.

"Well, Wade," Hadley said, "how does she compare to those fine Southern belles of Virginia?"

"Hadley" — both men used the other's first name for the first time — "by comparison, those so-called Southern belles pale and wither."

"Well," Hadley smiled, "how charming."

"And true," Rawlins added, his eyes still on Heather.

"Mister Rawlins has been telling me about the new place he's built."

"Yes, Miss Heather, we're duplicating Twelve Trees, every foot of it."

"Twelve Trees?"

"The home we had back in Virginia."

"I'm sure," Hadley said, "that this part of Texas has never seen anything like it."

"Well, you can come see for yourself, Hadley, you and your sister. We're giving a party next Friday. Sort of a house warming. Charlotte and I would be honored if you would both be there."

"I can't remember the last time we've been to a real party. May we go, Hadley?"

"Just lay in a good supply of bourbon,

neighbor." Hadley raised his glass. "We'll be there."

"And I do look forward to meeting your wife, Mister Rawlins," Heather added.

"My wi . . ." Rawlins laughed. "You mean Charlotte?"

Heather nodded.

"No. I'm happy to say that Charlotte is not my wife."

"She's not?"

"Charlotte *is* the mistress of Twelve Trees." Rawlins couldn't help making a little joke. "She also happens to be my sister." He laughed.

They all laughed.

And Heather couldn't help being more than a little pleased.

She didn't know about Twelve Trees, how it would look, but she knew that she had never met anyone who looked, dressed and comported himself quite like the Southern gentleman called Wade Rawlins.

Rawlins once more bowed slightly, affixed his wide-brimmed hat, and smiled.

"Well, if you two will excuse me, I'd best be getting back to Twelve Trees and sister Charlotte . . . and Charlotte and I will look forward to your visit next Friday, say around seven?"

"Around seven it is," said Hadley.

"Miss Heather." Rawlins tipped his hat and stepped off the veranda and walked toward the horse and carriage.

Pepper leaned against a rail of the corral, smoked a cigar and watched as Rawlins stepped into the carriage. He had been watching ever since Heather and Shannon rode in.

Hannah stood just inside the door, which had been left partially open. She had been listening ever since Heather and Shannon rode in.

From the stable, Shannon had been watching. He saw the three of them, Hadley, Heather and the man — particularly Heather and the man — nodding, smiling and laughing.

He had never before experienced anything like the stabbing sensation he felt as he watched Heather and the stranger nodding, smiling and laughing together.

As the elegant black carriage passed by the stable, with the handsome man at the reins, Shannon's face resembled a storm cloud.

Chapter Twenty-one

For the next few days not a word or even a look passed between Shannon and Heather.

He did everything he could, without arousing Hadley's suspicion, to effect even a fleeting encounter, a look or a word, but it was as if she were avoiding him, or so it seemed in his imagination — or *was* it imagination?

One day he managed to ride to Moon Rock. He waited until sunset and rode back alone.

He remembered a play he had read in one of Glenshannon's books. A play by William Shakespeare called *Othello*, where a dark outcast was consumed by jealousy. Consumed to the point of murder.

Shannon had seen the stranger only once, and as far as he knew, Heather had seen him only once. But in his soul was a monster begot upon itself, born on itself, and he imagined them together all during the day, and even more vividly at night.

In the stable he practiced with the hand-gun.

Hook. Draw. But he didn't fire.

Time and again.

Hook. Draw.

He pointed the Remington at a post.

But in his mind he saw the face of the stranger.

As the days edged ever closer to the Rawlinses' house-warming party, Shannon seethed within from an affliction he had never known before he saw the two of them together. He had seen something in Heather's eyes, something that made him shudder. Something playful, sportive, beguiling.

And the nation was edging ever closer to the inevitable — a nation that had sown a bad seed and was about to taste the bitter fruit.

The first fury of the storm had struck at Harper's Ferry, where a wild-eyed abolitionist named John Brown and his four sons, along with a fistful of followers, struck on the night of October 16, 1859. It was their mission to overtake the Federal arsenal and seize the weapons therein to provide arms enough to start an insurrection of slaves in the South.

The first phase of Brown's mission succeeded. He took possession of an engine house and held it for more than forty-eight hours.

The next phase proved his undoing.

Union forces, ironically led by General Robert E. Lee, Lieutenant J.E.B. Stuart, and a glory-seeking lieutenant named George Armstrong Custer, attacked, overpowered and captured Brown and his men.

Quick justice — if justice it was — was meted out. John Brown was hanged. But his truth went marching on.

In 1860 President-elect Lincoln became the sixteenth President of the United States — less and less united.

On December 20, South Carolina seceded from the Union — followed on January 10, 1861, by Florida and on January 19 by Georgia.

Texas would not be far behind.

Chapter Twenty-two

The last thing on Heather Glenshannon's mind was war.

Her most immediate thoughts were about the celebration that would take place in just a few hours at Twelve Trees.

Heather cupped her hands under her breasts and looked into the bedroom mirror as Hannah helped her into a party dress.

She was standing on the cougar pelt that Shannon had given her years ago.

"Hannah, do you think Cassie Higgins has a bigger bosom than I do?"

"I'm sure I don't know." Hannah Dean arched an eyebrow. "I've never paid any attention to Cassie Higgins' bosom."

"Well, all the *men* do. At parties, weddings, even at funerals. And she does her best to make them pay attention."

Heather tugged the neckline of her dress downward, exposing more cleavage.

"Is that what you intend to do?"

Hannah pulled the neckline up again.

"It all depends."

"On what?"

"Do you suppose Wade Rawlins has invited her to his party?"

"I suppose. From what I hear he's invited everybody who is anybody in Texas. And that old windbag father of hers does own the bank."

Heather tugged the neckline down again.

"She'll probably be wearing a newer and prettier dress than mine. Maybe from New Orleans or Atlanta or even New York."

"Probably from Paris," Hannah chided.

"Do you really think so?"

"I don't know, child, but I doubt if anybody will be looking at the label."

"No, they'll be looking at her bosom, the way she walks and thrusts them out. She jiggles in front and wiggles in back."

Heather studied herself in the mirror, even tried jiggling and wiggling some.

"Stop that!" Hannah admonished.

"Hannah, do you think this dress is pretty?" Heather tugged the neckline down again.

"It's pretty." Up went the neckline again. "What there is of it."

"I can't wait to see his . . ."

"His what?"

"Why, ranch, or plantation, or mansion or whatever it is. Wade says that . . ."

"Wade, is it now? Don't tell me you two are on a first-name basis after having met just once."

"Not yet, but . . ."

"But what?"

"But don't you think that Wade . . . Wade Rawlins, or Mister Rawlins, if you prefer, must be awful rich?"

"Awfully, not awful."

"Awful, awfully, what does it matter, so long as he's rich?"

"It matters the way you speak and the grammar you use. Remember, he's used to proper and genteel ladies, not illiterate cowgirls."

"I'll try to remember. But he's got to get used to a lot of different things in Texas."

"Why don't you just stand naked in front of him!?"

"There'll be plenty of time for that," Heather teased.

"Why you" — Hannah whacked Heather on her backside — *"Jezebel!"*

"That hurt!" Heather protested. "Oh, Hannah, I was only teasing."

"Just don't tease Wade Rawlins too much."

Heather looked in the mirror where she could see her own likeness and Hannah's.

She winked and tugged the neckline down only half as low as before.

"Not *too* much — just enough."

That morning Hadley had asked Gibbs to summon Shannon from the stable to the front of the main building.

Hadley stood on the porch and looked down at Shannon.

"My sister and I are invited to a party at a gentleman's house this evening. Mister Wade Rawlins. I expect the carriage to be spotless and the team to be impeccably groomed. Do you understand?"

Shannon barely nodded in acknowledgment.

"Good. Leave the carriage here in front of the house at six. Repeat the time."

"Six," Shannon said.

"Good. And you — after you've brought the carriage 'round front, leave it here and get out of sight. Go back to the stable and stay there. I don't want to see your dirty face this evening and neither does my sister. Do you understand that?"

This time Shannon gave no indication of acknowledgment.

He turned and walked toward the stable.

Shannon wasn't sure which one he hated

worse, Hadley or the man whose name he just found out: Wade Rawlins.

But there was enough hate in Shannon for both of them.

Maybe for the world.

At least for the world that now revolved around Glenshannon Hall.

At twilight Hadley and Heather were aboard a spotlessly bright and shiny carriage hitched to a pair of perfectly matched white-stocking mares.

Hannah and Pepper were standing on the porch as Hadley took a swallow from his silver pocket flask, returned it to his rear pocket, took up the whip from its sleeve, and flicked it just above the horses, who started off in perfect tandem.

Heather adjusted the front of the dress, smiled and waved at Hannah and Pepper, who smiled and waved back. Pepper's response was somewhat less enthusiastic than Hannah's.

As the carriage approached the stable, Heather saw Shannon standing at the entrance. For nearly a week he had wanted to meet or see her — to make eye contact, or speak even one word. But now he avoided even a glance from her. Instead, he turned and walked into the stable.

Heather couldn't help watching as he disappeared from her sight, and as he did she realized that for the first time in years, she hadn't seen him, talked to him, or thought about him for a very long time.

But almost at once, her thoughts went back to what she had been thinking about most of that time.

Wade Rawlins' party.

Shannon sat on a stool inside the stable, repairing a bridle.

Actually, he was cutting and punching with a sharp-pointed knife, more than repairing.

He realized that the bridle would never be repaired, at least not tonight. He slammed it against a stall, startling some of the horses, and let the bridle fall to the floor.

Someone had walked into the stable, and without looking, by just listening to the unrhythmic gait, Shannon knew who it was.

"Howdy, son."

Shannon neither said anything, nor turned toward Pepper. He just sat on the stool and looked straight ahead.

Pepper walked closer and sat on a bale of hay. In his mouth, a lit cigar. And in his hand, one that was unlit.

"Have one of Hadley's ceegars." He stuck out the unlit stogie. "They're a lot better than mine."

"The hell with Hadley and his ceegars."

"Look, son, I know how you feel."

"Do you?"

"I think I do, well, sort of, but I got to tell you somethin' — somethin' you got to hear and you might as well hear it from someone who . . . someone who's a friend. I hope, after all these years, *more* than a friend."

Shannon still neither spoke nor looked at Pepper.

"You might just as well face the facts — at least one fact — where she's concerned. You ain't got no more chance than a wax cat in hell."

"Nobody asked you."

"Nobody did, but I'm gonna say my say and you're goin' to listen."

Shannon looked up and locked eyes with Pepper.

"Now don't go givin' me that Kiowa look," Pepper said. "I love you like you was my own boy. Either you're gonna listen or you're gonna hit me. And I don't think you'd hit ol' Pepper."

He leaned in closer.

"Shannon, why do you stay around here

181

. . . around her . . . make yourself miserable over somethin' that can't ever be?"

Shannon stood and walked to a post, his back to Pepper.

Pepper rose and followed, summoning all the reason, all the persuasion he could muster in his voice.

"You're a strappin' young fella. Know more about horses than a brood mare. Shannon, pull outta here . . . get yourself a decent job on one of the other spreads . . . they'd be glad to have you . . . instead of stayin' around here, stinkin' of horseshit and takin' his insults."

"Maybe I like the smell of horseshit."

"And takin' his insults? You know you could break him in two with one hand. The way to beat him is to leave and make somethin' of yourself."

"If I left he'd win. That's what he wants me to do."

"It's not him that's keeping you here and you know it. Look, boy, I've got money. I'll stake you. There's nothin' keepin' me here. We could get a little spread together. I know a place. . . ."

"You know too damn much, Pepper. Get out of here."

Pepper looked at him for a moment and realized the futility of saying anything more,

182

at least for the time being. He shrugged, put Hadley's unlit cigar on the stool, then gimped out of the stable.

Shannon stood at the post until he knew that Pepper was gone.

He turned, walked to the stool, not fast, not slow, picked up Hadley's cigar, looked at it, then crushed it in his hand.

Chapter Twenty-three

The two-story structure did indeed look more like a transplanted Virginia plantation than a ranch in Texas. Twelve Trees was fronted by six square columns and in front of the columns, twelve Sycamores, standing like sentinals.

There were many fine carriages near the entrance. The first-floor rooms were brightly illuminated and there was the sound of music from within.

The lavishly appointed ballroom was filled with elegantly booted and bodiced Texans, gentlemen and ladies, doing their best to emulate the genteel refinement of the old South. Most of them just succeeded in displaying their social awkwardness.

As the music ceased, banker Amos Higgins stepped forward and raised his glass. Cassie Higgins stood at his elbow, her smile beaming toward Wade Rawlins, and so was much of her bosom. A little too tall, her canary coiffure a little overdone, and a face that had a somewhat unfortunate family resemblance to that of the man with the raised glass. Her bosom, however, was the object of many covert glances — and some not so covert.

Standing next to a semisober Hadley, Heather plainly was the most attractive of all the ladies in attendance.

A not-too-distant runner-up, Charlotte Rawlins wore the most elegant gown and possessed the true grace and carriage of a Southern belle.

Her brother, a portrait of a refined gentleman, smiled as Higgins began to speak.

"Ladies and gents!! Could I have your undivided attention here, please?"

"Alright, now," a voice from the crowd hollered. "Let's all listen to Amos Higgins!"

"Go ahead and say, Amos," another voice called from the crowd.

"I thank you one and all. Now, on behalf of all the fine citizens gathered here in these magnificent surroundings, I would like to propose a toast — matter of fact, a double toast. First, to our new neighbor and host, Wade Rawlins, and his sweet little sister, Charlotte . . ." Higgins sipped from his glass.

So did all the other guests.

Rawlins and his sweet little sister responded with smiles.

"And second," Higgins continued, "to this glorious day: February first, in the year of our Lord eighteen hundred and sixty-one, the day the great state of Texas seceded from the Union — the former Union — and joined the glorious Confederacy."

Immediately the orchestra struck up a chorus of "Dixie" amid cheers, laughter and general celebration. No one appeared to notice that the host's reaction was the most subdued in the room. The smile on his face seemed forced and his eyes betrayed a subtle uneasiness.

"I just want to say," Higgins went on, "that the Bank of Gilead will back the Confederacy with every resource at its command, and ladies and gentlemen, that's damn plenty!"

"Why, the whole shebang won't last a month!" somebody shouted.

"It'll be one big turkey shoot!" a tall Texan shouted louder.

"I'll drink to that" — Hadley raised his glass — "and to Jeff Davis!"

Another guest placed his hand on Rawlins' shoulder.

"Rawlins, ol' boy, how long you figure this war'll take?"

"I can't say, sir. Too long."

The guest removed his hand from his

host's shoulder, muttered something indiscernible, and moved away.

Higgins approached, escorting his daughter.

"Well, Wade, my friend, you sure know how to throw a party."

"Thank you."

"And I hope that we, Cassie and I, get to know you and your little sister much better." Higgins smiled expansively. "Both in business . . . and socially."

"I hope so." Rawlins nodded, touched Charlotte's elbow and escorted her toward another part of the room.

The orchestra segued from "Dixie" to a waltz and within seconds the booted gentlemen and their ladies were on the floor in step with the music.

A young man came close to Rawlins and Charlotte. He looked directly but uneasily at his host.

"Mr. Rawlins, my name is Donald L. Higley. Could I have the pleasure of this dance?"

"I beg your pardon?" Rawlins smiled.

"I . . . I mean with your sister. Miss Rawlins, my name is Donald L. Higley."

"My name is Charlotte Emily Rawlins and I'd be pleased to dance with you, Mister Higley."

As Donald L. and Charlotte Emily waltzed away, Rawlins looked in another direction toward Cassie Higgins, who was now in the center of a semicircle of swains, their collective attention mostly focused on her front and slightly above center.

But her attention was directed toward Wade Rawlins, who was approaching through the crowd. Her bosom heaved in anticipation. She was about to accept the as yet unspoken invitation — when Rawlins walked past her.

To Heather. Less bosom. More beauty.

"Miss Heather, would you do me the honor?"

Heather smiled and nodded. He escorted her to the dance floor past a breast-fallen Cassie Higgins, who promptly accepted one of the swains' invitation and pulled herself together.

If the world as they knew it was about to implode, nobody in the ballroom at Twelve Trees seemed to realize it. Even Wade Rawlins, with Heather in his arms, had cast aside his concern about secession and its consequences.

But there was someone just outside the ballroom who seemed to realize that the world as he knew it was about to collapse.

Shannon's face was pressed to a corner of

a window, his eyes straining to catch sight of what he did not want to see.

But he saw.

Heather in Wade Rawlins' arms, smiling a radiant smile. The handsomest, happiest couple in the room.

And that sight brought to his mind the words from Shakespeare's play: "Farewell the tranquil mind. Farewell content — it is the cause, it is the cause, my soul."

And to his face it brought a knot of bitterness. He wanted to turn his face away but did not, until a big hand rudely grabbed his shoulder and jerked him around. The big hand was attached to a big man named Redding, Wade Rawlins' foreman.

"Who are you?" Redding barked.

Shannon stared at the man but said nothing.

"I said, who are you? What're you doing around here? You don't belong here!"

Still Shannon said nothing.

"What's the matter? You deef and dumb? I asked you —"

Shannon knocked Redding's hand away. Redding swung, Shannon ducked and responded brutally.

Again and again he pummeled lefts and rights at Redding with savage strength, taking out on the foreman all his hurt and fury.

Redding smashed into the window, shattering it.

Inside the ballroom a woman screamed at the sound and sight of the bleeding man, half in and half out of the window.

The music stopped. Other women screamed. A half dozen men ran toward the window, but Shannon pulled Redding back outside and it seemed he would beat the foreman to death.

Now the men ran toward the door to stop the carnage.

Shannon braced Redding against the wall and hit him again without mercy as the Texans reached the two men. It took four of the biggest to grab Shannon and hold him.

Redding collapsed into an unconscious heap.

Rawlins, Hadley, Higgins and more than a dozen others, including Heather, were now on the front porch.

Tom Hill, one of Rawlins' top hands, went to the unconscious form that lay facedown. He stooped and turned the form faceup.

"It's Redding." Hill looked at Rawlins.

"He's my foreman," Rawlins said to nobody in particular.

"And he's damn near dead," Hill added,

and turned toward Shannon, who was still being held fast by the four men.

"Say, Hadley" — Higgins pointed at Shannon — "isn't that the redskin works for you?"

Heather stared at Shannon and he didn't avoid her look — a look of concern, contempt and pity.

Hadley walked up to Shannon.

"Bastard," he said, and slapped Shannon as hard as he could. "Get back to the stable with the other animals."

Shannon took the blow as if it were a leaf landing on his face. He pulled away from the men holding him, glanced for just a beat at Heather, then turned and walked away.

"Get Redding to the bunkhouse," Rawlins said to Hill. "See if you can get a doctor."

"I'm a doctor, Mister Rawlins." A portly man stepped out of the crowd. "Homer Kokernut. I'll do what I can for him."

"Thank you, doctor," Rawlins said as the men lifted Redding.

"I'm sorry, Wade." Hadley looked from Heather to their host. "I'll see that he's properly punished."

"Well, you ought to be sorry." Higgins put a cigar into his mouth. "Hadley, why the hell do you keep that heathen around, anyhow?"

Higgins lit his cigar. If he expected an answer from Hadley, he didn't receive one.

"Let's get back inside," Rawlins suggested. "And Miss Heather, I apologize for the interruption. May we finish our dance?"

Heather nodded and made an effort to smile — a vain effort.

"Well, I for one," Higgins puffed, "by God, need a drink."

"Make that two, Amos," Hadley said. "I can't, by God, let you drink alone."

The party went on. There was music and dancing and laughter.

But it was never quite the same. Hadley spent most of the evening drinking. Many of the guests spent most of the evening discussing the coming events between the North and South — an unpleasantness that would end quickly and decisively in favor of the South.

Still others continued their fascination with Cassie Higgins' bosom.

Heather spent most of the evening in Wade Rawlins' arms, dancing.

Shannon rode into the night on Black — not in the direction of Glenshannon Hall.

Chapter Twenty-four

The sun cast its long early shadows across the jagged outline of Moon Rock. Nothing moved except the creeping shadows.

There were no birds in the sky.

No reptiles on the rocks.

Nothing.

No one.

Except Shannon.

He lay where he had slept that night — what was left of it by the time he got to Moon Rock.

He had unsaddled Black and left him untethered and unhobbled, knowing the horse would not stray.

He lay on a blanket and looked up at the blue-black blanket of night, where thousands of God's eyes shone through and blinked at the speck floating and slowly revolving below.

He had been awake since first light and now sat up. He looked at his swollen and discolored knuckles, and thought for the first time of what those knuckles had done to the man who was unlucky enough to catch him trespassing.

And then he heard the sound of hoofbeats — and the beat of his heart — that told him without looking who was riding to Moon Rock.

And riding fast.

Heather galloped up the slope and leaped from Buttermilk into Shannon's arms — and a long, impassioned kiss. Then she took his bruised hands and put them to her lips.

"Shannon. Shannon. I knew you'd be here."

"Where else would I be?"

They moved to the throne-like stone and she sat close beside him as he took her into his arms again.

"Shannon, oh, Shannon. I love you . . . out here there's nothing . . . else . . . just you and me."

"You and me."

"But, Shannon" — she moved away a little — "where will you go now?"

"Go?"

She nodded.

"I'm not going anywhere," he said. "Except home to Glenshannon Hall. I just didn't want to go there last night."

"But Hadley . . . he . . ."

"What about Hadley?"

"You think he'll have you back after . . ."

"After what?"

"After what happened at Twelve Trees last night?"

"Did Hadley say anything this morning?"

"He's still asleep. But last night I thought he was going to throw a fit. You know he hates you."

"Sure he does, and I feel the same way about him, but you remember what he said while they were holding me and he slapped me just as hard as he could, which wasn't very hard . . . do you?"

"What do you mean?"

"I mean he didn't say get the hell out of Glenshannon Hall, did he?"

"I don't recall."

"He just said 'get back to the stable.' You recall that?"

"Truth is, I was so scared . . ."

"Well, that's it, Heather. Our little unspoken arrangement. His and mine."

"I don't understand."

"I'll keep to the stable, clean the manure and take what he ladles . . . but I'm not leaving Glenshannon Hall, 'cause I got me a hole card."

"What hole card?"

"Just never you mind, I'm staying."

"But Shannon, after the way he's done you all these years, why would you want to stay?"

"You damn well know why."

He took her again and she went willingly.

"But Shannon," she said, breaking away, "you know there's going to be a war."

"It's not my war."

"It's everybody's."

"Not mine."

"But don't you see how it could change things if you went?"

"All I see is I'd be gone from you."

"For a while . . . for a little while."

"What for?"

"Oh, Shannon, all those stories we used to make up when we were little — about you being an Indian prince and a warrior, being somebody important . . ."

"I'm not important now, that it?"

"I mean if you joined the Confederacy and went to a real war, made a name for yourself. If you were an officer with polished black boots, with a cape and sword . . ."

"Then what?"

"Then you'd come back a hero and they'd all look up to you because of what you did for Texas and the Confederacy."

"What the hell do I care about Texas and the Confederacy?" Shannon rose and moved away. "Fight for these damn people? All they ever did all my life was treat me like a slave, I'll be damned if I'd ever help them!"

Heather rose and followed him, speaking fast before weighing her words.

"You are nothing but a savage and you always will be! I saw you last night —"

"And I saw you last night, too."

"You'll never take your place with those people. You don't really care anything about me or what happens to us. You'll never be a gentleman like . . ."

"Like Rawlins!" He turned.

"Yes! Like Wade Rawlins! He told me last night he's going to apply for a commission in the Texas Army."

"He's a lily-faced piece of fluff with a powder puff for a backbone."

"He's a gentleman. And you're just jealous because he's got money and fine clothes —"

"Is that what you care about? Money and clothes?"

"And he'll be an officer!"

"If he's an officer, the North's got nothing to worry about."

"I won't listen to you talk that way about him."

"You don't have to listen to me at all!"

"No, I don't!"

She turned, ran toward her horse and mounted. She wheeled the animal and rode past Shannon.

"And you and your gentleman can both go to hell!" he hollered above the hoofbeats.

He didn't see that she was crying.

And she didn't see the Kiowa look in his eyes.

Chapter Twenty-five

Shannon's prediction to Heather at Moon Rock came true.

Hadley did not banish him from Glenshannon Hall — just back to the stable, where he bore whatever invective and insult could be heaped upon him whenever Hadley, drunk or sober, came within sight or sound of the stable hand.

And there was another sound — not yet heard in Texas. A faint rumble, gathering momentum across the Shenandoah, the Ohio, the Mississippi, the Missouri and toward the Red River.

While the sound and fury of fighting had not actually begun, the nation — now two nations — could hear and feel the drumbeat ever faster and louder.

One event piled upon another and anticipated the next, which came even faster and louder to a swelling chord of discontent, and would lead to the fighting — and to the crucible.

The beat had begun in November of 1860 with the election of Lincoln, and continued as South Carolina called a secession convention three days later. In December, lame-duck President Buchanan declared that it would be unconstitutional for South Carolina to secede from the Union. Sixteen days later, South Carolina responded by seceding from the Union, causing a chain reaction of secession by the other Southern states and leading to the election of Jefferson Davis and Alexander H. Stephens as provisional Confederate president and vice president. Meanwhile, Abraham Lincoln was inaugurated in Washington on March fourth, and began to form his cabinet, and he vowed to hold all Federal property, starting with beleaguered Fort Sumpter on an island near the mouth of Charleston Harbor. The fort was being menaced by Confederates under the command of colorful General P.G.T. Beauregard. Beauregard had been ordered by Jefferson Davis to bombard Sumpter into surrender and raise the flag of the South in the Confederacy's first victory. He succeeded in carrying out orders, and with the lowering of one flag and the raising of another, the drumbeat of war was drowned out by cannon fire. The war itself had begun — the war that beckoned Texas.

Sam Houston had been the savior of Texas, hero of San Jacinto, first president of the Republic of Texas and leader of the movement for Texas to join the United States. Then he'd been elected to the U.S. Senate, and at present he was governor of Texas and passionately opposed to secession. At almost seventy, he stood tall and brave, and issued, in a voice loud and clear, a warning to his fellow Texans of what was to come.

Your fathers and husbands will be herded at the points of bayonet. While I believe with you in the doctrine of states' rights, the North is determined to preserve the Union. They move with the steady momentum and perseverance of a mighty avalanche and what I fear is, they will overwhelm the South.

The prophet was not heard in his own land.

The news from the skirmishes and early battles between North and South was still good news for the South and for Texas and Texans who were eager to taste the sweet fruit of victory themselves.

They now flew the Confederate flag and they wanted to fight for — and under it.

★ ★ ★

None of them had realized it at the time, but the charge at Harper's Ferry would be the last time the commander and some of his officers who had graduated from West Point would ride side by side.

The commander, Robert E. Lee, had been the most distinguished officer in the U.S. Army. He graduated from the Point at the head of his class in 1829, served with honor and glory in the Mexican War at Vera Cruz, Churubusco and Chapultepec, became superintendent at West Point and saw frontier duty in Texas.

Robert E. Lee was offered command of the U.S. Army at the outbreak of the Civil War — causing a war within himself. Would he remain loyal to the Union — or to his native Virginia? Lee wrote to his sister in the North,

> With all my devotion to the Union and the feeling of loyalty and duty of an American citizen, I can not raise my hand against my relatives, my children, my home. My Virginia.
> I hope I may never be called upon to raise my sword.

But the call came.

And Robert E. Lee did raise his sword, however reluctantly, and was devastatingly effective against massive odds.

Other Union officers born south of the Mason-Dixon line pledged their allegiance to the Confederacy, and to Lee: Joseph E. Johnston, J.E.B. Stuart, P.G.T. Beauregard, T. J. Jackson, Jubal Early, and Albert Sidney Johnston, among others. Their swords also were raised against the North, and they inflicted terrible losses on their former comrades and country at Fort Sumpter, Lexington, Belmont, Shiloh and Fort Royal.

The last months of 1861 and the first months of 1862 resounded with victory after victory for the South.

Pepper was in the Emporium having a drink with Cherrie, who now owned fifty percent of the establishment. Baldy's luck was still bad and now so was his health. He came in later every day, took longer naps in the afternoon and gambled later every night.

But business at the Emporium was still good and Cherrie and her coterie were still thriving.

"Pepper," she smiled, "why don't we go upstairs to my . . . quarters. I've got some private stock up there that I think you'd enjoy . . . on the house."

"Cherrie, I've enjoyed your private stock before, and I will again, but not this afternoon."

"Why not? You not up to it?"

"That's never been the case with you."

"Don't I know it?! Then what?"

"Shannon's outside at Pierce's loadin' the buckboard with flour and airtights and we got to be gettin' back."

"Well, come when you can stay longer."

"I will."

"One more drink . . . and I'll walk you over."

"One more drink and I'll carry you."

Cherrie was already pouring.

Shannon came out of Pierce's General Store carrying a heavy bag of flour on his shoulders. He tossed it onto the buckboard already loaded with supplies.

Across the street the two Krantz brothers watched — and noticed that the young boy who had beaten the hell out of them had put on more than a few well-muscled pounds and a handgun.

It didn't take them long to decide to do nothing but watch.

But there was another man watching who had no such notion.

Tom Hill, who had worked for Wade

204

Rawlins until last month, walked toward the buckboard and Shannon.

As Shannon started to move close to the seat of the buckboard, Hill reached out and tapped him on the shoulder.

"You remember me?" asked the box-jawed, square-eyed man.

Shannon turned and looked.

"No." Then he started to move away.

"Look again."

"Why should I?"

"I'm Tom Hill. 'Til last month I worked for Wade Rawlins. Now I got my own spread."

"Congratulations." He started to turn again.

"Not that fast. Hank Redding's a friend of mine."

"Who the hell's Hank Redding?"

"Rawlins' foreman. You could've killed him that night."

"I could've . . . if I meant to."

"I think you did mean to. He's still —"

"Look, mister, I don't give a damn what you or anybody thinks." Shannon looked around at the crowd that was gathering and growing. "How about it, people? I'm here minding my own business 'til this horse's ass . . ."

"What did you just call me? Horse's ass?"

"Donkey's ass, if you like. What difference does it make? Just keep the hell away from me."

"Is that a threat?"

"Fact."

"Listen, Jasper, you might be pretty handy with your fists when somebody's not lookin', but how handy are you with that gun?"

"You don't want to find out," Shannon said, and then spoke again to the crowd. "Now somebody get the law, before somebody gets hurt."

Much of the crowd had already begun to back away. One of the citizens moved quickly toward the sheriff's office and the Krantz brothers were smiling and salivating at the prospect of what was likely to happen.

Tom Hill had a reputation. Fast draw. Crack shot. Trigger temper.

"Suppose we just move back a piece and find out who's the handiest?"

"That's it, Tom," Kurt Krantz hollered. "Don't let that dirtbag call you names."

"Bring him to his milk, Tom." Burt Krantz grinned. "He's just a waddie."

"Well, what about it, Jasper? Are we gonna step back and . . ."

Instead of stepping back, Shannon drew his gun faster than the blink of an eye and cracked Tom Hill across his skull with the barrel.

Hill fell backward and hit the ground stiff as a broomstick.

That's when Sheriff Joe Fox appeared through the crowd, which now included Pepper and Cherrie.

"Alright," Sheriff Fox demanded, "what the hell is going on around here?" He glanced at Hill in the dirt, then looked at Shannon standing by the buckboard.

"You again!" He recognized Shannon from his encounter with the Krantzes years ago. "What happened this time?"

"He was looking for a gunfight." Shannon pointed at the man on the ground who was coming to and rubbing at blood leaking near his temple. "I wasn't," he added, and looked around at the spectators. "Isn't that right?"

Most of the spectators nodded and murmured in the affirmative.

"Son," the sheriff said, "you . . ."

Shannon drew even faster than before and fired. The shot kicked up dirt right between Hill's legs, just south of his crotch. Hill's gun had barely cleared his holster.

"You know where the next one'll be." Shannon's gun was pointed directly at Hill's vitals.

Hill let his revolver drop to the ground.

"Well, I don't know what happened before, but I sure as hell seen that. Alright, everybody, break it up, move along."

A couple of the spectators helped Hill to his feet, stuck his gun back in its holster and helped him move away.

Both Krantz brothers shook their heads in disappointment and drifted down the street.

"Well, Sheriff," Pepper smiled, "I see you're still keepin' the peace."

"Will you keep a string on this stray of yours when you come to town, Pepper?"

"Sure thing, Sheriff."

Sheriff Joe Fox shook his head and walked in the direction of his office.

Amos Higgins had watched the proceedings from the entrance to his bank.

He turned and went inside.

"Mister," Cherrie smiled at Shannon, "you're sure as shootin' old enough to drink now. You want to step over and have one on the house?"

"Thanks, no, ma'am."

Pepper rubbed his jaw. "Boy," he said, "you didn't handle that like I taught you. When you pull a gun, kill a man."

"I guess I just didn't hit where I aimed." Shannon smiled.

"The hell you didn't." Pepper grinned.

Chapter Twenty-six

Amos Higgins took the first opportunity that presented itself to tell Hadley his version of the incident between Tom Hill and Shannon.

In the telling of Higgins' version it was no incident, but attempted murder — and why Sheriff Joe Fox hadn't slammed Shannon in jail was beyond the banker.

"Hadley," Higgins said, and shook his head in dismay, "why the hell you keep that damn savage on your ranch just plain stumps me. He's violent, not just violent, crazy — plain crazy. He's liable to murder the whole lot of you someday. Why the hell don't you get rid of him, answer me that?"

Hadley's answer was less than reasonable or articulate. He mumbled something about his father's dying wish that, among other things, was for Shannon to be allowed to stay at Glenshannon Hall. Then Hadley changed the subject.

Higgins knew that Glenshannon's dying wish didn't mean a hell of a lot to Hadley, who had already ignored certain parts of Glenshannon's will, but decided not to pursue the matter.

When Hadley questioned Pepper about what had happened, he received a more accurate account of the confrontation and of Shannon's prowess with a pistol.

Hadley decided not to pursue the matter but was no less temperate in his treatment of Shannon at the ranch.

In the ensuing weeks, with President Abraham Lincoln's cabinet in place and President Jeff Davis's cabinet completed, the adversaries went about the business of war.

Lincoln called for seventy-five thousand volunteers. Davis called for one hundred thousand volunteers. Lincoln proclaimed a blockade of Confederate ports from South Carolina to Texas; Federal troops were forced to retreat after the Battle of Big Bethel, Virginia. But the first great and decisive battle had yet to be fought.

From inside the stable, Shannon watched as one of Davis's one hundred thousand volunteers rode up to the main building.

Wade Rawlins, dressed in the immaculate uniform of a Confederate captain, dismounted and walked toward the entrance.

Good, Shannon thought to himself. *Maybe the bastard will go off to war and get killed. It can't happen too soon.*

Shannon himself had no such intention. He would stay in the stable and hope for the best — or weather the worst.

In the great room, Hadley poured himself and Rawlins a drink as Heather smiled with admiration at their uniformed visitor.

Hadley raised his glass and handed the other one to Rawlins.

"Well, here's to you, *Captain* Rawlins . . . and to the Confederacy."

"Thank you, Hadley."

"By the way," Hadley asked as both men sat, "how's that foreman of yours coming along?"

"Redding? It took some time but he's up and around, even back on the job."

"I'm glad to hear that."

"You heard what happened between Tom Hill and . . ."

"Yes, yes, I did." Hadley was not anxious to continue with anything more having to do with Shannon. "Will you be leaving soon? I mean, for active duty?"

"I hope so." Then Rawlins looked at Heather. "I mean, well, I'm waiting for orders. It could be anytime."

"Then" — and Hadley also looked toward

Heather — "you'd better make your time count . . . *Captain.*"

Hadley rose.

"I've got some business to take care of. It's a beautiful day. Why don't you and Heather go for a ride and . . . enjoy yourselves?"

"Heather," Rawlins asked, "would you like to do that?"

"Yes, I would," she nodded, "but I'll have to change."

"You go ahead. I'll have your horse brought 'round front," Hadley said.

Buttermilk was saddled and waiting next to Wade Rawlins' horse. Heather and the captain came out of the entrance, mounted, and rode away to enjoy the beautiful day, and themselves. Shannon watched from the stable.

They stood near each other beneath a tree at the bank of Willow Creek.

"Heather, somehow, when I'm close to you . . . I . . ."

"What is it, Wade?"

"I find that I can't tell you how I feel . . ."

"You don't have to say anything."

"Yes, I do. Look, Heather, I don't know what's going to happen. Nobody does . . . when I'm going to have to leave . . . but I want you to know that while I'm away, I'll be thinking of you all the time. In the meanwhile . . ."

"In the meanwhile?"

"In the meanwhile . . . I'd like to see you as much as possible. Is that . . . alright with you?"

"If it weren't, I wouldn't be with you now." She smiled.

"Heather, you don't know how happy that makes me."

"I'm glad to make a soldier of the South happy. Not just any soldier, though."

"Oh, Heather . . ." He leaned closer.

"It's quite alright, Wade. You may kiss me if you like."

As he did, Heather thought to herself that since she'd grown up, this was only the second man she had ever kissed.

It was nothing like the first.

The telegraph office, which also served as the post office, and press room of Gilead's weekly newspaper, *The Southern Cross*, was overflowing inside and out with citizens who were anticipating the results of the fiercest battle between North and South since hostilities had begun with the surrender of Fort Sumpter just over three months earlier.

Among those waiting as Brendan Bixby, the telegrapher-postmaster-publisher, sat scratching across a pad while the telegraph receiver clicked out the message, were Captain Wade Rawlins, Amos Higgins, Hank Redding and a whole herd of citizens of the Confederacy.

Early reports had Brigadier General Irvin McDowell's Union Army advancing upon Manassas Junction at Bull Run. The Confederate defenders — heavily outnumbered — were under the command of flamboyant General P.G.T. Beauregard. Among Beauregard's officers was Brigadier General T. J. Jackson, who at Bull Run was to gain the sobriquet "Stonewall" and be ever after known as Stonewall Jackson.

Over the clicking and scratching came overlapping voices from within the room and outside the open door on the boardwalk.

"What's it say?"

"What's the outcome?"

"Come on, Bixby, tell us somethin'."

"Did the Rebels hold?"

"How're we doin'?"

"Yeah, how're we doin'?"

"Did we stop McDowell?"

"Speak up, Bix . . . for God's sake!"

Brendan Bixby kept scratching and nodding but gave no clear indication of the results as a circle of spectators leaned over him trying to eyeball the news.

When the clicking stopped there were more questions from the eager crowd.

Bixby stood, paper in hand, and shoved people aside.

He made his way toward the open door where he could be heard inside and outside.

"Gimme room! Dammit, give me some room and shut up and listen. Here it is!"

The crowd went quiet with anticipation as Bixby proclaimed from the paper.

"July 21, 1861. The Confederate forces under command of General P.G.T. Beauregard, withstood, then repelled, the attack by General McDowell's Union Army at Bull Run, Manassas Junction. When last heard from, Beauregard was giving chase to the Yankees and was heading toward Washington, D.C. Hallelujah!!!"

Hats flew into the air. Pistols were fired. People pounded each other, laughing, and some were singing "Dixie."

Captain Wade Rawlins walked by the revelers onto the street, followed by Amos Higgins and Hank Redding.

"Best possible news." Higgins grinned at Rawlins. "Those Yankees can't take much more. They'll be suing for peace before you know it."

"I hope so, Amos," Rawlins replied. "I hope so."

"Hellsfire, Captain" — Redding shook his head — "the damn war's gonna be over before we even get in it. When we gonna shoot us some Yankees?"

"Right now," Rawlins replied, "our orders are to round up beef to supply —"

"I know the orders, Captain, but we're supposed to be in the army and we ain't even got uniforms yet."

"You don't need uniforms to herd cattle."

"The hell with herding cattle. We joined up to herd Yankees!"

There was more laughing and shouting on the streets of Gilead.

Sheriff Joe Fox just stood there while the celebrants laughed and shot, and sang "Dixie."

Pepper and Cherrie watched and listened to the proceedings from the batwings of the Emporium.

"Well," Pepper said, "looks like the Emporium's gonna do a land-office business for the rest of the day and night."

"Yeah," Cherrie said. "They'll be flocking in and I've got everything and everybody ready for 'em."

"Well, in that case I'd better drift."

"Hold on, Pepper, I thought we had an appointment this afternoon."

"Yeah, but that was before all this."

"The hell with 'all this.' An appointment is an appointment. They'll be fighting battles from now on. You're not going to let a little thing like a war interfere with . . . 'friendship,' are you?"

"Damn. You make good sense."

"That's not all I make good." She winked. "There's plenty of that private stock left."

"As a fella named Patrick Henry once said, 'Why stand we here idle?' "

"What did he do after he said that?" She smiled.

"I don't know about him — but, lady, we've got an appointment."

Word of the Confederate victory at Bull Run spread through the land, North and South.

And to North and South, war was no longer just a word.

It was a reality.

With blood and casualties.

With loss of life.

Soldiers were not just marching off to glory.

They were marching off to graves.

Shannon only wished that Rawlins and Hadley would march off with them.

Chapter Twenty-seven

Hadley had no intention of marching, or riding, off to war.

He would stay at Glenshannon Hall until the end of hostilities and ostensibly run the ranch, but Hadley didn't do much running. Pepper and Carson, along with Gibbs, Carey and the rest of the hands, ran the place.

There were times, more and more, when Hadley could hardly walk. He hadn't gone to bed sober since his twenty-first birthday.

He rode Bucephalus less and less — two or three times a week, and only for short distances.

He'd have one of the hands take the animal out for exercise and a good long run. But never Shannon. It was part of Shannon's duties to feed, groom and take care of Hadley's horse, but Shannon was not allowed to mount him.

When Hadley went in to Gilead, he would use the carriage because he had the good sense to know that he'd be drunk on the way back, and that a carriage was safer to sit in than a horse to sit on.

The purpose of his trips to Gilead was twofold. Business with Amos Higgins at the bank. Pleasure with a lady named Francine at the Emporium.

Hadley had sampled and compared half a dozen of the establishment's upstairs specialists before settling on Francine Almador for his visits to the Emporium's second-story pleasure dome.

Francine Almador would be considered a good-looking lady anywhere, and was arguably the best-looking working lady on the premises. She was blond, with deep blue eyes, high cheekbones, a cleft on her pointed chin, a long, slender throat, generous bosom, and a slim waist, rounding and tapering to lovely legs.

And of all the working girls, Hadley found her the best at her work.

Plying her trade, Francine spoke only when spoken to, and answered with words Hadley wanted to hear.

Cherrie had installed a private entrance at the rear of the Emporium, which led to a private room — presided over by a receptionist-bouncer — and a private staircase leading to the second floor. This was an accommodation for some of Gilead's more prominent citizens who considered discretion the better part of their reputation.

Cherrie was happy to accommodate them — for a price.

Hadley was happy to pay the price whenever he came to town.

One of the times when he came to town and paid an extended visit to Francine, Hadley was in no condition to make his way back to Glenshannon Hall — even in a carriage.

The next morning, after another session with Miss Almador, Hadley was pleased to pay the extra charge. And after that it was not uncommon for Hadley to make a night and morning of it.

When he didn't come home that first night, Heather, Pepper and Hannah became worried, even alarmed. But when he did come home he told them all that this would likely happen again and not to worry as he had business that would keep him overnight in Gilead from time to time.

Nobody much doubted what that business was, and everybody decided not to speak any more about it.

Even though Hadley always used the private entrance and stairs, while Pepper escorted Cherrie up the regular stairway, they did chance to meet more than once in the hallway.

Neither acknowledged the other's presence.

By now there was no doubt as to who was running the Emporium. Baldy's card games and siestas lasted longer and longer. He drank more and cared less. Pepper spoke to Cherrie about it more than once.

"Cherrie, you own fifty percent of the place and do a hundred percent of the work."

"Not a hundred percent. I do spend some time with you."

"You know what I mean."

"Pepper, I'm happy . . . aren't you?"

"Buy him out. Look, if it's the money, well, hell, I've got the three thousand the boss left me. It's sittin' right over there at the bank not doin' anybody any good. Why don't you take it and . . ."

"Pepper . . ."

"What?"

"Have I ever taken a plug nickel from you . . . for anything?"

"No, but . . ."

"No buts."

"You can pay me back if it'll make you feel better."

"That's not what makes me feel better, so

shut up and come over here. Besides, Baldy's not ready to sell — not yet."

"Well, when he's ready . . ."

"I'm ready right now." Pure seduction. "How about you?"

"Be right with you."

It was harder and harder to keep the hands at Glenshannon Hall. More and more they wanted to enlist and be able to come back with tales of victory and glory for the South. Most of the younger ones peeled off and left, all of them promising they'd come back to Glenshannon Hall when they got the job done.

A promise all of them wouldn't keep.

Carson, Gibbs and Carey were too old to enlist — and Pepper had fought his war.

So instead of pursuing Yankees, they would have to stay and punch cattle.

Pepper moved up alongside Shannon as Shannon stood by the gravesite on the hillside.

"Saw you comin' up here, son. Hope you don't mind some company."

"I've got company." Shannon looked at Glenshannon's grave.

"The dead don't make for good company."

"Better than most of the living."

"Includin' me?"

"I didn't say so."

" 'Preciate that, boy."

"What'd you come up here for, Pepper?"

"Same as you. Pay my respects."

"Uh, huh."

"Well, and maybe to have a little talk."

"About what?"

"The future."

"Yours or mine?"

"Both, maybe. I thought maybe you might change your mind about us partnerin' in on a spread."

"Nope."

"You know, Gleason and Perkins left today to join up with the 3rd Texas."

"So?"

"So everybody's got at least one war in him. I had mine, matter of fact, a couple of 'em."

"So?"

"So . . . I thought, maybe . . ."

"I'd join up with the 3rd Texas?"

"Well, somethin' like that."

"And get my head blown off? For what?"

"I didn't think I'd have to explain that to you."

"You and Heather, both of you so damn anxious for me to go and fight somebody else's war."

"Shannon! Listen to me. It's a way for you to get out of here, away from Hadley and all his —"

"No, you listen to me, Pepper. There's different kinds of wars. And I'm going to stay and fight mine right here. But thanks for the advice — and the company."

Shannon turned and moved toward Black.

Pepper shook his head, looked at Glenshannon's grave and shrugged.

For the first time since the War of 1812, when the British attacked and burned the U.S. capital, Washington was not only in harm's way but in great jeopardy of invasion, occupation, humiliation and destruction.

The nation had become a huge and bloody chessboard with Abraham Lincoln and Jefferson Davis the two chess masters.

But this was not a game. Every move caused crises and casualties, with repercussions that would last for centuries.

The players were not the familiar kings, queens, bishops, knights, and pawns. They had other names — a few, a very few, already famous. Winfield Scott of the North, Robert E. Lee of the South. But for the most part, the other players of North and South were relatively unknown except to their families and friends.

Their names would soon be etched in history and glory. Some were to die on the battlefield, others to return in victory or defeat, in triumph or humiliation — or even to the presidency of the United States.

Most of them, on both sides, had been cadets at West Point, many of them at the same time.

And many of them had fought under the same flag on the same side during the Mexican War. But now, just over a dozen years later, they fought under different flags on different sides, and would try to kill each other.

Both Heather and Pepper had urged Shannon to leave Glenshannon Hall, join the Confederacy and kill Yankees.

But as Shannon lay in the stable, in the stall that was his bed, the furthest thing from his mind was killing Yankees.

It was what was in his heart that kept him from sleeping.

Chapter Twenty-eight

Outside, the sun had already topped the eastern horizon and splashed the building with its first rays of light and warmth.

But the stable was still damp and dark as Shannon brushed down Bucephalus.

Despite the fact that Hadley seldom was seen outdoors before noon, Shannon would take no chances. Hadley's horse was always the first to be fed and attended to — just in case.

He would give the bastard no excuse to lace into him. So Bucephalus always came first.

Even though Shannon faced away from the entrance, he was aware that someone had entered the stable, and he knew it wasn't Hadley.

Heather looked at him for a couple of moments, then walked toward him. He paid no attention.

"Shannon . . ."

"You want your brother to come busting

in here? Have him start on me to where I can't take it anymore? Is that what you want, Heather? Because one of these times . . ."

"Hadley's still sleeping another one off."

Shannon kept on working with his back to her. She took a step closer.

"He's getting worse all the time — drinking and . . ."

"If you came in here to talk about Hadley, I just don't give a damn. You can save your breath."

"No, I didn't come in here to talk about Hadley. . . ."

"What is it, then? You want your horse? I'll saddle him up."

"No, I don't want my horse."

"It's not Hadley or the horse, what could it be, then?"

"It could be about you and me, Shannon."

He turned and faced her.

"You and me? Since when did you get around to you and me?"

"Shannon, you haven't talked to me since . . ."

"You got somebody else to talk to and ride with and . . ."

"And what?"

"I don't know, Heather. I don't know what. . . . But I can imagine. Tell me, Heather, did you ride with him up to Moon Rock and let him kiss you? Did you, Heather?"

"No! I've never been to Moon Rock with anybody except you. You ought to know that, Shannon."

"I ought to know a lot of things, but I'm not sure anymore. I suppose he never kissed you . . . tell me that, Heather."

She looked away.

"You can't, can you? You can't say he never kissed you, can you? What else did he do —"

"Stop it, Shannon! Stop it!"

"What's there for me to stop? I'm not doing anything different. I haven't changed."

"No, and you never will. You'll be content to spend the rest of your life in a stable."

"I'm not content, Heather, not without you, but it seems like you made a choice."

"I haven't done any choosing, Shannon, but you're not making it any easier!"

She whirled and started to run out.

He elbowed his way past the horse's rump.

"Go ahead . . . run to that posy-face with his fancy-pants uniform and toilet-water hair!"

Bucephalus moved, clomped a hoof down near Shannon's foot and whinnied.

"Watch it" — Shannon shoved the horse aside — "you whey-bellied bonehead!!"

★ ★ ★

That afternoon Shannon watched from the stable as Captain Rawlins and Heather rode off in the captain's carriage.

At least Shannon knew that they were not going to Moon Rock. The carriage would never make it up there.

But wherever they were going, they were going together, and Shannon would be alone — except for the horses.

He looked at the distant clouds far to the north, clouds that drifted in dark contrast to the clear blue sky, clouds that were filling, and sometime late that afternoon or evening would deliver their cargo of rain.

Good, Shannon thought to himself. He hoped that they would both be soaked through to their bones.

"Heather," Captain Rawlins said as they rode in the carriage, "you've never really seen all of Twelve Trees. Do you mind if we ride over there?"

"Why, not at all, Wade."

"There's something I want to talk to you about."

"I can't imagine what it could be." She smiled.

But she could.

230

★ ★ ★

The rain did come, right after sundown.

Hadley, Pepper and Hannah had eaten in the dining room, then Hadley had repaired to the great room and a bottle of bourbon, while Hannah and Pepper went to the kitchen. They could hear the grandfather clock in the hall strike nine times. There was no letup in the rain.

"Damn." Hannah looked up from her knitting. "Where could those two be?"

"Never mind where they be — what the hell are they doin'?"

"Oh, shut up, Pepper. You know Heather better than that."

"Yeah, but I don't know Rawlins all that well."

"Wade Rawlins is a perfect gentleman."

"Miz Dean, nobody's perfect."

"Oh, shut up!"

"You said that before."

Almost an hour later, Hadley still sat in the big chair staring at the flames in the fireplace — the bottle of bourbon on the side table next to him two-thirds gone.

He rose and grabbed the bottle by the nape. He knocked over the small table but managed to hold on to the bottle.

As Hadley threaded his way along,

Pepper came out of the kitchen.

"Say, Hadley . . ."

"What?"

"Can I get you anything? You didn't hardly touch your supper."

"No. I've got my supper right here." He held up the bottle. "I'm going to bed."

"Good idea. I'll help you off with your boots."

As Pepper guided him along, he thought to himself that in a way it was a good thing Hadley's father hadn't lived to see his son in this condition. Not just once in a while, but every night. On the other hand, if Glenshannon had lived, maybe his son wouldn't be in this condition every night.

Pepper knew that Hadley harbored demons, demons that would destroy him, unless something was done to help him. In spite of the fact that he had never had any great love for Hadley, he wished he could do something to dispell those demons. He also knew that there was little he could do except help Hadley off with his boots and put him to bed.

As he sat on the bed, Hadley's bootless right foot shoved Pepper in the backside and his left boot slid off his foot.

Hadley lay back on the bed, still wearing his clothes with the bottle on the nightstand next to him.

"Need anythin' else?" Pepper asked.

"Nooo . . ."

"Goodnight, Hadley." Pepper reached for the bottle.

"Leave it."

"Yuh." Pepper blew out the light and gimped toward the door.

In the dark Hadley reached over and took hold of the bottle.

The rain persisted.

In the kitchen, Hannah reached for the pot of coffee. She was about to pour herself another cup as Pepper poked his head in the doorway.

"No sign of 'em?"

Hannah shook her head, poured the coffee into the cup and returned the pot to the top of the stove.

Pepper walked in and lifted his yellow slicker from the back of a chair.

"Turnin' in."

"I'll wait up for her."

"Yuh." Pepper nodded. "Looks like it's gonna rain all night. Regular goose-drowner."

He put on his slicker and hat and headed out the kitchen door toward his rooms in the bunkhouse.

Shannon lay fully clothed, eyes open, on

his bunk in the stable, listening to the rain lash the roof and watching as the water hit and slipped down the window.

How long he had been listening and watching he did not know. What he did know was that Heather and her Captain Rawlins had ridden away in a carriage more than eight hours ago, and that he had wished they would both be soaked through to their bones.

And now he was afraid something worse had happened. The carriage might have turned over with them in it. Or maybe even worse than that — they were somewhere warm and dry in each other's arms.

Shannon heard something. Something he had been waiting to hear. He sprang out of the bunk and jumped to the window.

A carriage rolled up to the front of the main building.

Rawlins, dressed in a slicker, climbed down, then helped Heather — she wore a cape with a hood — step off the carriage and into his arms. He carried her up the stairs onto the porch and let her down slowly at the door.

They exchanged a few words, words Shannon could not hear but that nevertheless seared his brain.

Rawlins kissed her gently. She opened the

door and entered. He stood for a moment, walked back to the carriage and rode off in the rain.

As Shannon watched he almost smashed his fist through the window. But what he really wanted to smash was Captain Wade Rawlins.

Hannah rose as Heather came into the kitchen, still wearing the dripping wet cape.

"Heaven's sake, child, you're soaked through."

"I'm alright, Hannah."

"Take off that cape. Sit here near the stove and dry off. I'll get you some hot coffee."

Shannon made his way through the mud and rain to the enclosed rear veranda. He opened the door and entered.

He walked toward the kitchen door but as he came to an open window, he stopped, wiped the rain from his face, and leaned closer to watch and listen.

Heather had a saucy glint in her eyes and an enigmatic smile on her lips. She took a sip of coffee and looked at Hannah, who scowled at her.

"Young lady, do you know how long you've been gone? And without proper escort."

"He was very proper, but never mind that, Hannah. There's something I've got to tell you."

"I can't imagine what it is."

"Wade Rawlins asked me to marry him."

"I already guessed that part. What did you say?"

"What would any girl in her right mind say?" Heather teased. "He's handsome, kind, rich and generous. He'd give me everything I could ever want."

"Everything?"

"Yes."

"You mean everything he *has*. There is a big difference."

"Hannah, you're such a spoilsport."

"There's nothing sporting about this. You're talking about the rest of your life."

"He's the best catch in Texas. Any girl would be a fool to refuse him."

Shannon's face was still wet from the rain — and maybe more. He turned away and moved out of the open door.

"When are you going to marry him?"

There was a pause. Heather smiled.

"Oh, Hannah, I'm not."

"Why?"

"You of all people know why."

"Because of Shannon?" Hannah said.

"It doesn't matter what Wade Rawlins is,

or has." She nodded. "I couldn't live without Shannon. I *am* Shannon."

But Shannon had saddled Black and rode into the rain-splattered night — with a vengeance.

Chapter Twenty-nine

By morning Shannon had intended to be miles away — to the north.

But fate intervened in the form of a horseshoe.

As the rain stopped, Black's gait became uneven. Shannon dismounted and lifted the animal's left front leg. The shoe was loose and had lost two nails.

Shannon had no intention of trying to make it back to Glenshannon Hall.

He didn't want to be seen repairing the shoe. Not by Heather, Hadley, Pepper or anybody. There was only one alternative.

Gilead.

Shannon walked with Black over a dozen miles to the main street of Gilead, paused at the entrance of the barnlike building that housed the combination livery stable–blacksmith shop, and then entered.

By that time he looked like hell wouldn't have him.

"Beg pardon," Shannon said to the behemoth who had a hammer in one hand and was pumping the bellows with the other. "You the boss man?"

"Big Jake Trapp's the name. Who the hell are you?"

"Name's Shannon. Horse got a loose shoe. . . ."

"I'll fix it for two bits."

"Haven't got two bits, Mister Trapp, but I can fix it myself if you'll let me use . . ."

"This ain't no charity."

"I'll work it off however you want, cleaning or . . ."

"Bub, looks like you could use some cleaning yourself . . . get out of here and take your flies with you."

"Just a minute" — Cherrie stood near the entrance — "Big Jake." There was an implication in the way she emphasized the adjective proceeding the livery man's name.

"Oh, good day to you, Miss Cherrie, your horse and carriage are all ready for your Friday-morning ride."

"Never mind that, Big Jake. What's going on here?"

"Oh, this gypsy's got a horse with a loose shoe and no money to . . ."

"I'll tell you what you're going to do, Big Jake. . . ."

"Yes, ma'am."

Shannon couldn't believe the change in Trapp. He had become deferential, even submissive, seemed to bow slightly as she spoke and he listened.

"You're going to fix that horse's loose shoe and check the three other ones. . . ."

"Yes, ma'am."

"Then you're going to feed this gentleman's horse, curry him and deliver him to the Emporium, got that, Big Jake?"

"Yes, ma'am. What about your horse and carriage?"

"I've changed my mind, not going for a ride today."

"Yes, ma'am. I'll have that horse there in about an hour."

"Good. Now, young fellow," she addressed Shannon, "would you come with me?"

He nodded and walked with her to the Emporium. They sat at a corner table away from the half dozen early customers and she ordered him a steak with all the trimmings and a pot of coffee. He ate, drank and said nothing.

"You don't talk much, do you?"

"Thank you."

"Well, that's a start. You do remember me, don't you, from the times you came to town?"

Shannon nodded.

"Well, I sure as hell remember you. You make quite an impression no matter where you go — and Pepper talks about you quite a bit of the time. He and I are friends, you know."

"Yes, ma'am."

"Does he talk about me?"

"No, ma'am."

"I didn't think so." She smiled. "He's a gentleman. What're you doing, son, running away?"

"I don't call it that."

"Then that's all that counts. You know, you and I are both the same in some ways. Don't look at me like that. What I mean is, we're both misfits."

"You seem to be doing alright."

"That's the point. You mind if I tell you the story of my life . . . while you eat?"

Shannon shook his head. No, he didn't mind.

"I never knew my father. He died just before I was born. But he left my mother and me relatively well off in New Orleans. A comfortable house, with two servants — not slaves, servants.

"When I was sixteen I became engaged to a gentleman, never mind his name, who was very well off, very respectable. We were to be married when I became eighteen.

"But my mother became ill. We both knew she was going to die soon.

"On her death bed she told me something she thought I should know about my father — a secret, a dark secret. He was an octoroon. Do you know what an octoroon is?"

"Part Negro."

"One eighth. She thought it was time that I knew. What neither of us knew was that one of the servants was listening.

"And just after my mother died, the gentleman found a reason to call off the prospective wedding. It seems that the servant had received one hundred dollars for revealing, to the gentleman, what she had overheard.

"Soon the secret was no longer a secret among any of my friends in New Orleans — and my friends were no longer my friends.

"Time and again I looked into the mirror for any sign. Eyes, nose, lips, fingernails, all the same.

"But nothing was the same.

"Another thing my mother hadn't told me, the house was heavily mortgaged and there was little or no money.

"That's when I came to Texas, to the Emporium — and traveled through a land of men.

"Two of the finest I ever met were Shannon Glenshannon and Pepper.

"I never told the story of my life to anyone but Pepper, even though he never asked."

"Why did you tell it to me?"

"I'm not sure. Maybe because we're both misfits. Maybe because I like the look in your eyes and the cut of your jib."

"Miss Cherrie." Jake Trapp had entered the Emporium and stood near the table with his hat in his hand. "The . . . the gentleman's horse is outside and ready."

"Thanks, Jake."

Jake Trapp smiled, turned and left.

"Isn't he going to get paid?" Shannon asked.

"We exchange professional courtesies. Oh, not with me. One of the ladies upstairs. Now you're going to wash up. There's some decent clothes around here that ought to fit you, and you can be on your way."

"I'm not going back to . . ."

"I know that."

Half an hour later, Shannon and Cherrie stood outside the Emporium next to Black, who shimmered in the sunlight.

As Shannon started to mount, she touched him on the shoulder.

"Just a minute." She dropped five double

eagles into his palm. "This is to get you where you're going."

"No."

"Shut up, son, that's what Glenshannon gave me when he won that poker game. Take it."

"I'll pay you back."

"I know you will."

He mounted.

She looked up at him and smiled.

"Which way you heading?"

"North."

Without going into too much detail, Cherrie told Pepper of Shannon's departure. Pepper told Heather, who was disconsolate — and he also told Hadley, who was inwardly exultant.

Chapter Thirty

Under its brilliant generals, led by one of the most brilliant battlefield commanders of all time, Robert E. Lee, the Confederacy had early on succeeded in repelling the invaders and inflicting severe casualties.

At first, Lee, Johnson, Stuart, Beauregard, Jackson, Early, Longstreet and the rest seemed invincible — winning victories in battle after battle: Fort Sumpter, Lexington, Belmont, Shiloh, Fort Royal, Bull Run.

Lincoln had been heavily criticized for his conduct of the war and for his choice of generals in chief to lead the Union forces.

After putting his faith in a dozen generals, including McDowell, McClellan, Lyon, Scott, Fremont, Halleck, Hooker, and Meade, President and Commander-in-Chief Abraham Lincoln either discarded or demoted every one.

Lincoln finally found his general in chief, a man who just a few years before had been tossed on the ash heap of history, and before the age of forty, was looked upon as a flat-out failure: Ulysses Simpson Grant.

There was no more aggressive and determined officer in any army anywhere. His men loved him because he led them to victory after victory. Fort Henry, Fort Donaldson, at Shiloh and at the siege of Vicksburg.

Grant was now general in chief and poised at Chattanooga. His strategy for defeating the South depended on two of his most trusted generals, William Tecumseh Sherman and Philip H. Sheridan.

Sherman would invade from the west. If his Union forces could take Chattanooga, then he would cut a swath of death and destruction through Georgia, South Carolina, North Carolina, to the sea.

Sheridan would hit from the north through the lush Shenandoah Valley, destroy the Confederate supply lines, divide their battalions and force the Army of Northern Virginia to surrender.

When Shannon left Gilead and rode north, he had no idea that his destiny would be linked to General William Tecumseh Sherman's Army of the Tennessee.

But it all depended on whether Sherman could take Chattanooga.

★ ★ ★

Days, weeks, months went by at Glenshannon Hall. It became apparent to Hadley, who was pleased that Shannon had left for good, to Pepper, who had mixed feelings, and to Heather, who cried through many of the nights and days and often rode to Moon Rock, hoping.

There, the wind, vagrant and vocal, brought back voices from the past as she touched the rocks and remembered.

"Shannon, Shannon, I knew you'd be here."

"Where else would I be?"

"Do you know what you are?"

"I'm a stable boy."

"You will be king of all the Indians and I will be your queen, King Shannon."

"Indians don't have kings."

"We'll build a castle here at Moon Rock and live happily ever after."

"Where else would I be?"

"Shannon, oh, Shannon, I love you . . . out here there's nothing else but you and me."

"You and me, Heather."

"You know, there's going to be a war."

"Not my war."

"It's everybody's."

"All I see is I'd be gone from you."

"You'll never be a gentleman like . . ."

". . . like Rawlins?"

"I won't listen to you talk that way about him."

"You don't have to listen to me at all."

"I knew you'd be here."

But he wasn't. And Heather was giving up hope of ever seeing him again.

Pepper and Gibbs, in the buckboard, would pull up in front of the main building at Glenshannon Hall. Pepper usually debarked with some letters and a newspaper in hand, and Heather would run from inside toward him. But Pepper always shook his head no, and Heather walked past him toward the stable.

Two or three times a day, and sometimes at night, she would walk inside, lean against the stall where Shannon had kept Black, and cry.

If she stayed too long, Hannah would come to her, turn her around and silently lead her back to the house.

Too often, in the dining room Hannah would pass a platter of food to Heather, who would just look at it, then pass it on to Pepper. Hadley, noticeably more pallid, would pour himself another drink.

Whenever possible, Pepper would encourage Captain Rawlins to take Heather away from Glenshannon Hall.

Captain Rawlins didn't need any encouragement.

At Twelve Trees Charlotte played the harpsichord. Heather and Rawlins sat in a loveseat nearby. Rawlins smiled and took her hand. Heather did not resist, nor did she smile.

And one time, on the way back from Twelve Trees to Glenshannon Hall, Wade Rawlins stopped the carriage near Willow Creek.

Heather listened almost impassively as Rawlins, brimming with passion and emotion, talked to her for nearly half an hour.

When he stopped — after a long pause — she nodded.

"Heather, I'll treasure every minute of our life together. I'd give my life to make you happy." He kissed her.

Heather believed every word he said, but she looked out toward Moon Rock.

"You may kiss the bride."

And Wade Rawlins did.

Outside, the church entrance was flanked with people. Heather in her bridal gown and Captain Rawlins in his dress uniform hurried down toward the carriage bedecked with flowers.

They were all there: Hadley, Hannah,

Charlotte, Amos Higgins, Cassie Higgins and all the rest. All laughing or smiling, all except Cassie Higgins. All throwing rice as Rawlins helped Heather into the carriage, then climbed aboard and took her in his arms.

"I'm the happiest man in the world."

And this time Heather smiled.

There were shouts of "throw the bouquet," "throw the flowers."

Heather stood, laughed, and flung the bridal bouquet toward the crowd, making sure it would land in the arms of Charlotte Rawlins, her sister-in-law.

That night, in their marriage bed, Heather did her best to respond to the eager fumblings of Wade Rawlins' soft hands. She even closed her eyes and imagined she was with Shannon. But she knew she wasn't, and she could barely respond. Rawlins didn't seem to know or care. All he knew — or cared about — was that Heather lay beneath him.

Afterward, as Rawlins slept and Heather stared at the bed's canopy, she somehow had the strange sensation that she had not lost her virginity.

And probably never would.

Chapter Thirty-one

The Confederate Army of the Cumberland held good defensive ground atop the steep slope where the Union brigade charged.

Winning or losing the Civil War in the west largely depended on the outcome at Chattanooga.

The Yankee captain leading his troopers in the cavalry charge took the full impact of a deadly missile that tore his chest apart. In his right hand he had held a sword that fell to the ground as he crumpled from his horse.

The Union brigade took volley after volley from the Confederates entrenched above.

"Keep firing!" The Southern major shouted to his men. "We got their captain! They're scattering! Keep firing — we broke their charge! Fire!"

The few that were left of the Northern troopers were milling in leaderless confusion, then falling back.

Then, through the smoke and shells, one trooper, a superb horseman on a scarred and dirty black horse, grabbed up the fallen captain's sword and whirled around to face the retreating Union contingent.

Shannon's face had a savage, hateful look and his voice impelled obedience.

"Follow me!! Charge!! Dammit!! Charge the bastards!! Follow me!!!"

And follow him they did. Forward and up the slope over their own dead and through the holocaust into the Southern line whose ranks broke and fell back as their major lay dead on the bloody ground.

Shannon bled from a wound on the forehead. He held on until he knew that the Confederate retreat had become a rout, then he fell from his horse, still clutching the sword.

His head bandaged, Shannon lay in a tent at a field hospital, his eyes locked straight ahead, remembering the charge.

"There's somebody here to see you," the doctor said.

"I don't know anybody," Shannon replied with his eyes still straight ahead.

"He knows you." The doctor smiled and left.

Shannon turned his face.

A man in uniform stood by the cot. He

was of average height, with a short rough beard, small eyes, and catgut skin. There was no insignia on his uniform. A dirty cavalry cape covered his shoulders.

"How are you, trooper?"

"I'll be ready," Shannon said.

"I believe it."

"Who are you?"

"Name's Sherman, William Tecumseh Sherman, Army of the Tennessee."

Shannon tried to rise.

"General Sherman?"

"Lay back, trooper."

"General, I . . ."

"Lay back. You've earned some rest. You took some bad knocks, but you saved the day."

"All I did was . . ."

"All you did was rally a broken charge — ride like the devil incarnate and take a position which gave me just the advantage I needed. That's all you did, *Captain*."

"Captain?"

"That's right. They tell me they had to pry that sword out of your hand. Damn near had to cut your arm off."

Sherman touched the sword that leaned against the cot.

"It's your sword now, Captain. Don't let anybody take it away."

"I won't, sir."

"I believe that, too. You'll need it. At best, war is barbarous and I intend to be just that — to break bridges, tear up railroads, smash mills, burn and destroy all supplies and shelter from here to the Atlantic saltwater. And it's soldiers like you that'll help me do it. I'll be seeing you, Captain."

"Yes, sir."

Sherman started to leave, but turned back.

"I'm told your name's Shannon. That your first or last name?"

"My only name."

"Uh, huh . . . it's a good name."

General William Tecumseh Sherman nodded and walked away.

Sherman was the most controversial general in the North and the most reviled in the South.

Born on February 8, 1820, at Lancaster, Ohio, he was sixth in his class, 1840, at West Point and served in the Mexican War with distinction as brevet captain. He resigned from the army and as a civilian had little success at law, then banking. He became superintendent of the Louisiana Military Academy and when Louisiana seceded, Sherman went North, where he volunteered and entered the Army as a colonel. He fought at First Manassas as a brigadier general, suffered wounds and was even accused of being "crazy" because of his determination to "destroy, destroy, destroy — and win," but U.S. Grant believed in him and gave Sherman command of the Army of the Tennessee — and Grant's decision was vindicated at Chattanooga and beyond.

Chattanooga was decisive. Grant and Sherman were the undisputed heroes of the Union. The South had lost the war in the west. The Confederates had no choice but to withdraw into Georgia.

But Sherman would charge in after them — invade and destroy.

And Shannon would be one of the officers who led that charge — to invade and destroy.

Again and again, with a scar on his forehead, mounted on Black, at the head of his brigade as the bugle blew, Shannon raised his sword, then brought it forward screaming the command.

"Charge!"

Heather screamed as she lay in bed and the baby was delivered.

Hannah entered the parlor at Twelve

Trees where Captain Rawlins paced and Charlotte sat biting her lip.

"Captain Rawlins," Hannah beamed, "it's a girl. Beautiful little darling girl."

"Heather?" Rawlins asked.

"She had a hard time but she'll be fine."

"Thank you, Hannah." Rawlins smiled and embraced his sister. "And thank God."

What Hannah hadn't told Wade Rawlins and would never tell Heather, was that during the hard time of her delivery, when her life hung in the balance, she spoke only one word, over and over again.

"Shannon . . . Shannon . . . Shannon."

Chapter Thirty-two

Sherman's orders to his troops were to live off the land, then burn the land and everything on it, and move on. What was left behind was wasteland.

It was not easy to determine whom the South hated most — Lincoln, Grant, or Sherman. But in Georgia there was no doubt. There was a standing offer of one hundred thousand dollars to the soldier or civilian who killed William Tecumseh Sherman.

It was not specified whether the reward would be paid in Yankee or Confederate dollars. It was a moot point, since no one ever collected.

In the months that followed Chattanooga, Shannon twice again was wounded in charges that led to victory.

The second time he was paid another visit by his commanding officer.

"How you doing, son?"

Shannon just nodded.

"Hit bad?"

"No, sir, just creased the fat."

"There's no fat on you, Major."

"Major?"

"Now look here, Shannon, I'm going to quit promoting you unless you promise not to get wounded again."

"I'll do my best, sir."

"You always have."

January 1, 1863, President Abraham Lincoln had issued the Emancipation Proclamation. One of the two reasons the North had gone to war was officially ended: slavery.

The other reason was the preservation of the Union, and that mission was far from complete.

Before Shannon joined the Union Army he had never seen a slave. There were slaves in Texas, but not where he came from.

Along with Sherman's destruction of bridges, railroad tracks, mills, crops and plantations, he was destroying slavery. After Chattanooga, on his march through Georgia, Sherman had proclaimed that all the powers on earth could no more restore slaves to the Southerners than they could restore their dead grandfathers.

As Shannon and his brigade — the Tennessee 9th — plunged through Georgia, wherever they moved, they were followed by battalions of slaves, many of whom were not even sure of what the war was about.

Their fathers and grandfathers, along with their women and children, betrayed by their own tribal leaders, or taken by enemy tribes, had been herded by slave traders, white and black, into the bleak holds of ships for a one-way journey to the New World. Some with eyes bewildered, defeated. Others with tribal pride as ancient as history.

And that journey of hundreds of years had come to a conclusion with Sherman's march — and the Emancipation Proclamation.

Shannon and his 9th Tennessee had moved inexorably southeast toward Atlanta.

That morning he had led a charge at Three Forks and routed an infantry contingent of Georgia volunteers.

And that evening, officers of the Union Army under the command of Colonel Ned Sherman Crist, a cousin of General Sherman, had occupied a magnificent plantation.

Colonel Crist and several other officers, including Shannon, sat in the drawing room. The plantation, inside and out, was bullet-scarred and windowless, no longer magnificent.

"A good day's work, gentlemen. And so I shall record in my report to the general — with commendations for you all, and especially for Major Shannon. Your charge broke their spine."

Crist raised his glass. Earlier, plantation whiskey had been poured all around.

"To Major Shannon."

"To Major Shannon." They all toasted and drank — except Major Shannon.

"And now, gentlemen," Colonel Crist added, "I suggest we all get a good night's sleep in what's left of this fine old plantation, because when we leave tomorrow, there'll be nothing left but some fine old ashes. Good night."

The officers all said their good nights and started to leave.

"Major Shannon," Crist said. "Wait here a minute."

"Yes, sir."

When the door closed as the last of the officers left, Colonel Crist pulled open a desk drawer where he sat. He reached in and removed a large bandana tied in a knot at the top. He dropped the bandana on the desk and untied the knot, pulled back the corners of the cloth to reveal a pile of sparkling jewelry.

"Here you are, Major."

"What's that?"

"Spoils . . . for your war chest."

"I don't have a war chest."

" 'Bout time you did . . . like the rest of us."

"I guess I'm not like the rest of you."

"What do you mean by that?"

"I didn't join the Army to get rich."

"None of us did, Major." His voice was curt.

"I'm sorry, sir."

"Listen to me, Shannon. We can burn their food and supplies and houses, but this stuff won't burn. Neither will a lot of other valuables."

He rose from the chair at the desk.

"When the war's over you'll have the Army's gratitude but that's about all. Now, there must be something you want."

"There is." Shannon thought back to Heather and Glenshannon Hall.

"Well, Major Shannon." Colonel Crist pointed to the jewelry on the desk. "There's your first payment."

Those payments continued, with charge after charge, plantation after plantation —

victory after victory as Shannon's brigade fought, burned and looted its way through Georgia.

There were others, besides the unfettered former slaves, who followed the Union forces on the victory parade.

There were the "hookers," camp women named after General Joseph Hooker: "Fighting Joe" — handsome, cocksure, charismatic — a hard drinker, hard fighter, and all 'round ladies' man. Wherever he fought and drank, he enjoyed and encouraged their company. Other ladies soon emulated those who followed Fighting Joe and went along with other brigades who sought and paid for friendly diversion and companionship between encounters with unfriendly soldiers of the South.

There were occasions when Shannon availed himself of such companions, but mostly his mind and efforts were on two things: beating the Confederates and adding to his war chest.

Regarding the latter, there was a third group who followed the Union forces, besides the slaves and "hookers" — and that was the group that interested Shannon most.

This group was composed of Yankee traders — money men, moveable brokers —

who would purchase the loot from the officers' war chests, or whatever the enlisted men could steal from the South, in return for Yankee dollars.

This was the group that Shannon did business with. He had no use for silverware or necklaces, bracelets, rings or loot of any kind — except for Yankee dollars that someday would buy him anything in Texas that he wanted. If he lived.

And as the war progressed — or regressed — matters in Texas grew worse. The seaports were blockaded by Northern gun ships, and the Yankee Armies had cut off passage by road and rail.

Ranchers and town folk alike knew that there was a war going on — not like the Southerners of Tennessee, Georgia and Virginia who were losing their homes, but still, Texas was paying a price for not heeding the warning words of Sam Houston.

They had sent their husbands and sons to fight — rich and poor, from ranches and shacks, cities and villages — to heed the call of the Confederacy in places many of them had never heard of: Big Bethel, Bull Run, Wilson's Creek, Paducah, Cold Harbor, Glorietta and scores of other blood-bathed groves and basins.

Hundreds of miles away, sons of the Lone Star were being ripped to shreds and buried, if they were lucky, in fields or ditches that might as well have been on the continent of Europe or Asia.

Families in Texas read and too often wept at the casualty lists posted on bulletin boards or printed in newspapers.

Every day Texas knew more and more that there was a war going on, and that the Confederacy was losing.

Amos Higgins had called a meeting.

More than a dozen of the leading ranchers and citizens of the area sat at the conference table of the First Bank of Gilead, including a bleary-eyed Hadley and Captain Wade Rawlins still in a spotless uniform.

Higgins' voice was harsh as he leaned back on the chair and smoked his cigar.

"Gentlemen, I've called you all here collectively because you're all in about the same boat — although Captain Rawlins is somewhat better off. The rest of your spreads are all mortgaged to the hilt."

"Well, hell, Amos," one of the ranchers said, "you hold all those mortgages . . ."

"Damn right I do — and I couldn't collect ten cents on the dollar for the lot of them . . ."

"You wouldn't do that, Amos."

"I couldn't! Nobody's got the cash. I mean real dollars, or gold. The war's gone badly. Texas is virtually cut off from the rest of the South. That damn Sherman has burned a swath through Georgia and it looks like nothing's going to stop him."

"Amos," Hadley smirked, "I do recall you saying that the First Bank of Gilead would back the Confederacy with all its resources."

"Goddammit, Hadley, that's what I'm trying to tell you. The First Bank of Gilead ain't got any more resources — except your ranches, which ain't worth a damn."

"Jesus, Amos. We didn't realize it was that bad."

"Well, you better realize it now. Frankly, this bank and every other bank in Texas is overextended."

"In plain talk, what does that mean?"

"In plain talk it means that we're broke — busted. And the Confederacy seems doomed."

"The Confederacy was always doomed," Rawlins said in a quiet voice.

"What did you just say, Captain?"

"I'll say it again, gentlemen. The Confederacy was doomed from the start — from before the start."

The room reverberated with a swift chorus of disbelief, outrage and even threats.

"What the hell kind of talk is that?!"

"Sir, you are a disgrace to that uniform!"

"I demand an apology!"

"Some talk from somebody who hasn't done a lick of fighting."

"That's out-and-out treason!"

"No, gentlemen," Rawlins said calmly, "it's logic. There are over eighteen million people in the North, and nine million in the South, a third of whom are slaves. The North has nine-tenths of the nation's manufacturing capacity, two-thirds of the railroads and most of the country's iron, coal and copper. It controls the seas. The advantages are overpowering. The Confederacy *is* doomed, but there will be a last stand — and probably in my native state of Virginia. You're right, I haven't done a lick of fighting . . . not yet. But, gentlemen, I intend to."

Pepper had brought Hadley into town on the buckboard.

He had long ago withdrawn from Higgins' bank the three thousand dollars Glenshannon had left him, and had given it to Hadley to help pay creditors other than Amos Higgins. That helped, but not for

266

long. There was no income and Hadley even owed wages to all the ranch hands. Those who hadn't left to join the Confederacy.

When Hadley took the three thousand from Pepper, he merely nodded and didn't bother to express his gratitude. It was no more or less than Pepper had expected from the current owner of Glenshannon Hall, but Pepper did advise Hannah, who had gone to live with Heather, to keep the money that had been left her — for her old age. Hannah had exchanged the inheritance for double eagles and buried the booty where no one could find it.

While Hadley, Rawlins and the other ranchers were meeting with Higgins at the bank, Pepper paid a visit to the Emporium — and Cherrie.

As they sat at a table the conversation got around to Shannon.

"You think he's alive?" Pepper asked.

"Fifty-fifty. But, dead or alive, he's in uniform."

"Blue or gray?"

"Said he was heading North. What do you think?"

"Doubt if it's gray."

"So do I." She smiled. "If he is alive, you think he'll come back?"

"If he did come back" — Pepper puffed

267

on his cigar — "it'd only be for one reason — and it's too late now."

"Is she happy, Pepper? Does she love Rawlins?"

"She loves the baby, Hannah says. So she must love the baby's father."

"That's all you know about women."

"That's all I could know, not being one myself."

"Well, I am."

"So I noticed."

"And I saw something in Shannon's eyes that said he'd come back."

"If he does — God help us all."

Rawlins had made arrangements to join General Joseph E. Johnston's Army, almost halfway across the continent. If the war for the Confederacy were to be won — or more likely, lost — the conclusive battles would be fought in the Carolinas and Virginia.

His Texas brigade, including Redding, was mounted and waiting in front of Twelve Trees as the captain bade farewell to his wife and baby daughter, Angela. Hannah, as always, stood nearby.

"Come back to us, Wade." Tears filled Heather's eyes as she held the baby.

"I'll come back, Heather. I love you both. I'll come back."

For the first time, as Captain Wade Rawlins turned and mounted, he looked like a soldier.

Lincoln's re-election in 1864 looked doubtful, even to Lincoln.

The war-weary country — that is, the North — was resentful that the war had dragged on for years, instead of being resolved in months or even weeks. The North's casualties were appalling. Lincoln had called for a draft of another half million men. Because of Lee's brilliance, he and his generals had caused a prolonged stalemate between the Northern and Southern Armies. Neither Lee nor Johnston had been beaten and the Confederate Army had recently threatened Washington itself.

More and more people had begun to believe that a general ought to be elected President, a general who could lead the nation to victory.

The Democrats capitalized on that belief by nominating the ever-popular General George B. McClellan for President and General H. Pendleton of Ohio for Vice President.

Lincoln needed something decisive to bring him victory in the November election of 1864.

General William Tecumseh Sherman provided that decisive something. On September 2, he sent a telegram to Lincoln:

Mr. President, I give you Atlanta.

Shannon was there with Sherman, and with him as Sherman's dashing Yankee boys continued their victorious swath of destruction southeast to Savannah and Port Royal, then turned northward where they wreaked their most devastating destruction and revenge on South Carolina, "the mother of secession," the first state to secede from the Union and erupt the country into civil war.

Columbia, the capital, became a "howling waste" as Sherman torched the land and left two-thirds of what was a city in ashes.

And with each successive victory, Shannon — now *Colonel* Shannon — added to his war chest. He still rode Black, but less and less into battle and more and more on victory parades. He had other horses for the charges, but Black was still his favorite mount, and always would be.

On August 7, General Philip H. Sheridan took over the newly named Army of the Shenandoah with orders to destroy both Jubal Early's Army and the Shenandoah.

Sheridan did both, ending in a rout of Early's forces at Fisher's Hill; and the once green valley of the Shenandoah became a smoldering swath of waste.

In his report Sheridan wrote that if even a crow flew over the valley, it would have to bring its own provisions.

Phil Sheridan was not a man prone to exaggerate.

There was nothing left of the Shenandoah except victory for the North and defeat for the South.

Somewhere in Virginia a Yankee soldier stood guard at night as another trooper approached and barely spoke above a whisper.

"John . . . it's Dan."

"Yeah, Dan."

"Everything quiet?"

"Yeah."

"Tobacco?"

"Yeah."

There was a pause.

"Well?"

"Well, what?"

"Where's the tobacco?" Dan asked.

"Hell, I thought you was offerin' me some."

They both laughed.

"Well, Johnny, I got a feelin' if we can

make it through tomorrow we're gonna live to see the end of all this 'unpleasantness.' "

"Yeah, what with Grant, Sheridan and Sherman closin' in on all sides, Lee and Johnston can't last much longer."

"If Shannon can take Benton Ridge tomorrow, that'll cut them in half."

"Colonel Shannon could take hell on horseback," Johnny said.

"Specially if there's something in it for his war chest. He must be the richest officer in this man's army."

"Yeah, but I'm surprised he's lived this long. Never seen a man take so many chances."

"Those cavalry boys of his would follow him anywhere. They know he's too damn mean to die."

They both laughed until a voice came from the darkness.

"I wonder if the Rebels know that."

Colonel Shannon stepped into sight. He looked older, handsomer — even though his face seemed to be made out of hammered copper. The scar had blended into the upland of his forehead. His expression was colder than a December frost.

The two soldiers recognized him and were scared out of their belt buckles, but managed to salute.

"I . . . beg your pardon . . . sir," Johnny stammered.

"Colonel Shannon, sir . . ."

There was a moment of silence.

"What's your name?" Shannon asked the soldier who had spoken last.

"Dan, sir. Private Daniel Ross, sir."

"And you?"

"Private John Terhune, sir."

"I'm glad you two boys'll be with me tomorrow." He tossed something at Private Daniel Ross. "Have some tobacco."

Colonel Shannon returned their salutes, turned and walked into the night.

Chapter Thirty-three

"Forward at a gallop . . . ho!!!" Shannon commanded.

The bugles blew.

The battle for Benton Ridge began.

With the sun at his back arching into a heavy sky, Shannon, mounted on Black, reins in one hand, a saber in the other, led the cavalry charge from the flatland up the flank of the hill with rifles firing, guns blasting, and sabers gleaming as the battalion advanced.

The Confederates on horseback rushed to meet the charge.

Dust — smoke — yells — gunshots — hoofbeats — blood — broken bodies. Men and horses fell. Some rose. Others, wounded, gasped for breath and died.

Churning chaos among the Confederates, as the Yanks rallied around their wild-eyed Colonel swinging his saber toward the retreating Rebels as they broke and retreated on horseback and foot toward the deserted streets of Benton Ridge.

"Burn it!" Shannon commanded. "Burn everything!"

And burn it they did.

Within minutes, what had been a village became a pyre — then ruins.

On the other side of the ridge the enemy melted into the forest and disappeared.

The Rebels of Benton Ridge — those who died and those who lived — had fought and lost their last battle of the war for the Confederacy.

Lee and Johnston's only chance to seize the initiative and turn the tide had been to join forces and defeat Sherman in pitched battle.

But the key to joining forces was occupying Benton Ridge, and Benton Ridge was now occupied by Colonel Shannon.

Lee and Johnston were outflanked. With Sheridan down from the Shenandoah holding a road junction known as Five Forks, and Grant pinning down what was left of Lee's starving troops of the Army of Northern Virginia, the end was in sight for what would come to be the Confederacy's cruelest month — April of 1865.

At Benton Ridge, dozens of ragged captured Confederates, guarded by armed Yankees, were herded onto the charred streets. Smoke still smoldered from the burned and broken buildings.

Colonel Shannon walked with two of his officers, Captain Norman Wolfe and Lieutenant Robert Dumonte. They had been with him across Georgia, into the Carolinas, then Virginia.

"Our supply wagons'll be catching up to us before nightfall, sir," Wolfe said.

"Good, Norman. Double rations tonight."

"Yes, sir! The men'll be thankful."

"They've earned it — and so have you, Captain. That was a right smart maneuver on the left flank."

"Just followed orders, sir."

"There'll be a commendation in my report."

"Thank you, sir."

"Bob, have you made out a list of our casualties, yet?"

"Working on it, sir."

"Work faster."

"Yes, sir. Excuse me, sir." Lieutenant Robert Dumonte executed an about-face and disappeared double-time.

Shannon and Wolfe approached another officer, Captain LaRue, who was in charge of prisoners.

"Colonel Shannon," LaRue saluted.

"Everything secure, Captain?"

"Everything secure, sir."

"Our wounded been attended to?"

"Yes, sir."

"Very good."

"Uh, Colonel Shannon . . ."

"What is it, Captain?"

"There's a rumor. . . ."

"There's always a rumor."

"Yes, sir, but this one's awful persistent. . . ."

"So are you, Captain — what is it this time?"

"Well, sir, it's being rumored around that Lee and Grant are meeting at Appomattox Court House tomorrow — Palm Sunday, you know."

"Yes, I know."

"Well, sir, what do you think?"

"I think . . ."

Shannon recognized one of the Confederate prisoners, gaunt and dirt-smeared, who had been looking at the man in the colonel's uniform with utter astonishment, if not disbelief.

Shannon took a couple of steps toward Twelve Trees' former foreman, Hank Redding.

"You remember me?" Shannon asked.

Redding nodded.

"Well, I remember you too. Redding, wasn't that the name?"

Redding nodded again.

"Uh, huh. Well, Redding, how were things in Texas when you left?"

"Not . . . not good."

"So I've heard. Can't say it makes me sorry. You wounded?"

"Just hungry."

"And beat. Captain Wolfe, when the supply wagons get here, see that these men are fed."

"Yes, sir."

"Thank you," Redding said.

"My pleasure. And speaking of Texas, times must be bad for your former employer and mine. How are Rawlins and Hadley . . . and his sister, Miss Heather?"

"I don't know about Mister Hadley, but Miss Heather's married to Captain Rawlins."

It was as if a knife had pierced Shannon's chest, but he displayed no emotion, no change of expression.

"Is Captain Rawlins still in Texas?"

"He was at Benton Ridge this morning." Redding shook his head. "Don't know what happened to him."

"Sorry I missed him," Shannon said.

He turned and walked away.

"Miss Heather's married to Captain Rawlins."

All that night long, the words burned into Shannon's brain.

The image of the two of them dancing.

The sight of the two of them laughing in his carriage.

In the rain on the porch, Rawlins kissing Heather.

The thought of them at their wedding.

And then, the two of them — Heather and Rawlins — in their marriage bed.

At Benton Ridge Shannon thought he had fought and won his last battle.

"Miss Heather's married to Captain Rawlins."

But how could he fight and win this battle?

His only consolation was that maybe Captain Wade Rawlins had died at Benton Ridge.

Chapter Thirty-four

The meeting between Grant and Lee had been arranged by exchange of letters under flags of truce.

Palm Sunday, April 9, 1865, at Appomattox Court House in Virginia.

The battles on land and sea, in fields and streams, in cities and swamps — conquests and defeats, on horseback and foot, with all the fire and devastation — had led to the inevitable end.

Appomattox.

General Grant wanted his two most prized generals to be with him: Sheridan and Sherman.

But Sherman sent his regrets. He had Johnston boxed and would not leave his men until Johnston personally surrendered to him.

Instead, Sherman asked Grant for permission to send Colonel Shannon to represent his Army of the Tennessee.

Grant gave his permission.

Grant, along with Sheridan, Shannon, Colonel Ord and several of his staff, entered the room where Lee and his staff had been waiting.

Grant was dressed for the field in tunic, breeches, and mud-spattered boots.

Lee wore an immaculate uniform complete with dress sword.

There was some awkward hesitation as the two men exchanged greetings, then sat across from each other at a small table.

"I . . . suppose, General Grant, that the object of our present meeting is fully understood."

Grant nodded.

"I asked to see you," Lee continued, "to ascertain on what terms you would receive the surrender of my army."

General Grant put his hand to his forehead and tried not to look directly at Lee, tried to make the moment easier.

"The terms I propose, General Lee, are those stated in my letter of yesterday. That is, the officers and men surrendered, to be delivered up as captured property."

Lee nodded, not displeased.

"Those are about the conditions I hoped would be proposed."

"And I hope," Grant added, "this will lead to a general suspension of hostilities, sir.

And be the means of preventing any further loss of lives."

"May I suggest, General," Lee said, "that you commit to writing the terms you have proposed so they may be formally agreed upon?"

"Very well," Grant replied as easily as he could. He pointed to his manifold order book and addressed one of his officers, Colonel Ord. "Can I have that book and something to write with, please?"

This was not what Colonel Shannon had expected.

These two men had led great armies and ordered them to destroy each other — to kill and maim in brutal battle.

This somehow seemed too civilized.

Grant wrote rapidly and when he finished, rose and slowly took the few steps to Lee and handed him the paper.

"I have written that what is to be turned over will not include the sidearms of officers nor their private horses or baggage."

There were reactions from the Union officers, Sheridan, Ord, Parker, Williams and Shannon. And from the Confederates, Marshall and Babcock — and from General Lee.

"This will have a very happy effect on my army."

Lee had finished reading. He hesitated as if embarrassed to speak further, but did.

"There is one thing, General. The cavalrymen and artillerists own their own horses in our army. I know this differs from the United States Army."

Grant nodded.

"I would like to understand," Lee went on, "whether these men will be permitted to retain their horses."

There was a stilted moment.

"The terms do not allow this, General. Only the officers are allowed their private property."

"No." There was a regretful nod from Lee as he looked back at the paper. "I see the terms do not allow it. That is clear."

Grant would not humiliate the great general by forcing him to make a direct plea for modification of the already generous terms. He spoke as gently and respectfully as possible.

"Well, the subject is quite new to me. Of course, I didn't know that any private soldiers owned their own horses." He paused for just a beat. "I take it that most of your men are small farmers. I know that they'll need their horses to put in a crop to carry their families through next winter. I'll instruct my officers to allow all men who own a horse or mule to take the animals home to work their farms."

Lee's face was filled with manifest relief and gratitude. He looked directly into the eyes of the man who had defeated him.

"This will have the best possible effect on the men. It will do much toward conciliating our people."

"General Lee, of how many men does your present force consist, sir?"

"I am not able to say. My losses in killed and wounded are exceedingly heavy. Many of our companies are without officers. I have no means of ascertaining our present strength."

"I see," Grant said. "Suppose I send over twenty-five thousand rations. Do you think that would be a sufficient supply?"

"I think it will be more than enough," Lee replied softly, a soldier doing his best to hold back emotion. "And it will be a great relief, I assure you."

Shannon was dumbfounded. He had spent years doing his best to kill Confederates, and here was his commanding officer, offering succor to the survivors — most of whom had killed or tried to kill the Yankee invaders — and giving dignity to their leader.

He wondered what he would do in Grant's place.

But it wasn't his place to do anything — except wonder.

Then Lee stepped closer to Grant, readying himself for the final gesture of defeat. He spoke as he moved slightly in anticipation of giving up his sword.

"Thirty-nine years of devotion to duty has come to this . . . and this too, is my duty. . . ."

But Grant placed a restraining hand toward Lee's gesture.

"General," said Grant, "the war is over. You are all our countrymen again." And Grant extended his hand.

Lee did not hesitate. He withdrew his hand from the hilt of the sword; then he, too, extended his hand in a gesture of reconciliation and friendship.

Grant took it warmly.

The war was over. There would be a new beginning for the country.

For Shannon it would be a bitter new beginning — back in Texas.

Chapter Thirty-five

Months after the war ended — after Lee surrendered to Grant at Appomattox and Johnston to Sherman at Durham's Station, both with terms that almost everyone in the North considered too lenient — after Abraham Lincoln had been assassinated by John Wilkes Booth and Andrew Johnson had become President of the United States — after Jefferson Davis had been captured and thrown into a prison cell at Fort Monroe — after all of that, many of the Confederate officers and soldiers still had not returned to their homes, especially those whose homes were far west of the Mississippi — as far west as Texas.

A buckboard, battered and clattering, led by a gaunt and weary mare, pulled up in front of the main building at Twelve Trees.

Captain Wade Rawlins — in a uniform that was no longer spick-and-span, but worn and dirty — sat alongside Redding, who held the reins.

Redding helped the captain down from the wagon and handed him a pair of crutches from the bed of the buckboard.

Heather ran out the door, tears in her eyes, but laughing. Charlotte was close behind her, followed by Hannah, who held a little toddler in her arms.

Heather embraced her husband, crutches and all.

"Oh, Wade . . . Wade . . . why didn't you write you were coming . . . ?"

He kissed her and smiled as Charlotte came up to him.

"Don't trust the United States mail."

Heather looked at the crutches, then into his face.

"Oh, my darling . . ."

"Now don't you worry. These are just temporary adornments to get your sympathy. I intend to . . . hello, sister."

Charlotte kissed him but couldn't talk. She was crying.

"Now, come on. I want to see smiles, not tears. I . . ." He gazed at the little girl in Hannah's arms.

"Angela! Angela! Come give your daddy a welcome home kiss."

Heather took Angela from Hannah to her

daddy, who kissed his bright-eyed baby daughter.

Heather turned to Redding.

"Thank you for bringing my husband home."

Redding just nodded and smiled.

"Well, come on," Heather said, still sniffling. "Let's all get inside."

"Hannah," Rawlins said as he maneuvered along on his crutches, "it's good to see you."

"Welcome home, Captain Rawlins."

"*Mister* Rawlins. Heather, how's Hadley?"

"Hopeless."

They moved inside.

He was about to enter the First National Bank of Gilead as she came out of the door and almost bumped into him.

"Beg your pardon, Miss Cherrie . . . do you remember me?" Shannon smiled.

"My God!" She stared at him. "I can't believe my eyes! You look like the Emperor of the North!"

Shannon wore clothes that closely resembled a Union uniform, obviously tailored to his specifications, with a cape — all deep blue — and polished black boots. He had the looks and bearing of royalty, except for the outline of the Colt under his coat.

He tipped his hat, which also resembled that of a Union officer.

"No, Miss Cherrie, not an emperor. Just a soldier."

"Looks like you picked the right side, soldier. What was your rank?"

"Colonel."

"Is that all?" She smiled. "Had they made you a general, the war would've been over sooner."

"How are you, Miss Cherrie?"

"Well" — she nodded toward the bank — "I tried to do a little business with Amos Higgins, but it didn't work out."

"I see. Are you still at the Emporium?"

"On my way there now."

"I'll come by."

"You do that, Colonel." She smiled. "Yes, sir, it looks like somebody's come to town."

If Cherrie was amazed at the sight of Shannon, Amos Higgins was damn near paralyzed. He almost choked on his cigar, but sputtered and managed to invite Shannon to sit and visit.

Higgins could tell money when he saw it, and he saw plenty just by looking at the erstwhile stable boy.

It didn't take Shannon long to confirm Higgins' evaluation.

"I have here a draft from the First Federal Bank of New York, with a line of credit for fifty thousand dollars. Another one from the Philadelphia Trust, and another from the Union Deposit Bank of Chicago — all for the same amount."

"A hundred and fifty thousand?!"

"Yankee dollars, plus quite a large amount of cash I'm carrying on me."

"Well, well . . . then, Mister Shannon, you'll probably want to make a deposit. It . . . it's not safe to carry a lot of cash . . ."

"I wouldn't advise anybody to try and take it away from me, and I will most likely make a sizeable deposit later, but first I want to do a little business."

"Certainly, certainly," Higgins said with an expansive smile. "That's why I'm here."

"Oh, by the way, on my way in I ran into Miss Cherrie. She said she wanted to do some business with you, but it didn't work out."

"Yes," Higgins grunted.

"Would you mind telling me what that business was about?"

"Why, not at all. It seems that her partner, Jim Ritter — everybody calls him Baldy, you know . . ."

"Yes, I know."

"Well, Ritter finally's willing to sell his

share of the Emporium . . . and she wanted a loan of two thousand to consummate the deal, but . . ."

"But you refused."

"I did."

"Mind telling me why?"

"Well, you see, having a . . . a prostitute own part of a saloon is one thing, but being the sole proprietor is quite another, you understand."

"Yes, I understand."

"Besides, there's a rumor that she . . ."

"That she what?"

"Well . . . has negra blood in her."

"No!"

"Oh, yes."

"Well, Mr. Higgins, let's us get down to business."

"As I said, that's why I'm here."

"I understand you hold the mortgages on a lot of the ranches in the area."

"Not a lot — just about every damn one."

"Good. There's one I'm interested in . . . right away."

Cherrie sat at a corner table of the Emporium as Shannon came through the batwings. She motioned to him to come and join her.

There were about a dozen customers,

some drinking at the bar, the others playing poker at a couple of the tables.

Shannon noticed that two of the poker players were the Krantz brothers, now older, dirtier and uglier. They noticed him too. So did everybody else.

"How's Pepper?" Shannon asked as he sat and put his hat on the table.

"Still kicking." She smiled. "But not as high."

"You still see him?"

"When he's not playing nursemaid to his boss, Hadley."

"Hadley sick?"

"Drunk. You like a drink?"

"No, thanks. I see not much around here's changed."

"Nope. Joe Fox's still sheriff. Jake Trapp's still the blacksmith, Baldy's lungs are giving out and . . ."

"I see the two dirty dinguses are still around." He nodded toward Kurt and Burt Krantz.

"Worse than ever."

"Miss Cherrie, I . . . say, what is your last name? I never knew."

"Millay. That's what it is, Millay."

"Well, Miss Millay, I wonder if you remember these?" Shannon pulled five double eagles out of his vest pocket and placed them on top of the table. "You gave them to me before I left."

"I gave you five double eagles, but these aren't the same ones, are they?"

"They are."

"You mean you didn't spend them?"

"No, but it was a great comfort to know that they were there."

"If you want to take her upstairs," Kurt Krantz spoke out, "it won't cost you that much."

He laughed and so did brother Burt.

"Those two go to war?" Shannon asked.

"Got as far as Mississippi, got the measles and were sent back."

"Both of them?"

"Both."

"Excuse me."

Shannon rose and walked to the table where the Krantz brothers were playing poker. He looked down at Kurt, who was leaning back on a Douglas chair.

"Well, well, well." Kurt smirked. "If it ain't that Yankee-lickin' turncoat come back struttin' around like his boots was filled with somethin' special."

"Yeah," Burt added, "like he was some kind of war hero, like he, himself, killed J.E.B. Stuart and Stone Jackson."

"I'll tell you who the real war hero was, alright," Kurt said. "It was John Wilkes Booth, that's who it was — the man who killed that ape-faced nigger-lovin' sonofabitch, asshole Lincoln. I only wisht I'da killed him myself. What do you think about that, Yankee?"

"I didn't walk over here to talk about the war."

"Oh, yeah? Then why did you walk over here?" Kurt asked.

"Apologize to the lady, pig."

"She ain't no lady and you . . ."

That's as far as he got. Shannon kicked the chair from under Kurt and back-handed Burt, who joined his brother on the floor.

Shannon pulled out the Colt and aimed. "Stand up. Both of you. Up!"

They managed to stand.

"Walk over to the lady and apologize. Both of you." Shannon holstered the Colt.

Kurt's right hand began an almost imperceptible motion.

"Go ahead and draw — or go over and apologize, both of you."

They walked to her table, stiff-legged.

"Say it," Shannon commanded. "Both of you."

"I apologize," Kurt mumbled.

"Me too," Burt whispered.

"Louder. Both of you."

"I apologize!" Kurt shouted.

"Me too!"

"Now get out."

They did.

"There's some things about you that haven't changed." Cherrie smiled as Shannon sat. "I'm happy to say."

"Miss Millay, you've got some interest coming . . . on that loan." He pointed to the double eagles.

"What're you talking about? You didn't even use them."

"I said they were of great comfort, and that's worth something."

He pulled out a roll of greenbacks and placed twenty one hundred dollar bills on the table.

"Are you crazy?" she said.

"Nope. But you are now the sole owner of the Emporium. And I don't want to hear another word about it."

"I can't accept that money."

"Yes, you can and will . . . along with my gratitude, Miss Millay."

Shannon rose, put on his hat and walked out.

Chapter Thirty-six

Shannon stopped by the stable to make sure that Black was being taken care of. Then, as he crossed the street toward the Gilead Arms Hotel, he heard a voice that was faintly familiar, a voice he hadn't heard in years.

"Oh, Shannon, Mister Shannon! Would you hold up a minute, please?"

Shannon turned as Sheriff Joe Fox came closer.

Since the sheriff didn't extend his hand, Shannon saw no reason to extend his, either.

"I'd like to talk to you for just a minute, Mister Shannon."

"Sure, Sheriff — here? Or over at your office? Is this official, or . . ."

"Not exactly official."

"That's good."

"And not exactly unofficial. I heard you were in town. . . ."

"It's no secret, came in in broad daylight."

"Also heard about what happened at the Emporium with the Krantzes."

"From the Krantzes?"

"And others."

"Want to hear my version?"

"No need to, Mister Shannon, knowing the Krantzes as I do. 'Sides, Cherrie waylaid me and told me all about it . . . and about what you done for her."

"Then what's the object of this little conversation?"

"I understand you're carrying a sizeable amount of money."

"That against the law in Gilead?"

"No, sir . . . but . . ."

"But what?"

"There ain't much money around town . . . and you having fought with the North . . ."

"You think some of these Confederate patriots might feel tempted to relieve me of some of those Northern greenbacks?"

"I just thought I'd mention it, wouldn't want you to get jumped some night on a dark street."

"Well, I appreciate your concern, Sheriff, but I'm not going to be in town much longer . . ."

"You're not?" The sheriff seemed relieved. "Heading west?"

"Just a few miles."

"Oh."

"In the meanwhile — since the war's over — I wouldn't want to shoot any of those Confederate patriots . . . unless it was absolutely necessary. Anything else, Sheriff?"

"Not right now."

"I'll be over at the hotel for a couple of days in case you think of something. Oh, there is a little business I think you and I are going to have to take care of together."

"What kind of business?"

"Just a slight legal matter. Doesn't amount to a hill of beans. Good day, Sheriff."

Shannon touched the brim of his hat and headed for the Gilead Arms Hotel.

In the library at Twelve Trees, Wade Rawlins walked with a barely perceptible limp and with the assistance of only one cane, as the others in the room — Heather, Charlotte and Angela — watched.

Charlotte embroidered, Angela played with blocks on the floor, but Heather's attention was undivided, gazing at and encouraging her husband, who had discarded what was left of his uniform the day he came home and since then had dressed in more casual ranch clothes.

"Bravo! Bravo, Captain Rawlins!" Heather beamed. "Angela, clap your hands for Daddy!"

From the floor, little Angela clapped her tiny hands.

"Another month or so" — Rawlins smiled — "and I'll be running like a yearling."

"You just slow down, Wade Rawlins." Heather walked up and embraced her husband. "You've got no place to run to. You're staying right here."

"You're right about that, my dear. I've got no place to run to . . . and nothing to do."

"Wade, are we really so poor?"

"Not as poor as everybody else in Texas. At least Twelve Trees is clear. All of the other ranchers have had to borrow heavily."

"But Wade, all that cattle . . ."

Rawlins walked to a big chair and sat with the cane across the arms of the chair.

"Honey, there's cattle by the thousands swarming all over the plains, valleys and slopes of Texas. But there isn't any market for beef because there's no money in Texas . . . or anywhere else in the South. Some of the men are working for half wages. Some for no wages, just food and shelter."

"I had no idea," Heather said.

While Rawlins had been talking, there'd been a knock on the front door and now

Hannah entered, visibly upset, and whispered something to Heather.

"Charlotte," Rawlins said, "with all that embroidering, you're going to ruin your eyes."

"There's nothing to look at anyhow." Charlotte went on with her embroidery.

Now Hannah and Heather were both frowning.

"What is it, Heather?" Rawlins asked. "What's wrong with you two?"

"Nothing, Wade. Hannah, tell him we can't see him. Tell him to go away."

"Tell whom to go away?" Rawlins wanted to know.

"It's Shannon. He's back and he wants to come in here. Hannah, you tell him we don't want to see him."

"Now, wait a minute, darling. Maybe the fellow needs help. Let him come in, Hannah."

"Wade, I don't think . . ."

"Heather, this isn't like you. I said, tell him to come in, Hannah."

"Alright, Mister Rawlins, but he doesn't appear to need anything." She glared at Heather. "That is, anything we can give him."

Hannah went out the library door and into the hall.

"Wade, I think it's a mistake to . . ."

"Nonsense." Rawlins smiled. "If he's back we'll have to see him sooner or later."

"Why?"

"Why? Because it's only . . ."

The door opened and Hannah stepped inside, followed by the former stable boy.

But Shannon looked and sounded like anything but a stable boy.

"Good afternoon," he said, removing his hat.

He stood tall and magnificent in his dark blue suit, cape, and polished boots — self-assured, with the mien and bearing of a soldier-aristocrat.

Shannon looked first at the little girl playing with the blocks, then at Charlotte, who had lost interest in embroidering and couldn't take her eyes off of him, then at Rawlins — and finally at Heather, who was overwhelmed but restrained.

"Captain Rawlins," Shannon said, "it's good of you to see me."

Rawlins rose and stood, braced by the cane.

"Colonel Shannon, Redding told me of your kindness to the prisoners at Benton Ridge. Do you remember him?"

"Yes, I remember Benton Ridge."

"This is my sister Charlotte . . . our little

daughter, Angela . . . and, of course, Mrs. Rawlins."

Wade Rawlins sat. As he did he tapped his stiff leg with the cane.

"A little memento of Benton Ridge — still a little bothersome."

"Nothing permanent, I hope."

"No, not like many of the others who were there — and still are. I lay wounded in a ditch for two days and was found after General Lee . . . the day after Appomattox. I'm one of the lucky ones."

"Yes" — Shannon glanced at Heather — "I'd say you were very lucky."

"Would you care for some sherry? I'm afraid we're all out of brandy."

"No, thanks."

"Sit down, Colonel."

There was an empty chair close to Heather, but Shannon chose another — near Charlotte, who seemed half-mesmerized.

"Thank you, sir. And don't you think it's about time we all quit addressing each other by our former rank?"

"Quite right, Mister Shannon," Rawlins smiled, "quite right. The war is over. But much of the pain will go on for a long time — especially here in Texas."

"Are you just passing through Texas," Heather asked, "or will you go back to the

Army — or what are your plans, Mister Shannon?"

"No, I'm out of the Army for good . . . and I plan to stay in Texas."

"In Gilead?" she inquired.

"No, not in Gilead. I bought up a mortgage on one of the spreads. I plan to move in tomorrow. As a matter of fact, we're going to be neighbors . . . I'm taking over Glenshannon Hall."

Heather's heart was in her throat.

Wade Rawlins did his best to maintain his hospitable demeanor.

Hannah stiffened.

Charlotte lit up.

"It seems" — Shannon stood up — "the note was long overdue, and I paid it off with one commodity sorely lacking in Texas — dollars . . . Yankee dollars."

Chapter Thirty-seven

Most everything about Glenshannon Hall was in disrepair: the huge stone arch across the road, the road itself, the imposing Spanish-style main building with its tile roof, bunkhouses, corrals, small buildings and stable — even the hillside plot that held the remains of the once-proud owner who had carved out an empire in an untamed terrain.

During the nearly five years of war, not only had there been no improvements, but there had been no money for maintenance.

At one time, there had been dozens of hands working the ranch and range. By war's end there were only Carson, Gibbs, Carey and Pepper — and of course, Hadley.

A few of the former hands had straggled back since Appomattox and were allowed to stay, but they stayed without wages, only for food and a roof over their heads that leaked when it rained.

The only things that had grown and multiplied at Glenshannon Hall were cattle and wild horses. Herds of beef and mustangs roamed the hills, valleys and canyons, depleting the grass and quenching their thirst from the rivers that still flowed.

Such were the circumstances at Glenshannon Hall the morning that Shannon showed up.

Shannon did not show up alone. With him was Sheriff Joe Fox.

Hadley, Pepper and Carson were on the porch. About a dozen of Hadley's men, all armed, some still dressed in Confederate gray, flanked their grim and glowering boss. Carson, gripping a scatter gun, stood on Hadley's right with Pepper on the left.

". . . That's what this paper says," Sheriff Fox said for the third time. "And that's the way it's got to be and that's the way it's going to be, according to the law."

"To hell with you and the law! I'm not leaving! This is my place and nobody's taking it away from me. It's mine! Get off my land, Sheriff, and take that sonofabitch with you" — Hadley pointed to Shannon — "before I order my men to shoot both of you!"

"I've been the sheriff of this county for a good many years and better men than you have tried it and I'm still here. Now nobody's gonna shoot anybody. This . . . this man" — Sheriff Fox nodded toward Shannon, next to him — "he's got a clear title to the place and it's my duty, whether I like it or not, to serve this paper."

"Higgins!" Hadley screamed. "That dirty double-crossing bastard, Amos Higgins! It's all his fault! He didn't even . . ."

"Now that's enough, 'cause it won't do any good. Amos Higgins is a businessman trying to stay in business, so I guess you can't fault him too much. . . ."

"The hell, I can't! He should have warned me . . . protected me from this . . . this, this viper. Amos Higgins is a . . ."

"That's between you and him. Now, like I said, Mister Glenshannon, this man has clear title . . ."

"But . . . but, this is my home." Hadley's demeanor changed. He talked as if in a trance, dimly, pathetically. "I've always lived here. I can't leave. Please . . . where would I go? What would I do?"

Shannon spoke for the first time, evenly, unemotionally.

"You don't have to go anywhere, Hadley, or do anything. You were my host for a long time. It's only fair that I pay back your hospitality."

"What?" Hadley was stunned.

"And you won't have to sleep in the stable. You can have all the food and drink you can stomach, any horse you want to ride — anything. You're welcome as my guest at Glenshannon Hall."

"You mean . . ." Hadley, still in a daze, was not sure of what he had heard. "I can stay?!"

"For as long as you live or as long as you want."

Shannon looked at Carson.

"Put away that scatter gun and have his things moved into one of the guest rooms."

Carson didn't move. Nobody did.

"We might as well get this fixed," Shannon said, still evenly and unemotionally. "You can all stay. I pay thirty a month — Yankee dollars. Fifty to the foreman. But I expect this place to shape up and fast. Carson, do you want to stay on as foreman?"

"Alright, Shannon," Carson said. "I'll stay."

"*Mister* Shannon." He turned to Sheriff Joe Fox. "Well done, Sheriff. My compliments."

"Mighty peculiar," Sheriff Fox said as he walked toward his horse. "The way things turned out . . . mighty peculiar."

"Carson."

"Yes, Mister Shannon?"

"See that my things are brought in from the hotel."

"I'll do that, Mister Shannon."

"And don't overdo that *Mister* stuff."

"Sure thing." Carson smiled for the first time.

After Hadley turned and walked in the door, Shannon stood next to Pepper.

"Well, Pepper, how've you been?"

"How the hell you think I been? And what do you care? You didn't even bother to say so long."

"Didn't I?" Shannon smiled. "Must've been in a hurry. By the way, I forgot to ask you . . . are you going to stay?"

"I'll stay 'til the wheels come off."

"Good. Say, Pepper, what're we having for supper tonight?"

"What the hell else? Beef!!"

"Beats chitlins and Georgia goobers. Let's go inside."

That evening Shannon had changed into ranch clothes.

He held his sword in both hands, then placed it above the fireplace in the great room. He stepped back a couple of paces, turned and looked at Pepper, then at Hadley sitting not in the big chair but in a smaller

308

one with a drink in hand. He took a sip, then rose unsteadily.

"I'm going upstairs to my room." He had hold of the bottle of whiskey on the small table next to him.

"Hadley," Pepper said, "you ain't et."

"I've got my bellyful." Hadley sneered and staggered off.

"I guess he means me," Shannon said. "I think he sees my face at the bottom of that bottle."

"It ain't you, son — or at least not just you. There's somethin' been preyin' on his mind for a long time. 'Course, even as a kid he never was good company, not at all like his sister. . . ." Pepper was sorry he said it. ". . . Oh, I . . . I, uh . . ."

"That's alright, Pepper, you once told me I didn't have the chance of a wax cat in hell. . . ."

"Sometimes I talk too much."

"What about supper? We ain't et yet, either."

"I hired this new cook, Margarita. Would you believe she's a better cook than I am?"

"I'll believe it when I taste that steak."

Shannon spent money on paint, nails, tiles, lumber and whatever materials were needed, and the hands went to work on Glenshannon Hall, inside and out.

Missing stones were replaced in the huge stone arch. The main building was white-washed on the exterior and painted on the interior.

The corrals were reinforced.

The bunkhouses repaired.

The stable patched and painted.

Black was given his old stall and he seemed right at home in his middle age.

"What happened to Bucephalus?" Shannon asked Pepper.

"Got the 'numony and died."

"Got the what?"

" 'Numony, 'numony!"

"You mean pneumonia?"

"That's what I said. That damn fool Hadley come home drunk one night and left that poor hoss out in the rain instead of the stable — and that hoss took the . . ."

" 'Numony and died."

"That's what I said. Lookee, here come a stranger."

A boy about thirteen, dirty face and hands, tattered clothes on a bony body, barely dragging one foot in front of the other, approached the stable.

Carson, Gibbs, Carey and a couple of the other hands watched as the boy stopped, not too steady on his feet, in front of Shannon and Pepper.

"Whoa, there boy, you look a little wobbly," Pepper said.

"I'm . . . alright."

"Sure you are. What're you doin' around here?"

"Don't know."

"Where do you live?"

"No place."

"When have you et last?"

"Don't know."

"Where's your ma and pa?"

"Pa died in the war last year. Ma died of the fever last month."

"You got any kin?"

The boy shook his head no.

"I knew a kid like you once" — Pepper looked at Shannon — "a long time ago."

"What's your name?" Shannon spoke for the first time.

"Ben. Ben Hooper."

"Well, Ben," Pepper said, "this here's Mister Shannon. He's the boss."

"I'll work for food, Mister Shannon."

"What kind of work can you do?"

"Anything needs doing."

"I like your attitude, Ben," Shannon said, "but looks to me like you better eat first. Know anything about horses?"

"What I don't know I can learn."

"Well, here's the man who taught me — Mister Pepper. I can use a stable boy. Sleep in the stable. Eat in the bunkhouse. Pay's ten dollars a month."

"You mean *money?*"

"I don't mean manure, but you'll get plenty of that too. You want to hire on, Ben?"

"I sure do. Mister Shannon."

"Then you're hired. Pepper, take Ben into the kitchen and try to get some meat on those bones . . . then teach him about horses."

"I taught you, didn't I?"

"That's what I said. Say, Ben, what side did your daddy fight on?"

"The South, of course."

"Of course," Shannon said, then thought to himself, *Hell, I might've killed him.*

The new sign above the entrance read

CHERRIE MILLAY'S
EMPORIUM

That's the only thing that Shannon had insisted on. He wanted Amos Higgins and everybody else in Gilead to know that there was one, and only one, owner of the Emporium. Cherrie Millay reluctantly agreed.

After the sign was painted and placed, she admitted to herself that she approved of the looks of it.

The three of them, Cherrie, Pepper and Shannon, sat at the corner table and, from the best bottle of whiskey in Gilead, toasted the new sign.

"Here's to you, Miss Millay," Shannon said.

"And to you, Mister Shannon." Cherrie smiled.

"And to me," Pepper added. "If it wasn't for me . . ."

"If it wasn't for you — what?" Shannon wanted to know.

"Well, I'm the one who brung us all together — me and Mister Glenshannon — say, let's drink a toast to him — Shannon Glenshannon!"

They did.

"Pepper, there was one thing that you were wrong about."

"What's that?"

"Remember you said if Shannon ever came back, 'God help us all'?"

"I did?"

"You did."

"Well . . . it's early yet." Pepper smiled.

And so did Cherrie Millay.

But not Shannon.

There was one area of repair that Shannon allowed no one else to go near.

The hillside gravesite of Shannon and Maureen Glenshannon.

He polished the tombstone, cut the grass with a sickle, repaired and painted the picket fence that surrounded the gravesite and planted cactus roses at the head of the graves.

While Shannon worked, Ben Hooper, the young stable boy, walked from below to the side of the graves.

"Beg pardon, Mister Shannon . . ."

"What is it, Ben? What do you want?"

"Don't want anything, Mister Shannon — seeing you work up here all alone I thought maybe you needed some help."

"If I needed any, I could get all I want."

"Yes, sir. I'm sorry I bothered you." Ben started to turn away.

"Just a minute."

"Yes, sir."

"You come up all this way afoot?"

"Yes, sir."

"Well, a stable boy ought to have a horse, don't you think so?"

Ben Hooper just smiled.

"Well, I think so. You know that pinto in the last stall?"

"Domino?"

"That's right, Domino. Throw one of those old saddles on him and see how he sits. If you go for each other, you can have him."

"You can take it out of my pay, Mister Shannon."

"Alright, if it'll make you feel better. Fifty cents a month . . . from now on. That agreeable?"

"Yes, sir!"

"Now get out of here. Graveyard's no place for a young fellow."

"Yes, sir."

Ben Hooper turned and raced toward the stable and Domino.

Shannon turned back to the work on the gravesite.

He was the master of Glenshannon Hall, but the strange look in his eyes was not one of fulfillment, not yet. There was something missing — someone.

This was the beginning, but only the beginning. Shannon thought about what Pepper had said. *If he comes back, God help us all.* And he had also said something else. *It's early yet.*

That night after supper Pepper sat in the great room and smoked a cigar.

Earlier, when no one was in the room,

Shannon had made some changes in the gun rack, changes that Pepper hadn't noticed.

Now he turned from the gun rack with an old seven-shot Spencer in his hand.

"You remember this, Pepper?"

Pepper almost swallowed his smoke.

"You mean you still got that ol' thunderstick?"

"Brought it back with a few other items — newer ones, like this."

He reached back to the gun rack and removed two other rifles.

"One for you and one for me." He tossed one of them at Pepper. "This one's yours."

"God almighty, a brand-new Henry!"

"That's what it is," Shannon said. "Beautiful, if ever a gun was — well balanced, .44 caliber, fifteen shot, weighs nine and a half pounds with a brass breach. Load it on Sunday and shoot all week long."

"Shannon! I don't know what to say. . . ."

"Don't say anything. You gave me a gun once, didn't you? Matter of fact you gave me two. The other was a handgun — something like this."

Shannon reached back to the gun rack, picked up a revolver and tossed that at Pepper too.

"The hell it was!" Pepper said. "This's a new-model Remington — shoots metallic cartridges!"

"Yeah, be careful, it's loaded. We'll go out tomorrow and do a little shooting."

"You bet . . . I . . . I . . . want to thank you . . ."

"Save it."

"While you were gone all that time, you was thinkin' about ol' Pepper."

"No. I was just thinking about getting back."

The next afternoon, bottles and cans were flying off a fence as Shannon and Pepper fired their Henrys and then their new Remington revolvers.

It was hard to tell who was the more accurate, Shannon or Pepper, because there weren't many misses.

Carson, Gibbs, Carey and some of the other hands watched in awe from in front of the bunkhouse, and so did Ben Hooper from the entrance to the stable.

"I think you missed once," Pepper said as they started to reload from the boxes of cartridges.

"You do, huh? Well, I'll tell you one thing, Pepper, the last few years haven't affected your eyesight any."

"Wisht' I could say the same for my rheumatism."

"Mister Shannon." Ben Hooper had walked up from the stable.

"Oh, hello, Ben. How you getting along with Domino?"

"Just great, sir. That's what I wanted to talk to you about. You see, I've done most of my chores and I was wondering . . ."

"What?"

"You mind if I take him out for a little sprint?"

"Go ahead, Ben, throw a saddle on him and take him out for a little sprint."

"Thanks, Mister Shannon." Ben started to turn, but looked back and smiled. "Already threw a saddle on him . . . just in case you said okay."

While Shannon and Pepper were still reloading, Ben rode out of the stable on Domino looking like they had been born saddle mates.

As they started firing again at what was left of the bottles and cans, another rider approached on the road from the grand arch to Glenshannon Hall.

Both men ceased firing.

Charlotte Rawlins, smartly attired, with a basket in one hand and a glint in both eyes, reined up close to Shannon and Pepper.

"I thought the war was over." She smiled down from her mount.

"Not against cans and bottles." Shannon smiled up.

"Look's like you won again, Mister Shannon." She nodded toward the shards of glass and bullet-riddled cans.

"Let me help you."

He did as she dismounted.

"Miss Rawlins, I believe you know Mister Pepper."

"Hello, Mister Pepper."

"Miss Rawlins . . ." Pepper reached for Shannon's rifle. "Here, let me take that artillery. I don't think you'll be needin' it for a while."

As Pepper started to walk up the stairs, a bleary Hadley came out of the door.

"Goddammit! Who's doing all that shooting! Can't a man get some sleep around here?" he said to Pepper.

"Try gettin' up before noon," Pepper remarked, and went inside.

Hadley glowered at Shannon and Charlotte.

"How do you do, Mister Glenshannon?" She waved.

He responded by turning on his heels, going inside and slamming the door.

"It seems," Shannon shrugged, "that

319

Mister Glenshannon isn't receiving this afternoon. But I certainly am. Welcome to Glenshannon Hall, Miss Rawlins."

"Charlotte, please."

"Charlotte."

"The place looks beautiful."

"It's looking better all the time." He smiled. "You're the first visitor we've had. And I hope that this is the first of many of your visits."

"I just came by to drop off some preserves. I know that Pepper doesn't put any up and I thought you . . . and Hadley, would like them."

"I know we'll like them." He took the basket from her.

Charlotte made sure that their hands touched in the exchange.

"Thank you," he said. "Won't you come inside? Enjoy a beverage?"

"No, not this time." She smiled her most enchanting smile. "I'd better be getting back to Twelve Trees."

"If you don't mind, I'll have the carriage hitched and take you back."

"Oh, I don't want you to go to any trouble."

"I'm not going to any trouble." He too had an enchanting smile. "Just to Twelve Trees."

As the carriage pulled away with Shannon at the reins, Charlotte beside him, and her horse tied to the rear of the carriage, Carson came up to Pepper, who stood watching and smoking a cigar near the porch.

"It sure as hell does beat all, don't it, Pepper?"

"What sure as hell beats all?"

"The way things turn out."

"What things?"

"*Things.* Mister Glenshannon dead, Hadley drunk, Miss Heather married to that Virginia daffodil. Shannon, the ex–stable boy, with more money than Creosote, and . . ."

"You mean Croesus?"

"Don't make no never mind, he's rich and owns this ranch. And now along comes the best lookin' little filly since Cleopatra, flutterin' her eyelids and swingin' her hips, and off they ride like a couple of . . ."

"Look here, Carson, I ain't heard you talk so much since Bernard was a pup."

"Who's Bernard?"

"I don't know. It's just a name I made up."

"What's the point?"

"The point is . . . shut up and mind your own beeswax. Now leave me be."

Carson walked away.

"Damned if he ain't right," Pepper mumbled, "about things . . . and how they turn out."

And for some reason Pepper thought about the way things turned out for Sam Houston, and what Houston had predicted: "And what I fear is, they will overwhelm the South."

Sam Houston's fear had come true, but he hadn't lived to see it happen. On July 25, 1863, suffering from pneumonia, he stirred from a deep sleep as his wife Margaret held his hand.

"Texas! Texas!" he cried out.

Sam Houston had died that day at sundown. It would be a long dark night for Texas.

It still was, as far as most Texans were concerned.

Shannon's carriage headed back toward Twelve Trees. But not by the way that Charlotte had come.

Shannon took a different route.

"All this land belongs to you?" she marveled.

"That's what the deed says."

"You must be . . ."

"A former stable boy."

"And possibly a future senator or governor."

"No. Politics doesn't interest me."

"What are your main interests, Shannon . . . these days?" Her tone was as provocative as her smile.

"Well, this morning there were guns and rifles, but as of this afternoon . . ."

"Yes?"

"I've become fascinated by . . . brown eyes."

"Really? My eyes happen to be brown."

"Is that so? What a coincidence."

They both laughed.

"Oh, look!"

"I'm looking," he said, directly at her.

"No. I mean over there." She pointed. "What a strange formation . . . those rocks."

"Yes, very strange."

"But you're not looking."

"I've seen them before."

"Of course you have. How silly of me. Do they belong to you?"

"They belong to the ages. You've heard of the rock of ages. Well, there it is."

"Seriously . . . does that place have a name?"

"It's called Moon Rock."

"Yes, I can see why. It doesn't look like anything else around here, does it?"

"No. It doesn't."

"Have you been up there?"

"Yes."

"Would you take me up there some-time?"

"No."

"Oh . . ."

"I'm sorry," he said. "I didn't mean to be abrupt. . . . I just meant that I didn't think you'd like it up close. It's much better from a distance . . . unlike some things . . . and some people, Charlotte."

"I understand perfectly . . . Shannon."

Of course, she didn't . . . and Shannon didn't want her to.

As the carriage rolled away from Moon Rock, Shannon could hear voices from the past. Voices from the first time he saw Moon Rock — and other times.

"Isn't it beautiful?"

"I'm not sure."

"Why don't we go up there together?"

"Are you crazy?"

"It'll be our magic place."

"It's just a big pile of rocks."

"No, it's not, Hadley, it's beautiful."

"I'm not sure anybody owns it."

"Would you take us up there, sometime, Father?"

"Maybe sometime when you're older —
maybe next year."

"It is magic! Just like I knew it would be!"
"It's like nothing I've ever seen before."
"I could stay here forever . . . Shannon,
don't you think . . . ?"
"Let's leave. Now!"
"What is it, lad?"
"I can't explain . . . but I know we've got to
leave!"

"Shannon. Shannon. I knew you'd be
here."
"Where else would I be?"
". . . Just you and me."
"You and me."
". . . Why would you want to stay?"
"You damn well know why."
"You'd come back a hero."
"All they ever did was treat me like a
slave."
"You'll never be a gentleman like . . ."
"Like Rawlins?"
"Is that what you care about? Money and
clothes?"
"I won't listen to you talk that way about
him."
"You don't have to listen to me at all."
"No, I don't."

"You and your gentleman can both go to hell."

But those voices were all in the past . . . and now Heather was married to Wade Rawlins and he was riding beyond Moon Rock with Rawlins' sister, Charlotte, who wanted to go up to Moon Rock with him.

But Shannon promised himself that he would never go to Moon Rock with anyone except Heather.

Either with Heather . . . or by himself, alone.

At Twelve Trees Shannon had helped Charlotte down from the carriage and was untying her horse as Heather came out of the door and walked up to them. She did not bother to greet Shannon.

"We wondered where you had gone, Charlotte."

"Good afternoon," Shannon said.

"Yes," she replied, still looking at her sister-in-law, "good afternoon."

"I took some preserves by to Hadley and Colonel Shannon. Where's Wade?"

"In town — how is Hadley?"

"Oh, Heather, we went by the most beautiful place. It's called Moon Rock. Do you know it?"

"Yes." Heather looked at Shannon for the

first time. "I know it. I asked about Hadley."

"Well, I . . ."

"He's not too well, Mrs. Rawlins," Shannon interrupted. "You ought to pay him a visit . . . you and Mister Rawlins. It might cheer him up."

"It's very thoughtful of you, Colonel Shannon, to be so concerned about my brother."

"He really doesn't look at all well," Charlotte said, "but Heather, you should see Glenshannon Hall . . . what Shannon has done . . . it looks absolutely beautiful."

"Does it?"

"Yes, I . . ."

"I have no wish to see Glenshannon Hall. If Hadley wants to visit, he can come here."

"Too bad." Shannon started to climb aboard the carriage. "Seems like Hadley doesn't want to leave Glenshannon Hall and you don't want to go there. Too bad. Good afternoon, Mrs. Rawlins . . . and Charlotte, thanks for the preserves. I hope to return your thoughtfulness sometime."

Hannah stood on the porch and watched the carriage pull away.

Chapter Thirty-eight

"You ever hear a man scream in the middle of the night? Bang his fists against a locked liquor cabinet and curse you to hell because he needed whiskey and you cut off his supply . . . fall to the floor and curl up in agony, then plead — no, not plead, *beg* for a drink and threaten to cut his own throat unless you gave it to him? Did you, Cherrie?"

"No, Shannon. I've seen some men pretty bad off, but not like that."

"Well, that's how bad off Hadley is. Almost bad enough to be buried. So have somebody throw six cases into that buckboard out front. You and Pepper enjoy each other's company. I've got an appointment with Amos Higgins. Shouldn't take long."

"Take as long as you like." Pepper smiled. "Cherrie, did I ever tell you about that crooked card game I was in over in Dallas?"

"How'd you know it was crooked?" she asked.

"I was dealin'."

"I'll see you two later." Shannon rose from the corner table and walked toward the batwings.

But two men, oversize men whose faces were molded by somebody who never heard of handsome, blocked the exit.

"You the one they call Colonel Shannon?" the first man grunted.

"Used to be," Shannon said. "Not anymore."

"We heard about you and just rode into town."

"Looking for work?"

"No, lookin' for you."

"Why?"

"We heard you was at Altoona."

"So were a lot of people."

"Includin' our brother. He died there."

"So did a lot of people."

"We figure maybe you killed him."

"Maybe I did."

"Well . . . ?"

Shannon's revolver cleared leather and he fired twice. Two knobs — each in the center of a batwing — blew apart just behind the two men's heads. Then the gun was leveled between the two of them.

"And maybe I didn't. You want to let it go at that?"

"Well . . ."

"You've got three seconds to make up your minds." He thumbed back the hammer of the Remington. "One . . . two . . ."

Both men wheeled, pushed through the batwings and headed for their horses.

"You can put away your pistol, Pepper," Shannon said as he started out. "Thanks, anyway."

"Colonel Shannon, this is my daughter Cassie."

"Pleased to meet you, Miss Higgins."

"Oh, no. Cassie's a widow. Her husband, Caleb Kearny, died during the war."

"Sorry to hear that, Mrs. Kearny."

Cassie Higgins Kearny had put on weight since the housewarming party at Twelve Trees, and mostly in her already ponderous bosom.

"I've heard you've done wonderful things at your ranch, Colonel Shannon."

"A few minor improvements."

"I'd like to come out sometime and visit."

"Well, I'll make it a point to invite you, Mrs. Kearny . . . sometime."

The door was opened by Jeremy Pentwhistle, one of the bank clerks.

"Excuse me, Mrs. Kearny, you said let you know when your carriage arrived."

"Thank you, Jeremy." Cassie Higgins

Kearny rose, smiled and walked toward the door. "I look forward to your invitation, Colonel."

Keep looking, Shannon thought to himself as the door closed, leaving him in the room with Amos Higgins.

Higgins opened the lid of a box of cigars on his desk.

"Have a fine cigar, Colonel," Higgins said in his most solicitous voice.

"Thank you. I'll smoke it later."

"The last time you were here you said you were interested in some of the other ranches."

"We'll talk about the other ranches later. In the meantime, I'll be making some large deposits. I've secured a very substantial Army contract from General Sherman."

"Sherman?"

"William Tecumseh Sherman. My former commanding officer."

"Oh, yes, of course. You know we're here to be of service, Colonel Shannon. Will you be providing the Army with beef, sir?"

"Beef? No. There's no money in beef, Amos. Sherman can get all the beef he wants. You know what the Army needs most?"

"I'm . . . I'm not sure."

"Horses."

"Horses?"

"An army doesn't just move on its belly. And I've got an exclusive contract to provide the Army with horses. Did you know that there were almost as many horses killed in the war as soldiers?"

"No." Higgins was still solicitous. "I didn't know that."

"I killed quite a few myself. I like horses, Amos." Shannon rose. "You know I grew up in a stable."

He tossed the cigar on the desk, turned abruptly and moved toward the door, leaving Higgins with a banal look on his face.

The roundup began.

Shannon hired a dozen extra hands and ordered them, along with his regulars, to cover every foot of Glenshannon Hall: open range, hills, valleys, coulees and canyons. And to gather up every horse with four legs: roans, buckskins, overos, strawberries, sorrels and palominos — stallions, mares and colts with all kinds of markings: bald faced, snip, star-stripe, stockings, paint, pinto and blanket.

Horses that had been running free and wild — and multiplying — since the war began, would now be instrumental in another war. The war to secure and expand the western frontier — a war under the com-

332

mand of General William Tecumseh Sherman, along with other officers who had served in the Union Army: Philip Sheridan, George Crook, George Armstrong Custer and Nelson Appleton Miles.

Almost every day Shannon rode with his men, lassoing, gathering and herding the horses into Horseshoe Canyon, where there was plenty of grass and water, and where just a few men could keep them together until it was time to make the drive to Fort Griffin where Shannon would turn them over to the Army.

Along with Carson, Gibbs, Carey and the new men, Shannon had allowed Ben Hooper, the stable boy, to take part in the roundup. Ben and Domino did more than their fair share of the work.

There were already more than eight hundred horses within the rock walls of Horseshoe Canyon as a rider approached the narrow mouth of the enclosure.

Even from a distance, Shannon recognized Charlotte and rode out to meet her. Even in her riding clothes she looked perfectly groomed and elegant.

"Hello, stranger." She smiled.

"Hello, yourself. You look like something against the law."

"Shall I take that as a compliment?"

"That's the way it was given."

"Thank you."

"What are you doing out this way?"

"Well, I could lie and say I just happened to ride this way but . . ."

"But?"

"The truth is, since you haven't come by to see me, I thought I'd come out to see you . . . for just a minute. I heard about the roundup. How's it going?"

"Good."

"I thought maybe you were seeing some other brown-eyed lady."

"Only fillies, the four-legged kind."

"That's encouraging."

"As soon as this roundup is over, I'd like to see more of a certain brown-eyed lady, if it's alright with you."

"That's even more encouraging. Well, I'd better let you get back to work." She tugged gently on her horse's reins and the horse reacted. "I'll be waiting." She smiled.

"Not for long," he said as he rode away.

Shannon stood on the front porch, Pepper and Carson next to him. He looked down as a delegation of ranchers, about a dozen, dismounted with an aura of defeat and the odor of desperation. Their spokesman, Tom Hill, had asked for a meeting.

"All right, gentlemen, what can I do for you?"

"Well, we were told that you've got the contract to provide horses for the Army."

"That's right, Mister Hill. All I can get. So far we've rounded up almost a thousand head."

Shannon looked over at Ben Hooper, who had come from the stable and stood near the porch.

"Well, me and the men here've been rounding 'em up too. We've collected about five hundred from our spreads."

"Uh, huh. And what do you propose doing with them?"

"We . . . want to know if you'd buy 'em from us."

"I would, if they meet the standards . . . and for my price."

"They're good horses, all right. Uh, what is your price?"

"Five dollars a head," Shannon said.

There was a collective stunned impact as all the ranchers looked at each other and mumbled among themselves.

"Five . . . five dollars?!" Hill wiped at the dryness around his mouth. "Well, you got to be gettin' five times that much."

"I am."

"Well . . ."

"Well, what?"

"Well . . . that don't seem fair."

"It's not."

There was a pause, an awkward pause, for everyone except Shannon.

"We thought . . . ," Hill began.

"Mister Hill, save your thoughts. There's a lot of injustice in this world. I've found that out. It so happens that I've got the contract . . . and that's my offer. Take it or keep your horses."

"Could you make it —"

"I make it five dollars a head, coin of the realm. Talk it over and let me know. Now if you'll excuse me, I have to go inside and see about a sick friend."

Hill and the other ranchers knew that they had been dismissed. They began to saddle up.

"All right," Hill said as he mounted. "We'll talk it over and let you know."

They rode off.

"Mister Shannon . . . ," Carson said.

"What is it, Carson? What's on your mind?"

Whatever it was, Carson had already thought it over.

"Nothin', Mister Shannon. You're the boss." He stepped off the porch and headed toward the bunkhouse.

"Anything on your mind, Pepper?" Shannon asked.

"Plenty . . . and that's where it's goin' to stay, boss."

"You're a partner, Pepper. You get a percentage."

"That ain't the point."

"What is the point?"

"The point is . . . I'm hungry." He turned and walked inside.

Shannon looked at Ben, who still stood at the edge of the porch.

"Did you hear all that, Ben?"

"Yes, sir."

"I hope you just learned a lesson. Do you know what that lesson is?"

"I'm not sure, sir."

"The lesson is . . . when you are the anvil, bear . . . when you are the hammer, STRIKE."

"Yes, sir."

As Ben Hooper walked toward the stable, Shannon went inside to the hallway and saw Dr. Homer Kokernut talking to Pepper at the bottom of the stairway.

"I was just coming in to see you, doctor. How is he?"

"He's sleeping now. And I was just telling Pepper . . ."

"Suppose you tell me."

337

"I intend to. Mister Shannon, you've got to cut off his whiskey. I mean *off*. He's got to quit. His liver's turning to stone. He keeps drinking, he'll be dead in six months . . . or less."

"Did you tell *him* that?"

"I did . . ."

"And?"

"I might as well have been talking to a stone. He just stared straight ahead."

"Did you talk to him about going and staying with . . . his sister?"

"He won't leave here. Says this is his house." Dr. Kokernut shrugged in surrender. "Well, there's nothing more I can do."

The doctor started toward the front door, but turned back.

"But I'll say it again. If you don't want him to die, cut off his liquor."

"Thank you, doctor. I'll do everything I can."

Dr. Kokernut nodded and walked out, leaving Shannon and Pepper at the stairway.

"Well, Mister Shannon," Pepper said. "You heard the doctor. What are you goin' to do?"

"Well, Mister Pepper. You heard him too. If he keeps on drinking, he'll die. If I cut off his liquor, he'll go crazy and die. You said you were hungry. So am I. Let's eat."

"I just lost my appetite," Pepper said and walked away.

Gibbs and Carey brought him in at gunpoint. But he didn't look like he could do any harm. He could barely sit bareback on his pony.

He had been a Kiowa brave, but he was too gaunt and weak to be a brave any longer.

Still, he had been trying to prove his worth to the tribe by stealing a steer and taking it back to their camp.

Shannon thought he recognized the Kiowa from years ago when he was a part of Seccoro's tribe, but was not sure — the brave's face and body were like crinkled copper, but a yellowish pink.

"We didn't know what else to do with him, boss, so we brought him here. Don't think he could make it back to his camp, wherever that is."

"Help him down off that horse. Get him something to eat and drink." Shannon turned toward the stable. "Ben."

Ben Hooper came running.

"Yes, sir."

"Take care of this horse."

"Yes, sir."

★ ★ ★

In the next hour Shannon tried to think back and remember at least some of the Kiowa language he hadn't spoken since Seccoro died.

He remembered enough to converse with the brave who remembered Shannon as Tamonito who had lived with them years ago.

The brave's name was Nan-Tan-Lupan, which translated to Grey Wolf.

Grey Wolf had eaten more in the last hour than he had in the last week, and two shots of whiskey loosened his tongue.

Not understanding a word, Pepper listened as Shannon and Grey Wolf talked Kiowa.

But Shannon found out what he wanted to know.

Running Bear was still the chief but there were a couple of young bucks who wanted the title and the coup stick that went with it.

Grey Wolf was more than reluctant to disclose the location of the Kiowa camp, but another shot of whiskey turned the key of his reluctance.

Shannon and Grey Wolf, along with Gibbs, Carey and Ben Hooper, guided a half dozen steers into the mouth of Ghost Canyon.

From there, Shannon, Grey Wolf and the steers went through while the other three white men waited.

Rifles and arrows were pointed at Shannon until Grey Wolf made the sign of peace and friendship and nodded toward his companion.

Running Bear stood with the coup stick as Shannon dismounted and the other braves took a step closer.

Shannon looked around to the place where he had buried Seccoro, then spoke to Running Bear in the chief's language.

"Running Bear, these steers are for your people."

The chief's eyes were bullets of lead. His expression did not change, conveyed neither gratitude nor displeasure.

"I'm rounding up horses. I'm giving the ranchers five dollars for each horse they bring in. I'll give you and your people ten dollars — paid in cattle, flour, salt, wheat, sugar and other things you need — for each horse you bring in."

Still Running Bear said nothing, but the other braves and the women of the tribe stirred.

"Ghost Canyon is not a good place for your people to live. I have much land, better land than this. You can move to Grass Valley and live there in peace for as long as you like. There is water and good grazing. You can raise cattle and plant crops."

"We are hunters."

"Not anymore. You're the hunted . . . unless you change. Stay in one place. Grass Valley can be that place . . . your village. Your home."

"Why would you do this for me?"

"I'm not doing it just for you. I'm doing it for myself and for Seccoro. He saved my life and if it weren't for you, I would have stayed with the Kiowa. We're both better off that I didn't stay. That's why. Are those good enough reasons?"

What Shannon didn't want to mention in front of Running Bear's tribe was that they would probably starve to death or kill him and each other in internecine warfare unless they got some help. So he had given his old nemesis a chance to save face and his people, and himself a chance to pay back Seccoro.

He would pay back the Texans who had treated him as less than equal, less than human, in other ways.

"Running Bear, I ask you. Are those good enough reasons?"

Running Bear paused, folded his arms

342

across his chest, still holding the coup stick . . . and nodded.

"Two of my men will take you to Grass Valley tomorrow."

Shannon mounted Black and rode toward the mouth of Ghost Canyon without looking back.

The Kiowas were smiling, cheering, and even dancing.

All but Running Bear.

He and his tribe would survive, but at the sufferance of the white man.

Shannon rode up to Gibbs, Carey and Ben where they had waited.

"For a while there, boss," Gibbs said, "we thought maybe you wasn't comin' out."

"Is that so? What did you think, Ben?"

"Either you were coming out or I was going in."

"If that's true . . . you're a damn fool, boy." Shannon smiled.

Back at the ranch, Shannon told Pepper and Carson about the agreement made with Running Bear.

Carson shook his head, tilted back his hat and scratched his temple.

"Okay, boss, I'll send a couple of men out in the morning to take 'em to Grass Valley."

"Send Gibbs and Carey," Shannon said, "and let Ben go along with them."

"Yes, sir." Carson walked away, still shaking his head.

"What're you looking at?" Shannon asked Pepper, who had been listening and watching.

"Damned if I know." Pepper blinked. "After all these years, damned if I know."

That night Shannon walked into the stable.

"Ben. Here's another book I think you ought to read."

"Sure thing, Mister Shannon."

He handed the book to the boy.

"Written by a Greek fellow named Homer. It has to do with the Trojan War."

"The Trojan War. What was that about?"

"It was about a woman." Shannon turned and started to walk out. "Her name was Helen, but it might've been . . . anything."

Chapter Thirty-nine

What was left of the Kiowa tribe had moved to Grass Valley. They set up their wiki-ups near the stream and within days the valley had become a village complete with dogs, goats, women, babies and young and old men.

Running Bear walked through the camp like a lord in his fiefdom. For the first time in years he didn't have to worry about moving on to a better hunting ground.

The Kiowas planted corn and even rice at the edge of the stream. At first the young bucks were restless. They missed the excitement of the hunt. But after a few months they settled into the new life and spent more time with their squaws in the wiki-ups. And they found excitement in rounding up wild horses and herding them into the valley to be traded to Shannon for cattle and other chattel.

Running Bear had held on to his title as chief . . . and his coup stick.

★ ★ ★

Shannon was pleased with the progress of the roundup. He hadn't heard from Tom Hill and the other ranchers about their horses. He didn't care much either way and he knew that the ranchers needed the money more than he needed the horses.

But in the meanwhile he would attend to some unfinished business that was a part of his overall plan.

Willow Creek had always been an idyllic setting. Shannon knew that years ago Heather and Wade Rawlins met there often. There were times when Shannon, undetected, would watch the two of them from a distance. And, so, now, Shannon felt that there was no more fitting and romantic place to bring Charlotte.

As far as Charlotte was concerned, the place was of no matter. What mattered was that the handsomest, richest and most eligible man in the territory had chosen to be with her. And she wanted, more than anything she had ever wanted, to be with him.

All the years of being the little sister, prim and proper, with little or no prospect of being anything but a passive guest in her brother's house — all that would be left behind at Twelve Trees if she could become the mistress of Glenshannon Hall.

In the past months she had done what she had never done before. At night as she was about to change into her bed clothes, she had paused and examined her naked profile in the bedroom mirror. She was tall, almost five feet six inches, and undressed appeared less slender and more rounded than in her girdling apparel. And as she stood looking at herself, she thought of Shannon.

She thought of him as she lay on her goose down mattress and waited for sleep . . . and she trembled at the thought.

And now at Willow Creek she felt his arms around her and she stiffened as she waited to listen to the words she wanted to hear more than anything in the world.

Words that would lift her from the captivity of Twelve Trees to the unfettered freedom of Glenshannon Hall — and all that went with it.

"You can't do it!" Heather blazed.

"I can and I will," Charlotte said.

In the library at Twelve Trees, Heather and Wade Rawlins had listened as Charlotte made the announcement that she and Shannon were to be married.

Wade Rawlins sat stunned and silent as a rock.

Heather was even more stunned, but far

from silent — her face a thunderbolt storming at her sister-in-law.

"This is madness!"

"No, Heather, it's marriage. He's asked me and I have accepted. I thought you and Wade would be happy for me."

"Wade, talk to her."

"What is there to say?" Charlotte smiled. "We're in love and we're going to be married. Just as Wade and you are married."

"He doesn't love you!" Heather shouted. "I know he doesn't!"

"*How* do you know?"

Heather turned away and Charlotte took a step after her.

"Why, Heather . . . I do believe you're jealous."

"He can't love you." Heather turned back and faced her.

"Why can't he? I'm young and beautiful . . . or hadn't you noticed, Heather? And he's rich and handsome. Isn't that why you married Wade . . . because he was rich and handsome? Isn't it?"

Heather didn't answer.

"Any girl would be crazy to refuse Shannon, but he didn't propose to any girl, he proposed to me — to me, Heather."

"Wade, you've got to stop her." Even as she said it, Heather realized that her protestations were in vain, but she said it anyhow. "For *her* sake, stop her."

"He can't stop me. I'm free, over twenty-one. Nobody can stop me."

An armada of saffron clouds hovered over Moon Rock as if in a dead sea, becalmed, waiting for a favorable wind. Ghost ships without sails, without crew, without destination, without hope. Afloat to nowhere. The silent shadows, still as death, looked down on two specks, two scarred souls trapped between love and hate.

"I knew you'd be here," Heather said.

"And I knew you'd be here, too," Shannon replied, "when you heard . . ."

"Is that what you wanted, Shannon? To get me back here at Moon Rock? The two of us here alone together — and then what did you think would happen? Would that turn back the hands of the clock?"

"My life is a clock with no hands . . ."

"And no heart. Do you realize what you're doing to all of us?"

"And you, Heather, do you realize what you've done to both of us?"

"Whatever I did is done and it's too late to change it."

"Is it?"

"Yes! Yes! Oh, Shannon, why did you come back?"

"Don't you know?"

"No, I don't. You knew I was married before you came back, didn't you?"

"Yes. Redding told me at Benton Ridge."

"Then why didn't you stay away?"

"Why? To pay back what I owed. To every one of them. I helped beat them in the war and now they'll do what I want when I want and they'll call me mister while they're at it. I suffered their insolence, now they'll suffer mine — for as long as I want to heap it on them. It's my form of justice."

"No, Shannon . . . not justice. The word is revenge."

"That's another word for it. The Moor of Venice said it: 'Had all their hairs been lives, my great revenge hath stomach for them all.' "

"And for me, too? Is that the real reason you're doing all this — and marrying Charlotte? To punish me? Do you hate me, Shannon? Look at me and tell me."

He looked at her, but said nothing.

"You still love me, don't you, Shannon?"

Still nothing.

"We're here alone at Moon Rock. No one can see or hear . . . you're going to marry her, but do you still love me?"

"You made a choice, Heather. You sold yourself for worldly things. Money, position, power. I love you more in one heartbeat than that dandelion could in all his life."

"Then how can you marry Charlotte?"

"How could you marry *him?* You told me to leave and come back a hero with a cape and polished black boots and money. Well, here I am, Heather. But you didn't wait."

"And you didn't tell me you were coming back."

"Did I have to? I heard you that night telling Hannah that Rawlins asked you to marry him."

"And did you hear my answer?"

"I heard as much as I could bear. Would it have made any difference?"

"All the difference. But you left and you never wrote. You might've been dead."

"I am."

"I'm begging you." There were tears in her eyes. "Don't marry Charlotte."

"Who is there left for me to marry?"

Charlotte had a choice to make. They could wait until the roundup was over, and then drive to Fort Griffin — or they could be married immediately.

She chose immediately.

She didn't want to take the chance that something would happen to Shannon during the roundup, or on the drive, or that he might change his mind, or that Heather might come up with something that would impede the proceedings.

Charlotte and Heather had hardly spoken a word and Wade, as always, strove to be civil, but his displeasure, or at least disappointment, was not too well hidden. Much to Heather's chagrin, he did agree to give the bride away.

The ceremony, strained as it was, took place in the parlor at Twelve Trees with only the immediate family and a few friends, including Amos Higgins and Cassie Higgins Kearny in attendance — and, of course, Hannah.

Hadley had been invited but declined.

The minister, Reverend Groves, perfunctorily went through the motions of the ceremony, ate a slice of cake, drank a glass of punch, collected ten dollars from Shannon and went back to Gilead.

Shannon invited only one guest, Pepper, who after the ceremony also decided to go to Gilead and spend the night at the Emporium with Cherrie Millay and her private stock.

At twilight, the carriage with Shannon

aboard in his wedding suit and Charlotte in her wedding dress, moved in the direction of Glenshannon Hall, but Shannon looked back toward Moon Rock.

Charlotte didn't notice. She was too busy thinking about the future and gazing at the diamond ring on the third finger of her left hand.

Carson and Ben Hooper stood at the porch waiting as the carriage pulled up.

"Welcome home, Mrs. Shannon," Carson said as Shannon stepped down and back to help his bride.

"Thank you, Carson." Charlotte smiled.

"I'll see to the carriage, sir," Ben said.

Shannon escorted Charlotte up the porch steps, opened the door and waited for her to enter. She had expected to be carried across the proverbial threshold, but concealed her disappointment, smiled and preceded him inside.

As they walked into the hallway a voice came from the great room. Hadley's voice.

"Shannon!"

"You go ahead, Charlotte," Shannon said, pointing to the stairs. "Your things were taken up there this morning."

"Not *all* things." She smiled. "I'll be waiting."

"Shannon!" The voice came again.

Shannon entered the room. Hadley sat in the big chair, the chair he hadn't sat in since Shannon came back. There was a bottle and a glass on the table beside him. The glass was empty, the bottle full. And for the first time since Shannon came back, Hadley seemed stark sober and grim — and unafraid. He stared at the fire, then his eyes turned to Shannon.

Shannon came closer and stood directly in front of Hadley.

"Sorry you missed the ceremony, Hadley. It was a quiet affair. Your sister . . ."

"I want to talk to you."

"Go ahead and talk."

"And you're going to listen."

"I'll listen . . . but first . . ." Shannon walked to the small table, lifted the bottle and glass and poured himself a healthy drink. Hadley could hardly keep his eyes off the liquid, but gathered all his willpower. "I haven't seen you like this since . . . well, in a long time."

Shannon took a tantalizing sip, savoring the fluid, and returned the bottle to the table.

"You're a rotten bastard."

"Is that what you wanted to talk about?"

"That's just the beginning . . ."

"Well, go ahead. I'd like to see how it ends."

"Why did you have to come here?"

"Well, after the war . . ." Shannon took another sip.

"I don't mean after the war!" Hadley shouted. "I mean from the first!"

"I didn't come, I was brought . . . by a kind and gracious gentleman. You remember him, Hadley."

Hadley reached out, grabbed the bottle and took a deep swallow, then another.

"What right did you have?" He began to tremble. "You wanted to take everything."

"A little food maybe . . . and a place to sleep. Couldn't you have spared that much?"

Hadley drank again and was visibly shaking now.

"No! You tried to take everything away from me — the best horse — this house — my sister — my father . . ."

"No, Hadley. I didn't take your father from you. You remember that day . . ."

"I don't want to hear it!" Hadley hollered.

"You said you wanted to talk. Well, we've never talked about that, have we, Hadley?"

"Shut up!"

"There never was any need to talk about it, was there, Hadley? We both knew who set that fire. . . ."

"Shut up, I tell you!"

"You were weak and mean and selfish and you killed your own father because of it."

"I didn't kill him!"

"Yes, you did, just as sure as you're sitting there."

Hadley pulled a gun from the cushion of the chair where he sat.

"No! You're not going to take anything ever again. . . ."

Hadley stood with the gun aiming point-blank at Shannon. His voice crackled.

"Because I'm going to kill you!"

Hadley's hand trembled.

"Why, you puking weasel. You haven't got the guts to kill a chicken."

Shannon slapped Hadley forward and backward, grabbed him by the chest and slammed him against the stone fireplace, where he fell unconscious.

Shannon took the bottle from the table, placed it on the floor next to Hadley, then turned and walked toward the stairs and his bride.

Shannon opened the door to the master bedroom.

Charlotte had begun to undress, but turned at the sound of the door opening, and with mock maidenly modesty, held the dress up in front of her in an attempt to be saucy and cute — and at the same time, seductive.

"Why, sir, don't you know you're supposed to knock before entering a lady's chamber?"

Shannon ignored her, walked across the room toward the armoire. He had left the door to the bedroom open.

She walked to the door, closed it, and turned back, coyly.

"My, my. What will the servants think?"

Shannon opened the door to the armoire.

"Oh, darling," she said, "I'm so happy . . . and I'll make you . . ."

Instead of removing his clothes, Shannon pulled his cape out of the armoire and threw it over his shoulders.

Charlotte stood appalled, no longer coy.

"Shannon, what's happened? Shannon, what did Hadley say? Is there anything wrong?"

He walked back across the room, still not even looking at her, nor answering.

"Where are you going?"

He continued toward the door.

"You're not going to leave me . . . tonight?"

His hand was on the knob, turning.

"Shannon!"

He opened the door and walked out, leaving the door open.

She ran to the doorway and screamed after him.

"Shannon!"

"Who is it? Who's there?" Ben Hooper raised up in the bunk and looked toward the figure at the stable door holding a lantern in one hand and a gunbelt in the other.

"It's Shannon, Ben. Go back to sleep."

"What is it? What's wrong, Mister Shannon?"

"Nothing. I'm going out."

"Tonight?"

"Now. Going to saddle Black."

"I'll do it, sir."

"Alright, go ahead."

Shannon set the lantern on the ledge of the stall and strapped the gun and holster around his waist under the cape.

"Is somebody sick, sir?"

"No."

"Do you need any help?"

"Not where I'm going. You go back to sleep, Ben."

"Yes, sir."

When Ben was finished, Shannon swung onto the saddle.

"When will you be back, sir?"

"Good night, Ben."

Shannon, forked on Black, scudded out of the stable like a mounted specter, cape unfurled, riding into the cool, moonlit night.

It was almost as if Black knew their destination.

Ben stood at the stable entrance and watched as Shannon blended into the chocolate landscape. No one had treated him better. No one was closer — or more distant.

Hadley stirred on the floor, his mind still in a haze. He saw the whiskey bottle beside him and reached for it. He staggered to his feet, took a drink, then weaved toward his bedroom.

Charlotte lay in Shannon's bed, their marriage bed, alone and crying, Heather's voice echoing in her brain.

"He doesn't love you. He couldn't love you."

Shannon had dismounted and sat, shrouded in his cape, leaning against a boulder. The full moon splashed long shadows across Moon Rock. The whispering wind sounded like Heather's voice.

"Is that what you wanted, Shannon? To get me back here at Moon Rock?"

"Would that turn back the hands of the clock?"

"You still love me, don't you, Shannon?"

"You're going to marry her, but do you still love me?"

"How could you marry Charlotte?"

"I'm begging you . . . don't marry Charlotte."

Heather lay sleepless in bed, staring at the circle of moon through the window. She turned her face and looked at her husband asleep next to her. She pictured in her mind Shannon and Charlotte that same night, that same time, in each other's arms, making love in their honeymoon bed. She couldn't help wishing that it was she instead of Charlotte in Shannon's bed and Shannon's arms.

And she couldn't help thinking of Moon Rock.

Chapter Forty

It was no secret at Glenshannon Hall that Shannon had left his bride alone on their wedding night.

Ben Hooper had told no one, but Carson, Gibbs, Carey and some of the other hands saw Shannon riding back from somewhere while his wife had been alone that night.

No one said anything but there were whispers and Pepper heard about them.

"Is it going to be like that every night?" Charlotte asked her husband.

"If you mean am I going to leave every night, no I'm not going to leave."

"Are you going to stay in the same room?"

"Yes."

"In the same bed?"

"Yes. Don't ask any more questions about it."

"Just one more. Is this a marriage by day only?"

"If you care to put it that way."

"Why, Shannon? Why are you doing this to me?"

"To you, Charlotte? No, not to you."

"I don't understand. If I am so repugnant, why did you marry me?"

"No, Charlotte . . . you married me."

"Well, boss," Carson said, "between us and the Kiowas, we've rounded up more than we expected for the first trip to Fort Griffin."

"I think we'll add some more."

"Alright. I'll send the boys over to Gypsum Basin and see how many they can collect over there."

"No, Carson. You won't have to send the boys anywhere."

"What do you mean?"

"I mean, I think those horses'll come to us."

"What're you going to do?" Carson smiled. "Whistle 'em in?"

"Something like that."

The next day Shannon sat at the breakfast table with Charlotte. He was finishing his steak and eggs. Her breakfast remained untouched.

Carson stepped into the doorway.

"Beg pardon, boss. Tom Hill's outside. He'd like to see you."

362

Shannon nodded and rose.

"Excuse me, Charlotte."

Pepper was on the porch; Ben Hooper stood on the ground nearby.

Tom Hill had dismounted, and waited with the reins in his hand as Shannon came out of the door followed by Carson.

"Good morning, Mister Hill."

"Morning."

"Where're your friends?" Shannon asked as he looked around.

"They decided not to come, but . . ."

"But what?"

"Well, I'm here to talk for all of them."

"Talk."

"We've rounded up five hundred head."

"And?"

"Well, we've decided to sell you the horses. They're over at my place."

"Five hundred head at five dollars a head. That's twenty-five hundred dollars. I'll take a look at them this morning and pay you in town this afternoon, three o'clock."

"We'll be there," Hill said as he mounted.

"So will the money."

After Hill rode away Shannon looked at Ben.

"Hammer," Shannon said.

"What the hell's that mean?" Pepper asked.

"Ben knows."

★ ★ ★

The hands on the clock at the Emporium edged past two-thirty and the long hand began its upward creep.

The Emporium was much more crowded that afternoon than it had been for a long time during daytime hours.

More than a couple dozen ranch owners and cowboys stood at the bar and sat at the tables drinking, smoking and playing cards, but there was not the usual level of banter, laughter and noise. Instead there was a hushed anticipation and much more often than usual the customers checked the clock on the wall or their own timepieces.

Tom Hill sipped his beer and occasionally answered a question or nodded at Jim McCarthy, one of the ranchers, who stood next to him with an empty whiskey glass on the bar in front of him.

"Care for another?" the bartender asked McCarthy.

McCarthy, a tall man with a range-worn face and lean, hard frame, nodded.

Pepper and Cherrie Millay sat at their favored corner table, half-empty whiskey glasses in front of them and a bottle between.

"Your customers don't seem any too lively today," Pepper said.

"No, nor too happy."

"I reckon you wouldn't be too damn happy either if you were collecting less than a fifth of what your merchandise is worth."

"How much is Shannon giving them for the herd?"

"Five dollars a head."

"I know a place where you have to pay more than that for a steak . . . or a . . ."

"So do I. But that's his price and they ain't got no choice."

"They got one choice."

"What's that?"

"After they collect . . . he's liable to get a bullet in the back."

"You might not be too far from wrong . . . but that's the way it'd have to be. I don't see anybody here who'd face him."

"Maybe six of them would at the same time."

"They'd have to face both of us."

"I believe they would, Pepper, I believe they would. But after some of the things people have been saying about him . . ."

"Most of 'em are the same people who treated him like a dog before the war."

"Yeah, and now they say that dog's turned into a wolf."

"He sure as hell ain't no lamb."

The clock on the wall in Higgins' office

showed two thirty-six.

Both Shannon and Higgins smoked cigars, Higgins behind his desk and Shannon seated on the other side.

"I hear," Higgins said, "that Hadley's doing poorly."

"Not too well."

"I think it's most decent of you to allow him to stay at Glenshannon Hall, under the circumstances."

"I'm glad the circumstances aren't reversed."

"Yes." Higgins nodded. "I don't think he'd be . . ."

There was a knock on the office door.

"Come in, Jeremy," Higgins said.

The door opened and Jeremy Pentwhistle, the clerk, entered carrying a stack of currency.

"Here's the money you wanted, Mister Higgins," Pentwhistle said through his ferret lips. "Twenty-five hundred."

He placed the stack on Higgins' desk.

"Thank you, Jeremy. Now if you'll sign the transfer, Mister Shannon, then the McCarthy place is yours. That's a good piece of property, sir, plenty of water and . . ."

Higgins looked up at Pentwhistle, who was watching and listening.

". . . That'll be all, Jeremy."

Pentwhistle nodded and left quickly, very

quickly, with the door almost closing on his heels.

"As I was saying, Mister Shannon, that's a good piece of land. Adding that to your own spread is a good idea. Why, with the McCarthy place, that gives you . . ."

"Yes. I know, Amos." Shannon picked up the money from the desk.

"Why don't you sit for a few minutes and enjoy your cigar. We can talk about . . ."

"Yes, Amos." Shannon glanced up at the clock. Two forty-two. "I think I will enjoy this cigar . . . for just a couple of minutes."

Jeremy Pentwhistle raced into the Emporium, batwings swinging behind him, paused, looked around the smoke-clouded room, spotted Hill and McCarthy. He leaned in between the two men and whispered so both of them could hear.

Shannon came out of the First National Bank of Gilead, threw away what was left of his cigar and, out of habit, touched with his palm the butt of the Remington strapped around his waist.

"Shannon!"

The voice came from the direction of the Emporium.

Shannon turned and faced the men moving toward him from the saloon: Hill, a tall man next to him and the other ranchers close behind.

Pepper walked to one side, Cherrie stood at the Emporium entrance and Jeremy Pentwhistle's face peered from the saloon window.

"Shannon!"

The tall man stepped ahead of Hill and the ranchers, who stopped behind him.

"My name's McCarthy."

"My name's *Mister* Shannon."

"You're a thief, *Mister* Shannon."

Sheriff Joe Fox appeared, stood next to Pepper but for the moment said nothing.

"You stole my ranch, *thief!*"

"You're a liar. I bought it. But you can stay and work for me."

"Work for you? On my own place?"

"It was your place. It's mine now."

"Not while I'm alive, it isn't."

"You'd better think that over . . . and any of you friends of his here, better give him some sound advice."

Tom Hill took a step forward.

"Mister Shannon, I want to ask you something."

"Go ahead."

"Didn't you hold off paying us 'til after

you took over his ranch so's we couldn't pool the money and save it?"

"You'd better think about saving your own ranch."

"You're a bastard, Shannon!" McCarthy shouted. "You haven't even got a last name."

"And you haven't got a bullet in your heart . . . not yet." Shannon glanced at Joe Fox. "Now, Sheriff, aren't you going to do something about this?"

"McCarthy." Fox moved out a step.

"You stay out of this, Sheriff . . . it's between me and this bottom-dealing sonofabitch."

"No, it's not!" Fox said.

"We'll see . . ."

McCarthy drew. But before he could fire, he fell dead with a bullet in his heart from Shannon's gun.

Solemn silence. No one on the street moved. The Sheriff bent over the body, then looked up.

That's what McCarthy was . . . a body.

Shannon holstered the Remington, then took the packet of money out of the inside pocket of his coat and threw it on the ground not far from the corpse.

"There's your money, Mister Hill."

He turned toward the hitching post, untied the reins and started to mount.

The crowd stirred and murmured but nobody did anything sudden.

Pepper took the butt of a cigar out of his mouth and let it drop on the street.

Cherrie walked through the batwings into the Emporium where Jeremy Pentwhistle still looked through the window.

Amos Higgins stood at the open door of the First National Bank of Gilead, then disappeared as he closed the door behind him. He had seen all he wanted to see, and more.

As Shannon rode by, not fast, not slow, Tom Hill looked down at the money.

The town clock struck one, two, three times.

Chapter Forty-one

Carson, Gibbs, Carey and all of Shannon's men were dressed in their best clothes and mounted in front of the headquarters area.

Pepper gimped from around back. He, too, was dressed in a dark suit and string tie. A horse and buggy were hitched and waiting.

Shannon came out of the front door, but wearing ranch clothes. He looked at the other men, then at Pepper.

"We're going to a funeral, Mister Shannon. Jim McCarthy was a friend and neighbor to us for a good many years. Any objections?"

"No."

"Good, because we'd go anyhow." Pepper started to climb aboard. "I'll be seeing his widow and three kids. Anything you want me to tell 'em?"

"Yes."

"What?"

"Tell them the same thing I told him. They can stay there as long as they want."

"That's mighty generous of you, Mister Shannon, but they're already packed."

"Tell them . . . ask them to stay."

Pepper settled into the seat and picked up the buggy whip.

"Carson," Shannon called out.

Carson brought his horse closer to the porch.

"Yes, boss."

"We're still leaving for Fort Griffin with the horses tomorrow morning. Make sure we've got provisions for a couple of weeks."

"All taken care of, boss."

Carson's spurs nicked the flanks of his horse. Pepper and the rest of them followed as he headed away from the main building.

Shannon watched, then turned toward Ben Hooper, who stood at the side of the porch.

"Aren't you going with them?"

"No, sir."

"Ever see anybody dead, Ben?"

"My mother."

"Not a pretty sight."

"No, sir."

" 'Specially if you did the killing." He turned.

"Mister Shannon?"

"What is it?"

"Can I ride along to Fort Griffin with you?"

"Well, I guess we'll need somebody to help tend to the remuda. You can come."

"And Mister Shannon, just one more thing?"

"What?"

"Will you teach me how to use a gun?"

"Have you got a gun?"

"Not yet."

"Why do you want to learn how to use one?"

Ben Hooper looked toward the riders heading for Jim McCarthy's funeral.

"So I don't end up like him."

There were three or four other ranches that Shannon had intended to move in on through past-due mortgages that Amos Higgins held — ranches that would add strategically to his holdings.

His intention had been to do it right away. But since McCarthy's demise three days ago, and weighing the temper of the town and even his own men, Shannon decided to wait until after he delivered the horses to Fort Griffin.

Nobody was going to pay off his debt in the next month or so, and he didn't need any revolt among his hands between here and the Fort.

Tom Hill's place would be next, then the two spreads contiguous to Hill's.

The property Shannon coveted most was Twelve Trees.

If he couldn't have Heather, he'd have the place where she lived and slept. He already had one such place . . . her brother's . . . Glenshannon Hall. He intended to have another . . . her husband's . . . Twelve Trees.

He had looted plantation after plantation and taken bounty. What he wanted most from Twelve Trees was living bounty.

In his heart he hoped that Wade Rawlins would stand up to him like McCarthy did when Shannon took over his property, pull a gun. Then Shannon could take over Twelve Trees and all that went with it.

The trouble was that there was no mortgage against Twelve Trees.

Not yet.

Shannon walked into the great room. Charlotte sat in a chair and embroidered by rote. She never spoke to Shannon unless he spoke to her first. Her replies were brief and her eyes seldom locked onto his.

She had, of course, thought of leaving, going back to Twelve Trees, but she also thought back to Heather's face and voice.

"He doesn't love you. I know he doesn't."

"He can't love you . . ."

Better the humiliation here than there.

There was always the flickering flame of hope, hope that Shannon would take her in his arms and things would be different.

But with each passing day and night, that hope grew dimmer.

Take her in his arms? He hadn't even touched her. He had barely looked at her, or even spoken to her when they were alone — alone as they were now. But this time he did speak.

"Where's Hadley? I haven't seen him for days."

"He's in his room, dead to the world."

"Maybe the world's better off."

"Shannon?"

"What is it?"

"Are you leaving for Fort Griffin tomorrow?"

"Yes."

"How long will you be gone?"

"Ten days," he shrugged. "Two weeks."

"Would you like me to move into one of the guest rooms?"

"A wife's place is beside her husband."

He walked over to his desk, reached down, pulled open a double drawer and took out a holstered gun and belt, closed the drawer and started toward the door.

"Charlotte, why didn't you go to the funeral?"

She continued embroidering.

"A wife's place," she said quietly, "is beside her husband."

"What're you doing?"

Ben turned.

"Getting Domino ready for the trip," he said with a brush in his hand.

"What about you? You ready?"

"Yes, sir."

Shannon walked from the entrance into the stable, carrying a few items with him.

"Not quite," he said. "You'll need a couple of things. This bedroll, for one. Got it from the bunkhouse. And here's an old jacket of mine."

Shannon tossed the bedroll and jacket at Ben Hooper.

Ben caught them both but couldn't take his eyes off the gun and holster still in Shannon's grip.

"Oh, yeah," Shannon said. "And here's something else I used to wear when I was about your age. I think it'll fit. Take it and tie it on."

Ben did. His hand trembled nervously.

"Take your time, boy. Nobody's going to take it away from you."

"Yes, sir."

"How does it fit?"

"Good. Real good."

"Alright, we'll go out back and do a little practicing."

"Now?" Ben asked with an eager voice.

"Good a time as any. Come on."

Shannon began to walk and Ben fell in step beside him.

"You can take it on the ride to Fort Griffin, but there's a few things you ought to know first . . . just in case."

"Yes, sir."

"There are those who keep the hammer on the empty chamber. I'm not one of them. Might need that extra bullet. Now the most important thing is this . . ."

Chapter Forty-two

There hadn't been as many horses gathered together since the Mongols charged out of China.

"How many you think there's out there?" Gibbs asked Carson.

"I don't know," Carson said. "Count the legs and divide by four."

Tom Hill and the other ranchers had provided five hundred.

Running Bear and his Kiowas brought in another two hundred.

The cowboys from Glenshannon Hall had collected about seventeen hundred.

There were twenty-four hundred — more or less — on the hoof and headed to Fort Griffin. Shannon in the lead, with Ben Hooper often riding at his side, Carson overseeing the wranglers, Cookie at the reins of the chuck wagon with Pepper next to him, often with a cigar in his mouth.

"How you doing with the Trojan War?"

Shannon asked Ben as they rode at the head of the herd.

"Finished it."

"Learn anything?"

"A lot of strange-sounding names — Priam, Hector, Paris, Menelaeus, Achilles, Patroclus, Odysseus, and of course Helen, who launched a thousand ships."

"Anything else?"

"Well, after fighting over ten years and slaughtering each other by the thousands, the Greeks finally beat the Trojans with a hollow horse and their soldiers inside and using trickery to get through the gates."

"What did you say they used?"

"Trickery."

"Ben, in war that's called strategy. Say it."

"Strategy."

"That's right. In war and in life, you don't necessarily beat the enemy by storming the gates. You use strategy and gain the upper hand. Remember that."

"Yes, sir, I will. Strategy."

"But" — he pointed to Ben's hip — "keep that gun handy."

"Yes, sir."

There were close to two dozen horses tied to the hitch-rails in front of the main building at Twelve Trees.

In the parlor Wade Rawlins stood with an imposing man next to him. The owners of the horses, including Tom Hill, were assembled, sitting on couches and extra chairs. Some leaned against the walls.

Hank Redding was standing next to the imposing man and Heather stood unobtrusively near a door.

"I think everybody's here, Mister Rawlins," Redding said.

"Thanks, Hank. And I want to thank all of you men for coming here. I've called this meeting because, as Amos Higgins once said, 'We're all in the same boat.'"

"No, we're not, Wade," Tom Hill spoke out. "Your place is still clear."

There were nods and murmurs of agreement by the ranchers in the room.

"Now wait a minute, Tom, Twelve Trees is clear, but I don't have any cash to run it. In a few months I won't be able to . . ."

"You can always borrow from your rich brother-in-law."

More murmurs.

"Tom, we've been friends for a long time. I don't think I deserve such a remark . . . nor does my wife."

"No, I reckon not, Wade" — Hill was contrite — "and I apologize to you and Mrs. Rawlins. But I saw that sonofa— I saw him gun down my best friend."

"Tom, this isn't a court of law. Now, I've got a plan if you'll all just listen."

A chorus of affirmation came from the ranchers.

"Sure, we'll listen."

"Let him talk."

"That's why we're here."

"Go ahead, Rawlins."

"Let's hear this plan."

Wade Rawlins nodded.

"Thank you. The money Shannon paid you for the horses —"

"Don't amount to a spit in the well, excuse me, Mrs. Rawlins," one of the ranchers said.

"That's right." Rawlins smiled. "And we haven't a contract to sell horses to the Army. But we do have plenty of something else, something we can sell."

"What?" Hill asked.

"Beef."

"Ain't worth branding 'em," Hill remarked. "They'll bring a dollar a head."

"In Texas. But I'm talking about fifteen dollars a head — maybe twenty."

"Where?" Hill snickered.

"Abilene."

"That's in Kansas, last I heard. Almost a thousand miles from here."

"That's right," Rawlins agreed.

"Might as well be on the moon."

"Not quite. There's no trail to the moon. But there is to Abilene. A half-breed Comanche named Jesse Chisholm blazed it" — Rawlins pointed to the imposing man next to him — "and this gentleman has driven it."

Now there were murmurs of interest, even encouragement, to hear more.

"This is Mister Ethan Jones, the best trail boss in Texas — or anyplace else."

Wade Rawlins had their undivided attention.

"What do you want us to do?" Hill asked.

The other ranchers joined in in chorus, all anxious to know Rawlins' plan.

"Alone, none of us could make it. But if we banded together with one common herd — every man and boy that can ride — and with Ethan Jones leading the way to Abilene, then . . ."

"How many head?" Hill asked.

"Ten thousand," Rawlins said.

"At twenty dollars?" a voice boomed.

"Hell, that's . . ." Another voice.

"Two hundred thousand dollars!" Hill proclaimed.

"There ain't that much money!" someone shouted.

Rawlins took a step forward.

"There is in Kansas!!" He smiled, then

the smile faded and his face took on a different aspect as he held up both hands for quiet. "Now, wait a minute. It's not that easy. Let's hear what Ethan's got to say first. Go ahead, Ethan."

Ethan Jones was a man who commanded respect. Tall, spare except for stone shoulders, long hair, mustachioed. He had the look of a timber wolf: bullet gray eyes, Indian cheek bones, long aquiline nose and a chin carved out of granite. Around his slim waist was a black leather belt and a Colt butt forward in a fringed holster.

"The chances are, we won't make it," Jones said in a coarse voice.

There was sudden quiet in the room. The fevered enthusiasm of the ranchers cooled off. They looked at each other, then back at Jones and Rawlins.

"Then what's this all about?" Hill asked.

"It's about giving it to you straight," Rawlins said. "About telling you — telling all of us — what we're up against."

"We'll fight floods," Ethan Jones said, "fever, Kiowas, Comanches, border raiders and probably each other. At ten miles a day it'll take more than three months. Three of the longest, toughest months you'll ever know. And my word's got to be the law. There'll be no quitting or turning back if

383

you sign on. If we don't make it, I'll take nothing because you'll have nothing to give. If we do — and looking at you men here today, I think we just might — I'll take five percent of the market price. That's all I've got to say."

There was quiet in the room — a deep and absolute silence — until Wade Rawlins spoke.

"Well, what do you men say?"

The silence was smashed by cheering, clapping and near pandemonium. This was the outlet, the overflow of opportunity after years of pent-up frustration and defeat. They would sign on, every Texas one of them. No matter how slim the chances, how long the odds, it was better than the slow, incontrovertible, choking death of doing nothing.

Wade Rawlins shook Ethan Jones's hand. And Jones even smiled some.

Heather ran across the room through the cheering crowd and embraced her husband.

"Wade," she whispered, "I'm so proud of you."

But it had been a long time since she had said "I love you."

This part of Texas — or anyplace else — had never seen anything quite like it before. Cattle — hoof and horn, rounded up by the tens, the hundreds, the thousands, and branded with the rocking T.

T

Cows with the common brand of the common hope of every rancher in the territory — except Shannon — were moving and bellowing in an ever widening circle.

"Seems like we've branded every rump in Texas," Rawlins said to Ethan Jones.

"This is the easy part," Jones replied.

"There's one rump I'd like to brand," Hill said. "Clean through to the bone, and it's not on a cow."

"This is the best way to beat him, Tom," Rawlins said, "and keep him from doing what he did to Jim McCarthy."

"It's one way," Hill nodded. "But if it doesn't work, I've got another."

"Let's hope it doesn't come to that."

On the morning of the adventure, as the great herd milled and the saddled cowboys made ready, Heather, Hannah and Angela were aboard a buggy watching, waiting for the drive to begin.

Rawlins bowed his head unashamedly in prayer.

"Oh, Lord, bless us in this great endeavor

and help us to succeed, protect our loved ones while we're gone and guide the hand of Ethan Jones on our journey. Amen." His head rose and he looked at Ethan Jones.

"All right, Ethan. Take us to Abilene!"

Jones took off his wide-brimmed trail hat, waved it in a circle above his head and shouted.

"Yeeeeaaahhh!!!"

The rest of the cowboys took up the cry, and horses and cattle commenced the journey northeast to Kansas.

The stream of wagons and wagon trains moving westward had begun long before James Marshall found a glittering substance at Sutter's Mill in 1848, but once word of the discovery spread, the stream of wagon trains and "forty-niners" became a westward torrent moving across the landscape with men, women and children seeking their own manifest destiny.

Besides the natural barriers and obstacles — mountains, deserts, rivers — there was another hazard, or hazards. Living hazards.

Indians.

Indians who looked with disfavor on the trespassers, and did their damnedest to discourage them with bows, arrows, rifles, handguns and general bloodletting.

The United States government set up hundreds of forts throughout the western landscape to protect the travelers and those who decided to settle along the way — from St. Louis through Texas, Arizona, New Mexico and other states and territories to the north.

But cavalry men without horses were like infantry men without legs. Hence the need for horses.

Twenty-four hundred of those horses, shepherded by Shannon and his men, were within sight of the gates of Fort Griffin.

General William Tecumseh Sherman had been put in charge of quelling the querulous tribes — Apache, Comanche, Kiowa, Lakota, Cheyenne — and he intended to use cavalry men and horses as a major part of the quelling.

Shannon's herd would be converted to near fifty thousand dollars in Shannon's purse.

He knew that those horses would be used to defeat the Indians, some of whom he had grown up with, but he also knew their defeat, like the South's, was inevitable. And if Sherman, Sheridan, Crook, Custer and the rest of them didn't get the horses from him, they would get them from somebody else.

He would do whatever he could for the Kiowas he had grown up with.

Heather was polishing the silverware, working on a spoon, as Hannah came into the kitchen with Angela.

"Mommy" — Angela looked up toward her mother — "when is Daddy coming back?"

"Not for some time, darling. We'll have to get used to being without him for a while. I know it's hard, but will you be a brave little girl and try to do that?"

"Did he go to fight a war again?"

"Not exactly, dear." Heather glanced at Hannah. "But we've got to remember him in our prayers every night."

Angela frowned but nodded.

"What are you doing, child?" Hannah stepped closer to Heather.

"Just what it looks like. I'm polishing the silver."

"That's my job and I did it just last week."

"You did?"

"I did."

"Well, I have to do *something*."

"Heaven's sake, Heather, they've only been gone a few days. It'll be months before he's back."

Heather continued rubbing at the spoon.

"I know, Hannah. I'm just trying to keep busy."

"Well, you're going to wear out that particular spoon — try this fork for a while."

Heather smiled, then shrugged. Her smile turned into something else as she took the fork, looked at it for just a beat and set it down on the table with the other silverware.

"Hannah, come sit here closer to me." She glanced at Angela. "Angela."

"Yes, Mommy."

"Here's a nice shiny spoon you can sit on the floor and play with. Matter of fact, here are two spoons. Sit right down there."

Heather placed the spoons on the floor and Angela sat down in front of them and picked them up while Hannah took a chair next to Heather.

"Hannah, what do you think their chances are?"

"Chances?"

"Ethan Jones said they probably wouldn't make it. Floods, fever, Indians, border raiders . . ."

"If Ethan Jones didn't think they'd make it, he wouldn't have gone at all. Did you ever think of that?"

"I guess you're right."

"I'm always right. That's why I'm so beautiful." Hannah smiled. "Besides, Wade came through the war, didn't he? He'll come through this."

"This is a different kind of war. There you knew who the enemy was."

"You know damn well who the enemy is."

"Who?"

"He lives at Glenshannon Hall and I don't mean your brother."

"Shannon?"

"Shannon. Or don't you think so?"

"I hate him, if that's what you mean."

"Do you? Do you hate yourself?"

"What?"

"You once told me you *were* Shannon. What would you do if he walked into this room or into this house and you were alone with him?"

"What are you saying, Hannah?"

"What did you do the last time you were alone with him?"

"That was before the war. A long time ago," Heather lied.

"But you remember, don't you, Heather?"

Heather remembered.

It was at Moon Rock.

Chapter Forty-three

Ten thousand beeves moving at a slow pace can be seen from a long way.

Shannon and his men, riding back from Fort Griffin along with Pepper and Cookie in the chuck wagon, spotted the sea of cattle in the espadrille more than a mile in the distance.

Ben was the first to point them out.

"Look at that, Mister Shannon," Ben said. "Did you ever see anything like that before?"

"Let's have a closer look." Shannon spurred Black gently and motioned for the rest of his men to follow.

They did.

If they were surprised at the size of the herd, they were even more surprised at the sight of Rawlins, Hill and the rest of the ranchers.

Shannon reined up close to Rawlins.

"Mister Rawlins, I didn't know you had this many beeves."

"They're not all mine, Mister Shannon,

they belong to every rancher in this part of Texas — except you, of course."

"What're you planning on doing with them?"

"Selling them."

"For nickels and dimes?"

"Fifteen, twenty dollars a head."

"Where? Not in Texas."

"No, not in Texas. In Abilene."

"Abilene? That's a long way off, Mister Rawlins. Ever been to Abilene?"

"No, but" — Rawlins looked at Jones — "Ethan Jones has."

"I've heard of Mister Jones." Shannon nodded.

"I've heard of you too, Mister Shannon," Jones replied.

"Too many hazards along the way," Shannon said. "You won't make it."

"You better hope we do." Tom Hill spoke for the first time.

"Chew that a little finer." Shannon's eyes narrowed.

"Now, Tom, that'll be enough of that kind of talk." Rawlins looked back at Shannon. "Desperate times call for desperate measures. We're betting we get through."

"You'll need all the help you can get . . . and you look a little sparse on manpower."

"Shannon."

That was the first time the foreman hadn't called him Mister, and the oversight, if that's what it was, didn't escape Shannon.

"What is it, Carson."

"I'm drawing my time."

"Why?"

"You just said it. They'll need all the help they can get."

Shannon looked at the rest of his men.

"Any other crusaders among you?"

"I'll go," said one man.

"Me, too," said another.

Shannon looked at Gibbs and Carey. They both shook their heads no. Then at Pepper.

"What about you?"

There was a pause.

"I wouldn't be much help."

Shannon turned and rode off without a word, Ben Hooper next to him. The rest of his men, except for Carson and the two others, followed.

Pepper, Gibbs, Carey and the ranch hands pulled up near the bunkhouses. Shannon and Ben rode to the front of the main building where Shannon dismounted and handed the reins to Ben.

Shannon looked at Ben wearing the jacket

he had given the young man and nodded without smiling or saying anything.

With a weary walk, Shannon made his way up the steps of the porch and to the main door as Ben headed toward the stable with the horses.

He walked into the great room and stopped dead in his boots as if paralyzed.

Heather, wearing a black dress, sat in a chair, staring straight ahead.

There was a long moment. He was about to run to her when Charlotte came in from another room. She, too, was dressed in black.

Shannon looked from Heather to Charlotte.

"What's happened?"

"You're just in time," Charlotte said, "for the funeral."

Shannon didn't have to ask whose funeral. He realized that only her brother's death could have brought Heather back to Glenshannon Hall.

Her return had nothing to do with him.

"How long have you been here?" Shannon asked Heather.

"Long enough to be with him when he died. We didn't think you'd be back so soon."

"Sorry to have disappointed you."

Heather ignored the remark.

"He wanted to be buried next to his mother and father." Heather rose from her chair. "Even though he damned you with his dying breath, we didn't think you would deny him a plot of ground."

"He can have his plot of ground . . . twice as deep, if you like."

It was a bleak day promising rain that night.

Hadley's casket was laid in a fresh grave near his mother and father while they stood at the gravesite — Shannon, Heather, Charlotte, Hannah with Angela at her side, Pepper, Ben, Gibbs, Carey and the rest of Shannon's ranch hands.

Father Francis Shaughnessy was now in his late seventies, but he still stood straight and strong as his mellow voice intoned the familiar words.

The Lord is my shepherd: I shall not want. He maketh me to lie down in green pastures: He leadeth me beside the still waters.

The faces of the mourners were all bowed toward the grave. All but one face, Shannon's.

He restoreth my soul: He leadeth me in the paths of righteousness for his name's sake. Yea, though I walk though the valley of the shadow of death, I will fear no evil: for thou art with me; thy rod and thy staff they comfort me.

Shannon's eyes were cast straight at Heather.

Thou preparest a table before me in the presence of mine enemies; thou anointest my head with oil; my cup runneth over. Surely goodness and mercy shall follow me all the days of my life:

Shannon's thoughts were not of goodness and mercy.

and I will dwell in the house of the Lord forever.

His thoughts dwelled on Heather, and what might have been — what still might be.

Chapter Forty-four

Rain slashed. Thunder and lightning ripped through the cloak of night — pounded against the black sky, illuminated the main building, which seemed to shudder.

Shannon entered the bedroom and saw Charlotte standing in the shadows. Fleeting fingers of lightning revealed that she was naked. Wind-driven rain streaked onto the windows and dripped downward to the ledges.

She had seen the way that Shannon had looked at Heather in the cemetery. Now Charlotte looked at him in the same way as she came closer, naked and with only one thing in mind.

"Shannon . . . are you a man or the devil? Look at me. Look at what you have with you, here and now. Shannon, you and I are married . . . take me . . . take me in God's name . . . please . . . let me be your wife."

He cupped her face in his hands, felt her nakedness against him, looked into her pleading eyes illumined by bolts of lightning . . . and for a time it seemed he would respond to her.

But it was not *her* eyes he saw. Shannon was responding to something else.

His hands dropped away from her face.

He turned and strode toward the door.

Ben watched in silence as Shannon saddled the horse and galloped out of the stable like he had risen from hell with his hair on fire.

He rode Black through the storm-battered night — under the great stone arch, across the landscape — but this time not to be alone at Moon Rock. This time he had another destination and a different purpose.

The spent animal came to a stop in front of the main building at Twelve Trees. Shannon jumped off and waded through mud toward the entrance.

He crashed through the front door amid the cracks of thunder, closed the door behind him and moved toward the stairs.

Heather bolted up in bed, faced the door — and Shannon, framed in the doorway, dripping wet. He closed the door, flung off his cape and came toward her.

As he moved closer, neither said a word. He stood on the pelt of the panther he had killed years ago, the pelt Heather still kept in her bedroom.

She knew what was to come, and knew she couldn't prevent it — if she wanted to.

Maybe it was rape, maybe not. There was no witness — except the bizarre, volatile night — to what had always been inevitable. He took her for the first time, drumming heart against drumming heart. Dizzy, delirious, plunging, exploding — together.

But after that, there was no question of rape. They were in each other's arms, and she moved from sublime submission to joint, eager participation and serene rapture. Sensual, yet savage — after all the years, the promise of Moon Rock was fulfilled.

Shannon rode into the turbulent night and from a window above, Hannah watched and knew who it was and what had happened.

As she lay in bed after he was gone — for the first time, in her mind, body and soul — Heather no longer thought of herself as virgin.

Chapter Forty-five

Amos Higgins' meaty hands held the envelope out to Shannon.

"I sent word to you," Higgins said eagerly, "as soon as it came, Mister Shannon."

Shannon tore open the envelope and removed the contents.

"Thought I might as well have the draft mailed directly to the bank, Amos." He handed the contents to Higgins.

"Fifty thousand dollars!" Higgins gulped.

"Sometimes the U.S. Army pays off slow, but it always pays off."

"Yes, indeed." The banker stared at the draft.

"I've been carrying Sherman's marker for those horses around for over two months."

"Shall I deposit this draft straight into your account, Mister Shannon?"

"First I'd like to talk to you about something, Amos."

"Certainly. Anything."

"Tom Hill's place."

"Well, I . . . uh, well . . ." Higgins was visibly uncomfortable and upset. "You see, Mister Shannon, before they left on the cattle drive, Hill, Rawlins, and the rest of those ranchers came by to see me."

"They didn't come by to pay you off, did they, Amos?"

"No, no, Mister Shannon, but . . . well, you know I've been in this town a long time and done a lot of business with those fellows."

"You haven't done much business with them lately."

"No. No, unfortunately," Higgins laughed nervously, "but . . . well, I did more or less give my word that I'd hold off 'til they got back."

Shannon seemed surprisingly unperturbed.

"Well, Amos, I suppose you've got to more or less keep your word."

"I knew you'd understand." Higgins smiled.

"And I'll just more or less keep this draft 'til they get back."

Shannon took the draft from Higgins' hand and started toward the door. Amos Higgins stood stunned.

"Mister Shannon, I . . ."

"Now don't you worry, Amos. You and I'll be doing business again."

"We will?"

"Why, sure. That drive hasn't got any more chance of getting to Abilene than . . . 'a wax cat in hell.' "

Shannon opened the entrance door of the bank, stepped onto the boardwalk and almost bumped into Cherrie Millay.

"Hello, Handsome." She smiled.

"How are you, Beauty?"

"Fading."

"You? Never. Going in to see Amos?"

"Make a deposit."

"You still doing business with that pirate?"

"He's the only game in town. Don't like to keep too much money under the mattress . . . gets in the way of . . . well, never mind — so there's almost five hundred in this purse."

Shannon thought it unseemly to mention the fifty thousand in his pocket.

"In that case . . ."

"In that case, come on over and we'll have a drink. It's been too damn long and the deposit can wait."

"Confusion to the enemy." Cherrie smiled as they both drank at the corner table of the Emporium. "How's your wife?"

"What?"

"Charlotte. You remember."

"She's all right."

"Is she with child yet?"

"I . . . uh . . . don't think so."

"Well, what the hell are you waiting for? Don't you think it's about time you had an heir?"

"Hadn't thought about it."

"You better do more than think about it. You've got the biggest spread in Texas or just about anyplace else. You've got to leave it to somebody, Shannon, you can't take it with you."

"I know, but in the meanwhile, nobody's going to take it from me."

"I pity anybody who'd try." She smiled. "Say, how's ol' Pepper-pot? Haven't seen him lately."

"He's alright."

"You don't sound too enthusiastic."

"I think the ol' goat's beginning to believe he's my conscience."

"Why? Have you done something that preys on your mind?"

"Nothing I wouldn't do over again," Shannon said.

And he meant it.

A partially loaded buckboard stood outside the entrance of the main building at Glenshannon Hall.

Ben Hooper, carrying a bundle, came down the stairs into the hallway where Charlotte and Pepper were standing, then he went out the front door.

"That's the last of it, Miz Charlotte," Pepper said. "All loaded up."

"You're sure we've packed nothing of his?"

"Yes, ma'am."

"I don't want to take anything that belongs to him. Not anything. I'm leaving just as I came."

"Yes, ma'am."

"Except for one thing."

Charlotte turned, walked into the great room straight to the blazing fireplace.

Shannon's sword had been removed from its place above the mantel.

Charlotte leaned toward the fireplace where Shannon's sword rested with the blade directly in the middle of the flames.

She picked it up by the hilt with both hands, looked at the white-hot blade, then at Pepper, who stood at the doorway watching.

Charlotte smashed Shannon's sword against the stone hearth — one, two, three times — until the blade was bent and twisted and useless.

She looked at it in her hands as if she were

looking at Shannon, then threw it on the floor, walked out of the room past Pepper in the hallway and through the open front door.

Ben Hooper stood at the side of the buckboard as Shannon rode up, dismounted and watched Charlotte and Pepper walk down the steps of the porch. Pepper went past him without a word. As Charlotte walked by, Shannon took her by the arm.

She looked at the hand that held her, then at him.

He let go.

"A wife's place is . . ."

"I'm not your wife, Shannon." She was calm as a lily pond but with iron resolve in her eyes. "But neither is Heather and she never will be."

"Where are you going?"

"Home."

"To Twelve Trees? Sooner or later I'll have that, too."

"You can have every stone and snake in Texas. I'm going to Virginia. Even you can't take that away from us."

"Virginia?"

"On the other side of the continent, about as far away as I can get from you. Although at times I think you've been farther."

"What'll you do there?"

"I'll teach school or open a dress shop — or I don't care what. But I'll be far enough away from you to start living again."

She walked to the buckboard and Pepper helped her up, then got aboard himself.

"Good-bye, Shannon," Charlotte said. "You got everything and nothing. I pity you."

"Me too," Pepper nodded. "But I'll be back. Don't know when . . . or why."

Pepper whacked the reins and the buckboard took off, leaving Shannon by the porch with Ben Hooper close by.

Shannon looked at him.

"You got something to say?"

"Yes, sir."

"Say it."

"I'll take your horse to the stable."

"They tell me they had to pry that sword out of your hand," Sherman had said. *"Damn near had to cut off your arm . . . It's your sword now. Don't let anybody take it away."*

And nobody had. Not through the war, not afterward.

Shannon sat in the big chair, looking at the twisted steel blade in his hand for over an hour.

He resolved that somehow it would be

straightened and fixed again — and so would his life — or he would die trying.

Then he walked to his desk and drank for two hours while he wrote on two pieces of paper.

The first was his will — just in case he died trying.

The second concerned Charlotte, the fact that their marriage was never consummated and that they were never man and wife and in the sights of God and law — she remained unblemished.

He thought this might help her reputation and be of some help in her getting married again — along with the ten thousand dollars he'd make sure that she received.

Then he walked back to the big chair and took on the second bottle of whiskey as he stared at the twisted sword he had placed near the fireplace.

She did love him. If ever he had doubted, then that stormy night washed away all doubt — and not just because she kept the panther pelt at the side of her bed.

It was what had happened in that bed. No woman could make love like that without being in love.

The only thing that stood between them was Wade Rawlins.

How many men had Shannon killed in the

war? Why hadn't he killed Rawlins at Benton Ridge?

But Rawlins didn't die there.

A cat had nine lives. Did Rawlins?

He had used up one of his lives by surviving Benton Ridge.

Would he use up the other eight on the cattle drive to Abilene?

Nobody from Texas had made it to Abilene and back. Not with ten thousand head of cattle worth a fortune.

Shannon thought of what life with Heather would be like if Rawlins didn't come back.

Not only the marriage bed, but the days of sunshine and smiles with — as man and boy — the only girl he ever loved. With Heather in his arms, the world was his.

But if Rawlins came back . . .

Shannon's thoughts darkened as he drank. If Rawlins came back and found out what had happened between Heather and him, Rawlins would have no choice but to confront him with a gun — and Shannon would have no choice but to take Rawlins' life . . . and his wife.

And Shannon could make sure that Rawlins found out.

But he hoped it wouldn't come to that.

It would be better if Wade Rawlins died somewhere between here and Kansas.

For the first time, as Shannon rose and walked toward the stairs . . . he staggered.

Heather stood naked on the panther pelt at the side of the bed, her swollen breasts gleaming in the moonlight. She reached down toward her bedclothes lying atop the blanket, but stopped at the sight of the Bible on the bedstand near the headboard.

She reached down, took it up, walked the few steps to the window, opened the Bible at random and read by the circle of light in the sky above — read from *Hosea.*

For they have sown the wind, and they shall reap the whirlwind.

She closed the Bible, walked back to the bed, placed the Bible on the bedstand and started to put on her nightclothes.

But she stopped and stared at the pelt beneath her feet, the pelt where Shannon had stood, then took her, rudely at first, with hard hands at her breast, back, throat, waist, hips — consuming every curve, dip, and swell of her body — his ravenous mouth pressed to hers — and then the touch of his hands and body had changed from lust to love, as she too moved from fear and guilt to passion and, yes, she admitted to herself — love.

But she knew that that change was corruption in the eyes of the Lord and the law.

She was married, with husband and child. What might have been was found that night, but must be lost forever. It must never happen again.

Heather was afraid . . . afraid that it could happen again . . . and afraid that something else had happened that night.

Chapter Forty-six

Since Pepper drove the buckboard away from Glenshannon Hall with Charlotte and put her on the stagecoach, he had been staying with Cherrie Millay at the Emporium.

Never before had he stayed nearly as long. During all that time he had never mentioned Shannon's name. Neither had Cherrie.

But in the last few days Pepper had become more and more restless.

"That sonofabitch!" he suddenly blurted out.

"I was wondering when you'd get around to Shannon," Cherrie smiled.

"How do you know I meant Shannon?"

"Well, I didn't think you meant Judas Iscariot."

"In some ways Shannon *is* a Judas, he's betrayed . . ."

"I guess he was right in what he said about you."

"What did he say?"

"Let me see if I can remember it right . . . oh, yes, he said 'that ol' goat's beginning to believe he's my conscience.' "

"He did?"

"He did."

"That's because he ain't got no conscience."

"I don't know, Pepper. For years they played him dirty. Now he's playing them dirty. He lost the one thing he loved . . . besides you."

"Me?"

"That's why you're going back. Because you feel the same way about him, don't you?"

"I know how I feel about you."

"We never needed words, Pepper. Don't say anything you'll regret."

"I'm too old to regret. Cherrie, let's you and me get married."

"To each other?"

"Be serious."

"All right, you can have serious. Where would we live? In your bunkhouse, or here over the saloon? How soon before we'd both begin to rust — from boredom. This way it's kind of . . ."

"Kind of what?"

"Oh, wicked . . . and wonderful. Don't you think?"

"I think you're wonderful."

"Watch them words." She smiled.

"The hell with words . . . come here."

"Ben," Shannon said as they stood in front of the porch, "don't you think it's time you moved out of the stable?"

"How old were you when you moved out?"

"Things were . . . different then. You could move into the bunkhouse, take Pepper's place."

"Pepper'll be back."

"You think so, Ben?"

"His things are still there: Besides, you heard him say it."

"That was some time ago and he wasn't too convincing."

"He'll be back, Mister Shannon."

"Maybe, but Carson won't and I'm not so sure I'd want him back. Ben, you're near grown. Got gravel in your gizzard. Gibbs and Carey . . . and Pepper . . . can run the ranch for a time, but they're getting old and one of these days I'm going to need you to take over as foreman."

"Me? Foreman?"

"Why not? You're as good a cowboy as any of them and your head works. I'm upping your wages. Now do you still want to stay in the stable?"

"Let's give it another year, Mister Shannon, and see how the wind blows."

"Well, in the meantime, will you quit calling me Mister Shannon?"

"No, sir, Mister Shannon." Ben smiled.

Shannon started for the hitching post where Black waited.

"I'm going up and visit . . . up to the hillside."

"It's . . . peaceful up there." Ben looked up toward the cemetery.

"Well, when the time comes, that's where I'll be." He booted into the stirrup, then over the saddle. "There and another place."

"Another place?"

"Ever gone up to Moon Rock?"

"No, sir."

"Too bad." Shannon pointed Black in the direction of the cemetery. "But you will."

Heather stood on a stool adjusting the drapes as Hannah entered the parlor.

Hannah was beginning to stoop a mite. There were more and more stitches of white in her hair, still pulled back in a bun, and dark pouches under her eyes, but those eyes still conveyed confidence, and her voice authority.

"Well, I finally got that little angel of yours

to take her nap. She's just as stubborn as you used to be about —"

Heather had stepped off the stool, swayed and nearly fainted, but managed to compose herself.

"What is it, child? What's the matter?"

"Nothing."

"Nothing! That's the third or fourth time that you've —"

"I just felt a little flushed. Guess I've been working too hard . . . and worrying. I'll be all right."

"Of course you will, child," Hannah said, but sounded more than a little worried herself. Worried about something she didn't dare speak of . . . at least not yet. "It's just been too damn much for both of us around here with no men folk to help . . . just a couple of Mexican maids. Now I'll tell you what you're going to do, and I mean you're going to do it."

"What?"

"Go upstairs and lie down for . . ."

"Hannah! Oh, Hannah!! Look!!!"

Heather pointed out the window as Hannah rushed to her side.

In the distance through the window panes they saw what they had been waiting months to see . . . but not exactly the way they wanted to see it.

Wade Rawlins, Tom Hill, Hank Redding and about a dozen others on horseback plodded slowly toward Twelve Trees.

The men were bone-weary, dirty, some bandaged as if they were coming back from war — and in fact they were. The chuck wagon creaked behind, scarred and tattered.

Heather, followed by Hannah, ran out of the door as Rawlins stiffly dismounted.

"Wade, oh, Wade, my darling! Are you alright?"

As he nodded she flung both arms around him.

"Oh, Wade!"

She kissed him until he pulled away.

"Everything went wrong. We lost the cattle. Ethan's dead and Carson and . . . well, we're all that's left. Everything's gone."

"It doesn't matter, Wade. So long as you're here . . ."

"It matters, Heather . . . to all of us."

Hill, Redding and the rest had dismounted and came closer.

"All right, Rawlins," Hill said. "We're back now. Let's go inside and have that talk."

Inside in the library the air was thick as paste and the mood deadly.

Drinks had been poured and most of the men stared straight ahead.

Heather and Hannah listened from an adjacent room.

"If only . . . ," Redding started to speak.

"We got no time for if onlys!" Hill barked. "There's only one way to stop that bastard and that's to kill him."

"Don't talk that way," Rawlins said.

"There ain't no other way," Hill went on. "We ride over there right now and shoot him dead like the dog he is."

"That's right!" a voice growled.

"Nobody'll stop us and nobody'll blame us," Hill shouted. "Who's coming with me?"

"I'll ride." Redding nodded.

There was a unanimous chorus of "me too's" and nods, except for Rawlins.

"Hannah," Heather whispered, "they'll kill him."

"Let 'em."

"No. You don't mean that. Now listen to me. We've got to get him away from Glenshannon Hall. Now listen, Hannah, you hitch up your buggy. . . ."

Rawlins was desperate to stop the killing any way he could.

"Let's talk to Amos," Rawlins said. "I tell you, we'll be able to work something out."

"Higgins'll go with the money."

"Tom's right!"

"Listen to me. I'll borrow against Twelve Trees . . . I'll loan all of you —"

"No, Wade." Hill shook his head. "It wouldn't be enough. Not nearly. I'm not going back and tell my wife and kids we're all through." Hill pounded his fist on the table. "Not after all those gut-bustin' years on that place. How about you, men?"

There was an even more emphatic chorus of agreement.

"Kill the bastard," Hill repeated, "and be done with him!"

"Hold on!" Rawlins tried to reason. "Sheriff Fox'll charge you with murder."

"The hell with Sheriff Fox!" Hill sneered.

"We'll say he drew on us," Redding said. "They'll have to believe us because there'll be no —"

"No, wait!" Rawlins raised both hands. "Listen to me!"

"You listen!" Hill had it all figured out. "With Shannon dead your sister'll have everything. Everything he stole from Hadley and McCarthy — and she'll have all his Yankee money to boot!"

Rawlins grabbed Hill.

"No! I won't let you."

Hill pulled his gun and slammed the

418

barrel down hard on Rawlins' head; Rawlins dropped senseless and the men, led by Tom Hill, headed for the door.

Hannah had whipped her fat buggy-horse near to death, but she got to Glenshannon Hall and told Shannon that Heather was at Moon Rock waiting to see him now. That's all she told him.

That's all he had to hear.

Ben had saddled Black and brought him out front.

"Mister Shannon. What's wrong? You want me to come with you?"

"Stay here. Look after that woman in the buggy."

As they galloped under the great stone arch, Shannon spurred Black in the direction of Moon Rock, but only once. It was as if the horse knew their destination and every pounding hoofbeat hammered the same fixation deeper into Shannon's brain. She had sent for him. She was waiting at Moon Rock. They would be together, nothing else mattered. He would hold her in his arms and woe be to any son of a bitch — including Wade Rawlins if he was alive — who tried to take her away from him.

By the time Shannon came within sight of

the ghostly formation, Hill and the ranchers were at Glenshannon Hall.

"Where's Shannon?" Hill asked Hannah.

"He's gone to hell and you can go there too."

"We're gonna find him and kill the —"

"Tell it to somebody else," Hannah said.

When they left, Ben Hooper saddled Domino.

At Moon Rock, Heather waited as Shannon dismounted and moved to take her in his arms, but before he could . . .

"Wade's back."

Shannon stopped dead.

"But they lost everything," Heather said.

Not everything, Shannon thought to himself. Wade Rawlins hadn't lost his life.

"I had to get you away from Glenshannon Hall. They blame you for everything. They're coming to kill you."

"Let 'em come."

"Wade's trying to talk them out of it, but he won't be able to."

"Why would he try to talk them out of it?"

Heather paused for just a moment.

"He wouldn't . . . if he knew I was going to have your baby."

Her words resounded like a cannonade in his brain — *"going to have your baby."* His

420

baby . . . their baby . . . a living bond between the two of them. His baby.

Shannon reached out to bring her to him, but Heather pulled away.

"No! Shannon, you blamed me for wanting worldly things. Now the only thing I want in the world is for you to leave us alone."

He took her in his arms and held her close, pressing his body against hers.

"Heather, you know I love you . . . that we love each other."

"You . . ." She tried to pull away. He allowed her to, just a little. "You can't tell your love from your hate anymore. You've paid us all back, Shannon. You've won."

"Everything and nothing. There's only one way I can win. I know you love me. I knew it that night and so did you. I know it now."

"No! No, I don't!"

He drew her closer again.

"Don't you?"

She tried to resist but couldn't.

"I've got a husband and a daughter!"

"And my baby. Now there's you and me and the baby, Heather. And we're here at Moon Rock. Nothing else matters . . . we're the only people in the world."

"No! No, we're not!" she cried out.

"Shannon, I'm begging you! Go away and leave us alone!"

"I'll leave *them* alone if you come with me."

"No . . . no . . . no!"

She tore herself away.

"I don't ever want to see you again!"

"You'll see me every time you look at our son or daughter."

Heather slapped him hard again and again.

"I hate you! Shannon, you've made me hate you! I hate you!"

Shannon locked into her eyes.

"Hate me all you want . . . but I'll hold on to you until we're both dead . . . and after."

"I wish to God I were dead now . . . and I hope they come and kill you!!!"

She ran to her horse and rode away in rampant rage, whipping the animal as if it were Shannon she was hitting — bolting recklessly down the rocky curves, the horse's hooves clattering on the flint-hard slopes.

Shannon leaped on his horse and rode after her.

Hill, Redding and the rest of them trudged back from Glenshannon Hall as

Rawlins, his head still bloodied, rode toward them from the direction of Twelve Trees.

He reined up close to Tom Hill.

"Tom?"

Hill shook his head.

"No. Your wife sent Hannah to warn him. He was already gone, but we'll find —"

"Mister Rawlins . . ." Redding pointed.

Far off to the west, Heather was galloping away from Moon Rock and far behind her, riding like a wild Indian, was Shannon.

She spurred the horse as tears welled from her eyes, blurring her vision.

And Shannon spurred Black, narrowing the distance and crying out for her to stop before she killed herself and the baby.

"Heather! Heather!"

The two of them racing again as they did when they were young, but this time racing toward destiny — destruction.

Her face agonized, she rode and remembered, the ground bouncing in front of her, the sound of his voice and supplications spurring her faster and faster. Her brain was a whirling wheel of love and hate, of remembrance and regret, as he narrowed the distance between them to about twenty yards.

"Heather!"

Her eyes were blind with tears, she was insensate but still racing — until the horse stumbled and with brute force smashed her to the ground.

Shannon's horse was close behind, about to trample her. He ripped back the reins, the bit tore into Black's mouth and the horse twisted, pawed the air as its back legs went out. Black whinnied, buckled, and fell. Shannon hit the ground on his feet and ran toward Heather, who lay unmoving.

Rawlins and the rest were still in the distance but galloping toward them, and in the distance even farther away a lone rider now spurted toward them in a fury.

Shannon knelt, took her close to him and wiped the dirt that streaked her face.

"Heather . . . Heather . . . I'm sorry . . . for everything . . . Heather."

He kissed her face and lips.

"Don't die . . . live, Heather . . . live . . . don't die . . . I love you, Heather . . . don't leave me alone . . ."

She opened her eyes and looked at him. She saw the tears on his face and she smiled, turned her face toward Moon Rock . . . and she was dead in Shannon's arms.

Rawlins, Hill, Redding and the rest reined up a few yards away. As they dismounted, Hill pulled a shotgun out of his saddle boot.

Shannon, with Heather still in his arms,

stared at the formation of Moon Rock, ignoring the men who walked closer.

He lifted Heather's lifeless body and began to carry her, moving toward Moon Rock.

"No! Hill, don't!" Rawlins screamed as Tom Hill lifted the shotgun and fired.

The blast ripped into Shannon's back. He crumpled, still holding Heather.

"Hill!" It was Ben Hooper, who had been trailing them from Glenshannon Hall.

Tom Hill turned, the shotgun in his left hand, his right hovering over the gun in his holster.

"Hill, you murdering sonofabitch. Pull!"

He did, but Ben Hooper's bullet had already hit Hill's heart.

Wade Rawlins walked to the bodies of Heather and Shannon, his head bowed for a long moment, then he looked up and to the west, to the eternal monument.

Moon Rock.

Shannon and Heather were buried next to each other on the hillside and Ben planted a cactus rose between the two mounds where they lay.

Pepper stood next to him as Ben remembered the words that Shannon spoke not too long ago.

"When the time comes that's where I'll be . . . there and another place . . . ever been to Moon Rock . . . too bad, you will . . ."

Moon Rock, a place holy and horrible, serene and savage, bleak and beautiful.

There are those who still say that on certain moonlit nights when the vagrant wind searches through the buttes, voices can be heard.

Shannon, I knew you'd be here . . .

Where else would I be . . .

About the Author

Andrew J. Fenady has spent most of his adult life in the badlands of Hollywood creating, writing and producing motion pictures, television series, Movies of the Week, stage plays and songs, including the classic "Johnny Yuma Was A Rebel."

Fenady has received a passel of awards, among them The Golden Boot for Westerns, The Edgar Award for *The Man With Bogart's Face*, The Christopher Award for *The Green Journey* and three Emmys for *Confidential File*.

He's worked with the toughest top stars, such as John Wayne, Robert Mitchum, Charles Bronson and many, many more.